Jonathan Trigell was born in Welwyn Garden City in 1974. In 2002 he completed an MA in creative writing at Manchester University.

He has spent over a decade of winters in the Alps, working right across the ski industry, from bar work and holiday repping to journalism and organising major events. In the summer months, he has worked as a TV extra, an outdoor-pursuits instructor and a door-to-door salesman, among other things.

Jonathan Trigell's first novel, *Boy A*, won the prestigious John Llewellyn Rhys Prize for best work in the Commonwealth by an author under thirty-five, and also the Waverton Award, for best first novel of 2004. It has subsequently been made into a film by Channel 4.

Praise for *Boy A*

'A compelling narrative, a beautifully structured piece of writing, and a thought-provoking novel of ideas' Sarah Waters, Chair of the John Llewellyn Rhys Prize Judges

'A fine and moving debut novel...Harrowing at times, this compulsively readable novel is more optimistic than it sounds...a rare treat' *Independent*

'A thought-provoking commentary on human nature...A gripping and disturbing read, *Boy A* is a carefully cultivated work that challenges readers while also being entirely gripping' *Good Book Guide*

'The book bristles with issues of personal responsibility, social justice and the reformative value of prison life. It would give reading groups much to ponder over' *New Books Mag*

cham

Jonathan Trigell

A complete catalogue record for this book can
be obtained from the British Library on request

Published in 2007 by Serpent's Tail,
an imprint of Profile Books Ltd
3A Exmouth House
Pine Street
London EC1R 0JH
website: www.serpentstail.com

ISBN 978 1 85242 458 4

Designed and typeset at Neuadd Bwll, Llanwrtyd Wells

Printed and bound in Great Britain by Clays, Bungay, Suffolk

10   9   8   7   6   5   4   3   2   1

The paper this book is printed on is certified
by the © 1996 Forest Stewardship Council
A.C. (FSC). It is ancient-forest friendly.
The printer holds FSC chain of custody SGS-COC-2061

FSC
Mixed Sources
Product group from well-managed
forests and other controlled sources

Cert no. SGS-COC-2061
www.fsc.org
© 1996 Forest Stewardship Council

In memory of Rob Coates and all the others chosen by the mountain.

To my one-monkey menagerie and my own faithful Fletcher.

Acknowledgements

Amanda Preston.
Pete Ayrton.
John Williams.
Anna Davis.
Tally Garner.
Robin Wilkins.
Neil and Andy.
Baz and Bass.
Jamie Strachan.
Johny 'Midnight' Reid.
Natives.co.uk.
Erna Low.
Chamonet.com
Chamonix Mont Blanc, for which even superlatives are inadequate.

The great object of life is sensation, to feel that we exist, even though in pain; it is this craving void which drives us

Byron

Every day confirms my opinion on the superiority of a vicious life – and if Virtue is not its own reward I don't know any other stipend annexed to it

Byron

December 12th, 2.30 a.m.

He's just dragged her from the carpark. Her skin's luminous in the confines of the lift. Someone's smashed the ceiling panel off again, leaving the glare of three bare strip-lights to bounce off the snot-smeared mirror and marker-tagged metal walls.

There's something a little like fear in her eyes. Blue eyes. Young eyes. But he can see the desire in them too. He can always tell when they want him.

His fingers find the top button on the control panel behind his back. Floor 6. Must be. He doesn't want to stop looking at her. You don't know what they're going to do if you look away. Have to mesmerise them. Like a snake charmer. Like a snake.

'Please, no, I've got a boyfriend,' she says, as he starts to kiss her neck.

Of course she has a boyfriend, she's just arrived, they all have boyfriends.

When the lift stops at floor 6, he pulls out the roll of duct tape from his pocket, and tears off the first fastening of the season.

Thou hast a voice, great mountain, to repeal
Large codes of fraud and woe – not understood
Percy Bysshe Shelley,
Mont Blanc, Lines Written in the Vale of Chamouni (1816)

December 12th, 11 a.m.

It was thanks to Shelley that Itchy ended up in Chamonix. Shelley and Byron and Dr Polidori. Poets with about as much relevance to the blood-grudge struggle that marks life for most of humanity as the practice of sliding down snowy slopes on planks of wood.

The others have gone riding. Itchy's alone in the apartment. Nineteen square metres to himself. The sink is full of plates, bowls and the dumb, brown-glass beakers that all French flats have as standard, too small to quench your thirst without three refills. The floor, already covered in beer stains and baguette crumbs, is at least free from other people's pants. They're still in the early, tidy, phase.

He climbs out of bed, from under the comfort of the Union Jack duvet he brought with him, and looks out of the battered patio doors over the balcony. He can't see Mont Blanc for cloud. But he can picture its smooth saddle. He knows it's there and that's enough. When you can see it, the mountain doesn't look so big from Chamonix, though the distance is farther than from Everest base camp to summit. It's from everywhere else that Mont Blanc looks big. From the Three Valleys or the southern

Alps or Val d'Isère, hanging in the background, like Mount Fuji in a Samurai painting. You can love it or hate it, but you can't ignore it; it's there staring you in the face like an angry drunk. Come and have a go if you think you're hard enough. So you do.

If you're in advertising, sooner or later you will move to New York, to be the best you have to. Finance London. Fashion Paris. If you're an actor you go to LA. Where at least, when you fail and flounder, you will have the sympathy of a city that knows how tough a business it is. You can swallow your pride and leave, or stay and throw your genes into the pool; add to an even more beautiful next generation, just as doomed to prescription drugs and disappointment. If you like winter – if you like winter so much that you like even the word 'winter' – if you long for snow and are willing to work at whatever keeps you in it, then sooner or later you come to Cham. That's just how it is.

The first time Itchy came here even the road up was like a call to arms. It's raised on great soaring stone pillars, which look like they were looted from the temples of the Titans, but it feels as if it was made before even those pre-gods. As if it surged from the centre of the Earth with the same unfathomable energy that forced up the crag-ragged ridges on either side. It's like a magic road, a way that leads you to Narnia or the Misty Mountains of Middle-Earth: suspended halfway up a valley; immersed in cloud and expectation; leading learned and unwary alike to pray at pitiless Mont Blanc. Chamonix is indeed a mythical place, a mystical place: where civilisation confronted the wilderness and for once they agreed to differ; undefeated; the undisputed free-ride capital; the death-sport centre of the world. All the first mountains ever assailed were climbed from here. The history of Alpinism itself is a history of Cham. Chamonix is where it all began.

Even Itchy isn't sure where it began for him, why he leads this life he leads. Most of his mates work in London, earning a lot of money, or else not nearly enough. When he looked on the Friends Reunited website, to see what the lost majority from his year at school are doing now, he saw a lot of teachers, a lot of accountants, a lot of kids and cats. A lot of people planning to leave England 'soon'. No one was doing much spectacular with their lives. He's not sure there's much left to do for this generation.

Itchy's grandad won the war. No doubt others helped, but it was mostly him. He hardly talks about it, but he was in one of the finger-countable 7th Armoured Division tank crews that survived all the campaigns that roll off the tongue: the siege of Tobruk; El Alamein; the invasion of Italy; D-Day. He returned with no job and few prospects, to a wife and soon a baby son. He walked out of a prefab every morning for months on end to look for work, walked till his demob shoes were walked right through. He built from the nothingness he was given a stable home. One day bought his own home.

Itchy's dad, that man's son, the only one, that baby, got school scholarships, became head boy, went to university, a family first, and got a first. Worked for a blue-chip company and then started his own company. Turned the stable home he had been brought up in into a wealth his own father could hardly comprehend, an ease of living and a spending power completely alien. He is highly intelligent and took some gambles, but mostly he grafted. For years, maybe since his first day at a school he hadn't the social prerogative to attend, he worked harder than anyone else around him.

And Itchy? What meaning did they leave him? Where was there left to go? To turn a comfortable life into an even more comfortable one? To come from an affluent background and make himself even wealthier. To outdo his father, to become ludicrously, obscenely rich. To throw parties with ice sculptures costing thousands of pounds which will drip into nothing by morning. To have a car so fast there is nowhere left to drive it. To find a trophy wife so beautiful it hurts just to look at her. When you come from what is perfect, where are you supposed to journey to? All Itchy can see to do is to try out a different life, which they weren't able to. And sometimes he thinks his dad understands this.

He necks a stubby from the sallow, food-stained fridge to kill his hangover. Ignoring the nagging worry that this willingness to drink from the start of the day is the first slip towards alcoholism. Booze lurks at the periphery of everything he does, but he doesn't see it as controlling. He blasts through it like the snow, he chooses the direction, he stops when he wants. Anyway, Itchy isn't the sort of person who gets addicted to things. He doesn't have those genes.

Not that he's some kind of a predestination freak, quite the opposite – but when he's gone to one of the discount supermarkets in Moutiers, Cluses or Bourg, or any of the dark, deep-valley, dirty industrial towns out in the Alps, he's seen people who clearly never stood a chance. Thin-necked, chinless spindles, whose family trees can only have survived at all through charity, and the cripple's exemption from military service.

The Derapage has been in Jean-Paul's family for generations and it looks like it has remained unchanged for most of that time, though apparently it started out as a butcher's shop. It's a cellar bar now, down stone steps; it's small, but long on wood panels. It could be used as a film set for wartime France – if you knocked one of the walls out, otherwise there's not enough room for cameras.

Jean-Paul's a short man, lean and haggard in a way that suggests a slow taxidermy from filterless fags. If he was English you'd suggest he see a doctor, but there's nothing strange about looking like that in Cham – the mountain sun corrugates in age the same skin that it kissed in youth.

The first time he met him, Itchy thought Jean-Paul was himself a doctor – most of the Brits call him Doc. It's a joke, though: JP, his nickname with the French, is pronounced GP to English ears.

It's only Itchy's fifth night at the Derapage now, and it's slow. Working in a bar is painful when it's as quiet as this. He polishes the pumps, though it seems unlikely that he and the solitary half-pint nurser in the corner can have produced much by way of dust since the last time he did it. A couple of shots of Fernet Branca's goodness make him feel a little wholer. Fernet is a liquor like the cigarette-tar that causes a cough and the syrup that cures it, distilled into one.

It's getting near closing-down time when they come in: gendarmes, out of uniform, drunk. He recognises them from when he worked at Wild Wallabies, coming in to catch staff not on the books. They never did. Which is not to say that there weren't any. They come to the bar to order, unusual for the French – most expect you to wait on them. Which is fair enough, it's their country.

They spot he's English, even through the haze of their session and in a frog bar.

'Two aleves of beeer, please, siir,' one says, in an accent that could be a clowning exaggeration, or simply slurring, but which makes them laugh.

They both have the large moustaches favoured by gendarmes and comic-book Gauls and one has a booze-pocked nose, bubbling like the head of the beer Itchy pulls him. They switch straight back to French, and a previous conversation, as they prop up the bar – presuming Itchy can't understand, or not caring.

'*So you think we're going to catch him, this rapist?*'

The word 'rapist' draws Itchy's ears; it's *violeur* in French, sounds like a musician or his instrument.

'*We will eventually. These guys, they always get caught eventually. But usually just from luck. Someone passing by, something they drop. We can't keep the whole carpark under watch and he knows it.*'

'*Probably a foreigner, English.*' Pock-nose nods his head slightly towards Itchy with this; who feels a scald of shame, moves farther away to restack unused glasses.

Sean, one of his flatmates, sends a text message just as Itchy's locking up.

```
ichie, in Dicks.
So r nu Ski
Planet nannys...
Ugly but gr8ful. C u
here l8er. ];-)>
```

Sean has a scar he tells girls he got in a knife fight in Mexico. They must have stabbed him right in the appendix if so. He likes to make curry so hot that his eyeballs sweat.

His offer is not overwhelmingly tempting bird-wise, but then Itchy does fancy another beer. Itchy generally fancies another beer, even if the prices in Dick's Tea Bar are predatory.

The streets are quiet in a way that only normally busy streets can be. He sees corners he's never really noticed before. Snow is falling but not settling or coming hard enough to promise a powder day. It just leaves the cobbles wet, and a white dusting on the hair of the few people he passes. In the mirror of a blackened window Itchy catches a glimpse of what he might look like as an old man. A silver-crowned, wiser him, grown out of the sins of youth. But that seems unlikely. Sometimes even living to be old seems unlikely. And he'd probably be bald like his dad.

Sean's got black slicked-back hair, like a Prohibition gangster. And he looks a bit like one: lolling at the bar in Dick's; arms around a couple of molls. But Sean's a holiday rep, he deals in cheese instead of bootleg liquor, and these girls are slappers, not flappers.

The one Sean tries to palm off on Itchy has big cheap-gold earrings, which swing gently – chavertising – she's called Bryony.

'But my friends call me Britney,' she says, ''cos of these.' She squeezes her arms together to exaggerate her prominent but unremarkable cleavage.

Itchy agrees that she does appear to have exactly the same number of breasts as Miss Spears, the sarcasm missed by a mind well washed with Bacardi Breezer.

Truth is, he's never really seen the attraction of overly large breasts. OK, they look good in tight tops, jutting out, supported by more wires and straps than a flying Peter Pan at the Christmas panto. But unlike Peter, they are exceptionally susceptible to age and gravity – they should come with a best-before date tattooed on an underside. Even when they're young, it's hard to get them in exactly the right place: pendulous in doggy; slumped in missionary. Sure, they're fun, but no more so than a small pair; and you always feel like you should be doing more with big tits, when there isn't really anything else to do.

He can't decide whether shagging Bryony is going to be worth listening to any more of her drivel, but when she says she's off to Meribel for the winter tomorrow, that they were just in Cham for training, he decides it probably is. At least he'll never have to see her again. Besides, it's always safer to do things; things Itchy didn't do are infinitely more regrettable to him – except for that one thing. The ghosts of all the girls he never fucked haunt Itchy – the nearlys and the maybes, the wastage – because one day, he knows, he will lie on his deathbed and wish he'd had more sex.

He unlocks the Derapage and fucks her on a table. He has no idea where Sean went with the other one. The table has a funny wobble, he should stick some folded paper under one leg to make it level – like they used to for exams his first year of uni. Itchy dropped out after that first year. He focuses on the wobble to avoid coming too soon, not because he much cares about Bryony's pleasure, and she's not going to talk to anyone he knows, just because he's enjoying himself.

Bryony can't remember where she's staying, so he ditches her in the middle of town. That's the best thing about shagging the homeless – you can drop them off anywhere. She's shameless drunk, knickers in her pocket, screaming at him across the square that he's a bastard. As if he doesn't know. But it's snowing hard now, coming down in great globs like the money shot from a porno, and he can't stay out too late, because it's looking like a powder day tomorrow.

> Dangers which sport upon the brink of precipices
> have been my playmate; I have trodden the glaciers
> of the Alps and lived under the eye of Mont Blanc.
>
> *Shelley*

December 13th, 8.32 a.m.

The best bit about sex is the static just before the first kiss. Anticipation. Likewise Itchy loves preparations for powder: strapping on his knee brace, testament to a ligament-shredding fall four seasons back; wrapping the corset-belt of his armadillo spine-protector; buckling into place his avalanche transceiver, the click and half-twist of the fasten, the light that flashes against slick blue moulded lines – the James Bondness of it; filling his camelback with tap water, fresh as Evian; checking that his collapsible shovel and probe are in place in his pack; and throwing in three Mars Bars, because there is no time to eat on a powder day.

Powder is what it's all about. More than birds. More than booze. More even than mountains. Because powder is the medium the mountain uses to play with you. And it comes so infrequently, lasts unsullied by sun, unblasted by wind, untracked by people for such a brief instant, that it is purity and transience and pleasure distilled.

Aussie Mark, the other flatmate, has a car. It's a short-wheel-base Landy that looks as though it probably did service driving various charities, mercenaries and militias around African starvation spots, before retiring to the Alps. It's got a rack, bolted and rusted on to the spare wheel on the back, and Itchy and Sean shove their skis in. Aussie Mark's a boarder and a bum, he's a diamond driller – whatever the fuck that is – Itchy knows it's to do with construction and not jewellery; he makes a bundle in London in the summers anyway.

Aussie Mark has a scar above his right eye from a punch he took defending a stranger and he likes the way his climbing harness squeezes in his trousers, making his packet look really big.

The Landy guffs out of inertia, and Aussie Mark executes a perfect seven-point turn, pulling out of the cramped underground parking space, around the scabby Renault van that has all but blocked him in and a Guy Fawkes pile of broken wood and cardboard boxes.

The carpark is massive, runs under the whole of Chamonix Sud – the ghetto. It is a warren, though that sounds too pleasant, of interlinked tunnels and small isolated bays, all covered in crude graffiti, oil, ancient urine and squares of smashed-in windscreen glass. It is home to rubbish bins and rats, and now it would seem something worse.

Sean is building a spliff as they drive along the postcard road up to Argentière. He does it the French way: crumbling herb into his cupped hand and using this as a mixing bowl to meld it with tobacco from a Camel Light. Aussie Mark taps on the steering wheel, even though there is no music playing; he's always tapping or fidgeting, too much energy. Itchy watches the trees out of the window. They are bowing to the car, bent under weighty ermine robes from the first big valley floor dump. It's hard not to feel like a hero today, hard not to imagine you are a gladiator, helmed and armed, about to do battle for nothing but glory and love of the fight.

Sean's mobile rings, with two tinny lines from an old Sade track – 'Smooth Operator' – and breaks Itchy's shallow abstraction.

'Snow Spirit Holidays, Sean speaking, how can I help?' he says, though he has just checked out the caller ID so knows who has rung. 'Oh, hi, boss. Yes, going round doing my health and safety checks. Yeah, it does look great up there, doesn't it? How could you think that? I know how important it is to get everything sorted now. Yeah, I don't mind – there will be plenty more powder days.'

Sean lies with a glibness and fluency that Itchy had never before encountered. He seems proud of it, lies unnecessarily and extravagantly. Lying is of course in a rep's remit, but you can't help admiring someone who takes so much pleasure in their work.

There's a queue for the lift up at the Grands Montets. They haven't opened the cable car yet, waiting for the pisteurs to finish detonating avalanches. Occasionally a volley, as if from a lone Luftwaffe bomber, reverberates around the valley. On big blasts the vibrations judder up into the legs of the crowd stood waiting. There are no punters in the queue; all season workers, or bums, or locals. Pupils glossy with expectation. There is tangible camaraderie, smiles, stranger chat. This is what it was like in the Blitz, when that spirit of the Londoners was everywhere and the good old Queen Mum could look the East End in the eye

– though no doubt they were expected to stoop to the ground, to make this easier from within an armoured Bentley.

Itchy's muscles ache with readiness, but his hangover lungs retch on the thin cold air and his gut churns with every early morning movement. His skis feel heavy in his hand. He has one of his Mars Bars while he's waiting. What he could really do with is a beer.

There is a cheer when the cable car engine churns into life, in its one gear. The lifty might be bunking off school to stand at the turnstile letting people through, he looks about fifteen. He's got sparse and soft blond bum-fluff, and a grin like he wouldn't want to be riding the hill because looking at lift passes is so much more fun.

The guys get in the third cabin to go up, which is not bad for when they arrived. It'll be different when the season really kicks off in a week or so's time.

The doors are closed and cranked in place with a metal bar, like the French Foreign Legion use to hold the fort gates when the Arabs charge. The lift system in Chamonix is antiquated and unapologetic. They never spend money on it. Why bother? The town's always full anyway. They don't care about investment, or competitiveness, nor about advertising, nor customer service. Even by French standards, they don't care about customer service. The problem with Chamonix is that it knows it's Chamonix.

Itchy is by the cabin front window, separated from the other two by a throng of Scandies, all wearing helmets and earnest expressions. One of them is about eleven feet tall. Itchy looks at the cable from which the 'bin hangs, twisted like a liquorice stick, barely the girth of your arm, but spiralling off unsupported up the mountain.

A friend who had never skied came out to see him at the end

of last season, and Itchy was amazed by his reaction to these lifts. You could sense his adrenalin, the urge to jump – if only to end the spin-giddy fear of looking down. Humans very quickly become complacent about such things, though. Have to keep upping the dose of danger to get high. To Itchy, the view is pretty but the cable car not in the least bit exciting – except for what is promised at the end of it.

The riding is out of this world. They do two laps of the Lavancher bowl, barely stopping, in deep untracked powder. Relishing the sprays of snow hitting their faces as they turn. Dancing in the order they descend. Shouting and laughing like kids. Serious as saints.

For Itchy, deep powder is a near-religious experience. It is absolute freedom, because you can ski where you want: rocks are blanketed; tree stumps blister-packed; pitfalls filled. And it is merciful, the snow allows you mistakes and welcomes them, envelops them in its love. It liberates, lightens the load, lifts even the everyday burden of your own weight. It lets you fly with an abandon that you couldn't hope to get away with on normal snow. It is forgiving and allows him to feel forgiven. Drops that would jar his spine, or smash his knees into his chin, instead catch him and cradle him. And everything is as white as the light that Itchy may one day walk towards in that final drop, where he would not hope to be forgiven as fully.

'Spot on,' Aussie Mark says, just the three of them in one of the Bochard bubbles, 'today is totally spot on.'

He wipes off the snow stuck to the top sheet of his board with his big, gloved hand and watches it drop to the rubber-matted floor. Then looks up with a smile that splits his Labrador's face into toothy mayhem.

He's a funny-looking sprout, Aussie Mark, there's no doubt about it. Has a curly ponytail, like some eighties wide boy, and wears his jeans drainpipe tight when almost everyone else in Cham still buys them about five sizes too big. Not that he's wearing them now, of course. Only Parisians and teenagers wear jeans for skiing. It's not a good look. And you're not paying respect to the mountain if you aren't wearing waterproof and properly insulated gear. You have to remember, the mountain can crush you at any moment. It's not exactly hankering to, it doesn't even notice you're there. To a mountain that has existed since the continents formed, a human being is not even as significant as a micro-organism is to a sperm whale. But Itchy is in no doubt that when it's going about its business – of eating giant squid and being enormous – a sperm whale regularly destroys whole congregations of micro-organisms. And it is certain that the ill-prepared, badly dressed ones die first.

Sean wears this bright yellow jacket, which is top of the range, double duck down, but still makes him look like a motorway maintenance worker. Aussie Mark wears a mishmash of makes, but all black; his board's black too, with a naked lady and dragons on it – like the album cover from the rock band he seems to want to be in. Itchy has worn Billabong for years, but only because it's always the best looking of the technical gear, he has no brand loyalty. What's that line he read in *Moby-Dick*?: 'I have no allegiance but to the king of cannibals, and I am ready at any moment to rebel against him.' Moby-Dick, now there's a sperm whale. Moby-Dick would be Mont Blanc.

'Are you dreaming again, Itchy, son?' Sean says, as he straightens and then lights the spliff he built back in the car.

Overpoweringly sticky fumes fill the bubble. Itchy opens the window.

'Nah, bro, keep it closed. Let's hot-box it,' Aussie Mark says.

'Piss off.' Itchy laughs. 'I'll be sick.'

Sean and Aussie Mark pass the joint between them for the rest of the journey. Itchy doesn't have any. He doesn't smoke at all now. Used to have the odd fag, when he was young. Smoked a lot of draw his first year at university, that only year at university – but stopped after that. Dope makes you get introspective; he didn't want to get too introspective after that.

They click into their skis again. Itchy has fat black Factions, with the contours of a mournful girl for their graphic. Sean rides plain white, unbranded test skis, which he bought off a pisteur. They wait while Aussie Mark ratchets his boots down on to his board. Snowboarders are always on their arses. The Scandies call them seals, and you can see why: sprawled over the slopes in little colonies, flapping and clapping about on mittens and knees.

There's no animosity between skiers and boarders now, though, never should have been, maybe there never really was. Only in the minds of gromets and middle-aged billys.

As if to prove it, Itchy and Sean team up to drag Aussie Mark to the start of the traverse into the bowl. Him holding on to one of each of their poles as they skate along. There are a few more tracks around now, a few more whooping riders. But the snow is still light and perfect powder. Insubstantial, weightless; and yet the most substantial, the most important thing in the world; iridescent in a thousand colours, all white.

They carve long arching turns through the billowing mass, riding at the very edge of their ability to stay upright. Short swings and neat bootlace tracks are strictly for punters. Tracks don't survive long enough in Chamonix to be admired.

They cut over to drop down into the Dream Forest, named years before Itchy arrived on the scene. On a powder day it is truly a dream – a series of banks and pillow drops, twisting through the trunks. Occasional sink holes which emerge only at the final second. Sudden escape manoeuvres and small boulder hucks. All among spruce trees, the dark green of bottled wine, sugar-coated like a witch's cottage.

Even though it's one of the first days on the hill, and Itchy and Sean are knackered, they keep going till the lifts close. Aussie Mark is built like a bull mastiff and never tires. The home run in one shot is almost more than Itchy's thighs can take. They are shrieking at him to stop, screaming with the burn of lactic acid. But pride bites even more strongly and he follows the others down, face scrunched in pain like a screwed-up bill.

There's a stag do in the bar later. Brits, of course. One says they are from Yorkshire, but they don't sound Northern, probably all work in London. Why they've come to Chamonix is obvious: an hour from Geneva airport – easyJetsville. A bit of skiing, though it is doubtful any of them will be going tomorrow, and plenty of boozing. Why they've chosen the Derapage is more confusing. They are overwhelming the place; would have scared off the other customers, if there were any. At least they're all amiable for the moment. Some are standing on the chairs, all joining in rugby songs about accommodating virgins and biblical figures. It is only a matter of time until someone gets naked.

The groom, for whom getting stripped in the centre of town was probably always on the cards, is numbing himself to the various horrors to come by doing shots of green chartreuse; maybe that's just another one of his forfeits, though. He's got sweaty, curly blond hair and something piggy about his eyes: possibly that they have blond lashes, but they are very round as well. Actually he reminds Itchy of the pink hippo from *Rainbow*,

George. Was George gay? The posh rugby boys are constantly calling each other 'poof' and 'bender', as if this is the most unarguable assertion of their own manliness. Though as the evening progresses it becomes clear that they think nothing of drinking beer from each other's arse-cracks and other acts that many hardened homosexuals might shrink from.

Itchy has never played rugby, but he used to be pretty hot shit at football. Had trials for a few local teams, played for his uni side that first year. What happened with that uni team is why he can't stand these rugby boys: so drunk and arrogant. He keeps smiling, though, keeps laughing at the jokes, keeps pulling the pints and pouring the shots. He's a barman, after all. A barman who can't be nice to drunks needs to look for a new job.

The First Semester

S HE WAS THE zenith. The pinnacle. Tina. A bit of bright
Beverly Hills heaven in the beige of Sheffield. A voice crying
in the wilderness. The Star of India among cubic zirconia.
Tina. And while doodling her name, like a lovesick teen – and he
was still a teen, just, anyway – he noted that she must be the girl
for him. Tina: There Is No Alternative.

She was blonde, with dark eyebrows, which framed her face
like question marks; made him wonder whether her pubic hair
was dark like them. He could have roofed a cottage in the time
he spent wondering about that thatch. But even clothed she was
a goddess: Venus in Guess jeans and shell-toes. Breasts large
enough not to need a Wonderbra, still small enough to sometimes
not wear a bra at all. He watched, he knew.

Tina studied English too, was his only reason for going to
lectures – he did not attend those she didn't have. She was also
his reason for excelling at the Romantic period: she was in his
tutorial group and he wished to demonstrate his intelligence,
or at least to be sure he had something to say. He found, with
application, he could expound at length on the pathos in Keats's

poetry, when he had previously thought that Pathos was one of the musketeers. He studied harder at the Romantics than all the rest of his work put together. Shelley and Byron and Keats and Tina.

Itchy's tutor, Dr Ragworth, had an earnest and candid passion for his subject, without a trace of intellectual snobbery. He loved the Romantics with the clumsy evangelical charm of a pigeon fancier or Morris Minor restorer, a hobbyist who knew he could never explain what bliss his mistress offered the devotee, and still couldn't help trying. He was also the author of a surprise bestseller; what his publisher described as 'a dramatic history of the life of Lord Byron'. A book that he shyly plugged and the other lecturers slyly denigrated, as lacking in both literary and historical merit.

It was for Tina that Itchy worked and read, but perhaps Dr Ragworth's enthusiasm aided the process, showed that genuine ardour could bud. Because, rather as in an arranged marriage, what at first was duty if not drudgery for Itchy turned in time to an act of intimacy and unshammed love. He stroked the minor Romantic works, licked the fragments, lingered in favourite passages, suffered even the most outlandish theories. He gorged on poetry, wallowed in it; but through all Tina was present; flickering and faint at the edge of Itchy's feast.

Dr Ragworth persuaded his publishers and the department, to which his book had brought much prestige in public if not academic acclaim, to jointly fund a creative writing competition. The challenge: to reproduce one of the three lost Gothic ghost tales from the infamous summer at Villa Diodati.

The prizes were significant, sufficient to tempt cynical students into writing a piece that would not affect their degree. The entries were nameless, only prison digits handed out by the department recorded their creators, to ensure the judging Dr Ragworth's strict impartiality; although the majority of students wrote their piece from the perspective of Byron, knowing full well where Dr Ragworth's strongest affections lay. A smattering chose to create Shelley's tale. Only a couple the eternally neglected Polidori. Itchy wrote all three. Each mentally dedicated to Tina. Love poems in faux-old prose.

Even at this age Itchy was no novice with girls. He had an innate sense of the appropriate thing to say, the cad's self-confidence and moral autism. He had butchered his way through a succession of neighbours and acquaintances within the first few weeks of term. Acquiring a reputation in the process, which encouraged far more women than it put off.

'Chicks love players,' his wingman, Marty, a biology student, told him once, 'the same self-destructive bent that makes elephant-seal females flock to a male, so hugely blubbered he may well suffocate what he fucks makes women flock to philanderers. It's about the genes, you see: offspring of a successful mater will have a higher probability of being successful maters, scattering their mother in their seed just as much as Daddy-pops. There is no nurture, man – it's all about the genes.'

Marty was tall and good looking, despite some facial chickenpox scars that an overindulgent mother must have let him pick to his detriment. He still liked to pick. Even through trousers, Itchy would see him worrying a scab on his knee, from football on the hard court. They were both in the soccer team. Marty was a good partner for pulling and drinking, and seemed like someone who wouldn't let you down – even though he was mono-browed and plucked the centre, which Itchy felt to be inherently untrustworthy.

Itchy wasn't convinced by his theories, though; the only reason women like players is because they don't like to feel they're missing out on something. Fuck genes, it's fashion.

Nothing worked with Tina, though. Itchy rarely got close enough to her to work his charm. When he tried, it slid off unnoticed. His carefully practised smile, with that hint of Tom Cruise hiding in the curl, raised not even a parting of her pulpy lips. Her mouth was amazing: teeth American in their even, milky equidistance; lips plump like red-plush scatter cushions in the sanctum of a courtly lover. Sometimes she had a tired air about her, which on another girl you might think was a sign of nights spent clubbing or shagging, but Itchy could sense that in Tina it came in fact from the opposite of this: from a weary ennui at the hedonistic student world with which she was surrounded. Her skin was pale and healthy, washed with soft pink beneath her cheeks, either not made up or made up so delicately and finely that even close observation could not reveal it. And Itchy observed just as closely as one could, without coming across like a stalker.

'Do you fancy a coffee?' he'd asked, after class one day, propped casually against the door, as she was leaving with her books held hard against her womb.

Only she hadn't looked up at the right moment, which somehow sent his question sailing past her to land on some grubby plank behind, who it turned out did very much fancy a coffee; only decaf, because he didn't like his drinks too lively – or his conversations.

Usually Itchy's nerve left him anyway at such opportunities. Something about her kept his confidence low. She was out of his league, he knew it. Not in a self-depreciating way – just that she was out of everyone's league. You looked at her and couldn't imagine there being a guy alive who deserved her. If he'd had her, it wouldn't be for a drunken shag. She was girlfriend material. Marriage material.

Another time Itchy had followed her home. Slinking through

student mobs striped with peroxide and Adidas. Creeping half a street back when the crowds thinned. Running to catch her when he lost sight, then loitering at road ends and under weeping trees when he got too near. A temporary agoraphobia. Constantly a clutching sickness in his stomach, a slip knot sliding tighter inside. A sudden panic when she stepped into a chemist's, leaving him stranded on a long open avenue. He ducked down on to a bus-stop bench and found an abandoned copy of *The Times*, penetrating the paper with his fingers, punching twin eyeholes in it, to watch for her leaving, like a film noir spy.

So he found where she lived, which in all its end-of-terrace glory was no different to where a thousand other students lived. Though a princess inhabited this tower, it looked almost as though her chamber could only be the same as the countless, slightly damp, second-hand-shop-smelling bedrooms that Itchy had already woken up in that year; stealthily trying to locate his clothes without waking the conquests; forearmed with an excuse of football practice, if they should stir. Girls Tina's age, usually blonde like her, but also-rans, bit-part players.

And with this new knowledge, life went on exactly as before. Him eyeing from a distance. Her unaware of his existence – except, he could only hope, as that guy in the Romantics tutorial, who was so sensitive and insightful. He didn't go back to her house. Never hung about in the park opposite at night, hoping to catch her undressing. Waiting to see a silhouette of slim nakedness sketched against a sixty-watt bulb. He never pushed anonymous love letters through the stiff black brushes of her letterbox. Didn't type them, didn't cut out words from the magazines that sprawled around his bedroom floor and Pritt-stick them to faint-lined sheets ripped with raggedy-lace edges from a spiral-bound A4 pad. He never broke in through an ill-locked window, slid down like a serpent on his belly from the sill, wrinkled his way through the contents of her drawers, read her diary, ate from her plates, sniffed her soaps and shampoos. Itchy didn't do any of these – but he thought of them all, and more.

But he still went to the union with Marty. Still found himself embroiled at the end of the night with spares, or single birds. With Metro-Goldwyn-Mayer hourglass figures or little boy-girls with hard tits and tight asses; a shaven-headed darling he took for a lesbian until she pulled him into a corner and covered him in Lemon Hooch kisses; sullen; smirking; sometimes grindingly cheery; a black girl, who really leaned into her moaning, like she was on audition; a flat-chested ging with a tattoo of a barcode and a glint in her eye that said she'd be as much fun to fuck as she was; even a chubber or two, when it would be rude not to; some had names, some didn't; some made him bag up, sometimes he remembered, usually neither of them cared. One girl made him go to the family planning with her the next day, for the morning-after pill, or was it to a doctor's? Itchy no longer remembers, but he can picture leaflets on giving up smoking, browned at their corners by the dirty fingers that had popped them back in the box after all, and posters peeling up the walls where Blu-tack couldn't stop their urge to curl back into themselves. Same as the people: desperately pretending not to be there, on those road-cone-red school chairs; staring at the one spot of dirt on the wall or floor that might make them invisible. Maybe it was also an STD clinic.

Tina came into the tutorial one day with charity raffle tickets to sell, Amnesty International, not animals. He might have loved her a little less if it was animals. There was a middle-aged woman who used to come round and collect for a charity called Only Foals and Horses in the pub, which he'd found ridiculous.

'How can you collect for animals when people are dying?' he'd asked her once, drunk beyond manners.

'I like horses more than people,' was her reply. She was brittle looking, not sturdy and chunky-thighed like horsey people are supposed to be. She looked like she wouldn't even want to impose on her equine friends enough to ride them, just to look at them galloping around in the fields she'd helped to buy.

Tina liked people, though, which made Itchy suspect that the slight sleepless rings beneath her eyes stemmed from another night spent worrying about others. She explained very briefly, almost hesitantly for a girl usually so self-assured, that anyone who wanted a ticket could get one afterwards. Itchy realised, sand-mouthed, that he had no money on him, and rather than try to explain, he slipped away at the end, with most of the others in the group. Emerging into the sunshine outside the English block – which always aggressed his eyes, like after an all-nighter, and forced that same weird awareness that the world continued even when his own attention was elsewhere – he decided to immediately track down the student Amnesty branch and join up.

Tina wasn't at the meeting he attended – two weeks later, twenty-one pounds lighter, in a room that smelt of sick – few people were. A girl he'd slept with in Freshers' Week was, though, and she slipped him very unphilanthropic fusillades of death stares throughout the fairly tedious proceedings. When he wormed a look, Tina's name wasn't even on the membership list.

Man, being reasonable, must get drunk;
The best of life is but intoxication.

Byron, Don Juan

December 19th, 8.51 p.m.

Wednesday is Itchy's night off, so he heads over to the Jekyll, a short walk from the apartment. Like most barmen in town, he spends most of his free evenings in bars. The Jekyll is a little piece of Chamonix legend, at the south end of Cham Sud, hanging in the dark, backed up against Mont Blanc. It's rock-walled, timber-framed, steep-roofed, and seems to loom over the compressed old street it's set on. A relic of a street really; far from the blocks of the ghetto, though only a few hundred yards away. Looking down that long straight road you look into the past, a sometimes murky past, shaded even from the moon by hanging frontages. The Jekyll; the name is ominous. Dr Jekyll, of course, a good guy, but one who starved for the strength and the freedom of his darker self; one who couldn't resist the call of the wild. There is only a small single doorway into the big black building, no windows. This is what drinking dens should be like.

Inside it's bright, though, if anything too brutally so, after the dim street. A girl clatters down the stone stairs from the first-floor bar, somehow managing to make the noise of high heels with only her trainers. Music follows her, also coming from upstairs.

Itchy's mouth is dry from lack of drink. He hasn't eaten much either, but eating's cheating. The walls on the way up are lined with old Guinness adverts; framed, and nailed in place to stop drunken thievery. In theory it's an Irish bar, though the owners are Brits and the staff mainly Scandies. Even the Guinness is brewed in France. Itchy's not big on Guinness – too much like hard work – but the creamy top on the hoardings makes him think that maybe a White Russian is in order.

Josey is working at the bar, a good girl. Sometimes Itchy's fall-back shag. Eyes the brown of Baileys. She's pretty, but slightly too squared off, like Mr Strong. She's a posh girl, who did a season and stayed too long. Josey loves this life, though. She likes to think that one day she'll go back and get a permanent job in London, but she won't. The ones who think that don't, it's the others. She has her own name tattooed just above her bum, which is kind of sexy, because it is there so relative strangers can remember it while they're fucking her from behind, or learn it. And Itchy likes that, he likes that there are women who pluck what they want from the world as readily as guys do. As carelessly as guys do. He likes the fact that one day he will be fucking a girl and find out that she has 'slut' tattooed above her arse, and that the joke will be on him not her.

Josey has a scar on her finger, from where an engagement ring got caught in a slammed car door. Itchy sees the scars in everyone. Maybe because his own scars run so deep. He likes sleeping without dreams.

She takes pride in making the White Russian. Itchy nods to her his satisfaction at her workmanship, and smiles at the extra shot or two of vodka that goes in. The bar is busy, with a buzz that makes him think something special is going on tonight. Before he can ask what, Josey backs off to serve another customer. Blowing a kiss, ringing the bell and rattling Itchy's change into the tips jar simultaneously, so that it seems like she must have had one extra hand.

They've built a small stage at the end of the room, but there is no sign of a band. Just a lone microphone, standing one-legged, like a steel flamingo. Itchy notices that several people around the room are wearing numbers on their chests, badges of card, circular, the size of the Wagon Wheels he used to eat in the days when E-numbers were not given a thought. Not that they exactly plague Itchy's conscience now. Some of the girls' badges are decorated: with felt tip, glitter, tinsel and faux-fur. Children's things that make them look like jailbait. Mostly the guys have just got a number, drawn in marker.

He sees Daniel and Suzi standing by the stairs that lead to the crow's-nest top floor, and edges through the crowd to get to them. He kisses Suzi on both cheeks, so natural out here, so pretentious at home, and clasps Daniel's hand hello. Suzi always drinks gin and lemonade, Daniel is on Ricard; Itchy thinks that he might switch to Ricard after this White Russian.

'How's it going?' Itchy asks.

'Good,' says Daniel, 'real good.'

Suzi smiles. She's a knockout, a ten. She and Daniel have been going out for years, though. Itchy holds them up as the best couple in Cham. He briefly wonders whether one day he will know what it's like to be them, but he doesn't really believe in such things. Some people just fool themselves better than others.

'Are you not in the auction?' Suzi asks, prodding Itchy's shirt where a card badge isn't. 'I thought it would be right up your street, you dirty slag.' She winks to show that she means no malice. Which is doubly unnecessary: since Itchy does not consider *slag* to be an insult, and knows that Suzi is in any case incapable of deliberate offence.

He is bothered by her words, though. 'Auction?' he says. His brows kink and he cannot help cocking his head slightly to one side, a habit he formed, after over-employing it in flirtation, which has evolved into a sign of nervousness.

'There's a slave auction on tonight, didn't you know?' Daniel says. 'For the British disabled ski team.' He says this as if there could be no worthier cause imaginable, but then Daniel is a ski instructor. He's ridiculously fit, goes running every night when he's finished skiing; good looking too, if a bit overqualified on the chin front; and went to Cambridge, though it's not something you would ever hear him mention. So far as Itchy is aware, he has no scars at all. Suzi has only a tiny scar where a belly-button piercing got infected, which Daniel likes to kiss and blow raspberries on. Normally Itchy is easy in their company, but the abrupt knowledge that he has stumbled into somewhere he doesn't want to be makes him struggle not to flinch or flee.

He has a swig of his White Russian, amazed that so far he has not so much as sipped it, and now needing the fortitude that a good drink can give him. He wipes off the milk froth that probably isn't there on his upper lip, but he does it like old men play with their pipes: to buy a little time before his response.

'Slave auction, huh,' he says to them, already calmer. 'Not sure I'm going to stick around long if that's going on. Not a big fan of that stuff.' Then he adds, possibly a bit too obviously, as an afterthought, 'It's racist, if you ask me.'

Sean comes over, with four slammers on a tray; he must have seen them from the bar. Daniel groans in good-natured protest, but takes one with the others. This is ritual, it's these things that bond them, remind them of all the other times they've done these things. Three swirls, three bangs, swallow. The rules don't need saying between old friends, so no one does. They do it together on the six inches of shelving that flows around the walls of the room like it should have a Hornby train track on it. The lemonade explodes into the tequila as they bang, spumes lather up their noses as they down it. Itchy likes to hold it in his mouth a moment, so he knows he's got it, before he swallows. He likes to feel the harshness of the liquor burn his throat; imagining a land so sparse and arid that tequila and chilli are the softest pleasures.

The MC comes on stage, in a Natives hoody and baggy jeans, rather than black tie. He's a cocky pretty-boy that Itchy doesn't have much time for, but always sees around.

'Hi, guys, thanks for coming,' he starts, his face filled with a grin so cheesy that even most reps would consider it overdone. 'If you don't know already, tonight we're having the second annual Jekyll Slave Auction...'

His babble continues, with the excessive enunciation of a daytime quiz-show host, but Itchy has stopped listening. He's planning the move to extricate himself from this situation with a minimum of fuss. Just a few quick goodbyes and he can be off, or maybe see whether the others want to come with him, hit South Bar.

The MC has got all the girls up for auction to get on the stage now, ten or twelve of them. A few Itchy recognises, veterans, but new faces too. Some are swaying hips to offbeats of the background garage music, playing coquettish eye-catching with the audience. Some nervous like on the first day at school, wondering what they're doing there. Only one stands impassive: not nervous and not trying to tempt. The bearing of a real slave. Standing like a martyr. Like she had. Like Tina.

Itchy realises that he can't hang around for this, heart beating like he's drunk a gallon of espresso. He nudges Sean and mimes going for a piss. Then he turns and forces his way through the crowd behind and down the stairs, but past the toilets and through the heavy wood door, out on to the cheek-freezing street.

He's glad he's left the others behind now. Daniel is the sort of friend whose presence in his life makes Itchy believe there must be some goodness left in him. But sometimes he doesn't want to feel like that. Sometimes there is a comfort in being absorbed by the bad.

A break in the clouds is letting through the ember-light of a single, marooned star. Itchy gets his beanie out of his back pocket and pulls it down low over his eyes, so that a thick brow is settled over his vision, hiding the star and even the streetlight. He can see only the road in front of him as he zips up his coat and marches back towards the ghetto and the carpark. South Bar first, though. Another drink.

The ghetto isn't a real ghetto. It isn't a ghetto in the sense of a slum, though any holidaymakers who stay there are definitely 'slumming it'. It isn't a ghetto in the sense of state-provided flats, but all the apartments are built around a series of central squares, looking inwards like American housing projects. It isn't a ghetto because of social problems, though it is covered in graffiti, there are always drunks wandering the corridors and the lifts often smell of piss and sick, regularly don't work at all. It's not a ghetto in the sense of drug dealings and death, because, though drugs are easy enough to get hold of, most of the deaths occur up the mountain. It isn't even a ghetto because of crime, though it has to be said that most of Chamonix's relatively little crime is focused there. Most importantly, it's not a ghetto because people aren't trapped there, they have chosen to move there and they like it.

The ghetto *is* a ghetto by the dictionary definition: Cham Sud is *segregated* from the rest of town, separated by the river and by its own high walls; you have to pass through alley entrances or the Hades carpark to enter; those who live there are overwhelmingly *foreigners and minorities* and they do so for *economic and social reasons*, because it is far and away the cheapest area of Cham, and to be with their own kind; and it is an area *characterised by a single type of resident*, because they are all here for the mountains and the snow and the partying.

South Bar, in the heart of the Cham Sud square, is busy with Scandies. Actually, it's always busy with Scandies, it's a Scandie bar. Tonight, though, it is bustling and busting out at the seams with them. They are drunk to a blond-bonced man and chick. Bellowing above the music in their incomprehensible hurdy-gurd. Itchy wishes he hadn't bothered, by the time he's fought his way to the bar. He gets a demi, to get out quick, but the barman does a shooter with him and so Itchy buys one back. By which time he has started into conversation with the girl next to him.

She's a Stockholm student, Sophia, feathered hair, brown, not unusual actually, but against stereotype. She is short and from his higher vantage he can see quite a lot of the little couloir between her breasts. Which seems like the kind of place he'd like to be right now. So he gets more shots, for him and her and the barman, and then just for him and her. Her English is great, but he's only really listening enough to seem interested, to ask the right questions. Charm is just a gambit. She has never been abroad before on her own. Not that she's on her own, but her friends seem to have gone, she explains. He wonders vaguely whether he seems exotic to her, in the way that she would have to him, at her age. She can't be any more than nineteen. He doesn't ask, though, because to introduce the question raises the possibility of incompatibility. The decade that sits between them, among the empty glasses.

He starts getting the shots in lots of six; to save time wasted trying to catch the barman's eye, when he would rather be staring into hers. They do sambuca – cheap and quick. A finger licked, dipped and set on fire, which you can't blow out until you down your shot. He's seen someone's eyebrows singed away, with that pungent, death-camp, hair- and flesh-burning smell, when they blew too soon, mouth still full of spirit. Gas chambers next, staying on a theme, sucking caustic fumes from beneath the upturned glass with a straw. Pure alcohol, vaporised, atomised and absorbed into their bloodstreams in all its forgetting warmth. Then basketballs, sealed to their hands by the vacuum of evaporated spirit. Hands that are often brushing now, as they pass. Then lit in their mouths, her eyes dewy in their hesitancy, her lips well licked against the burn, by a tongue bubbled and pink like champagne. Head tilted back to hold the flame in place while he drops a pinch of cinnamon from above, which splutters into sparks like shooting stars, like sparklers. This evokes a craze among the other revellers – sambuca is now the dealer's choice. But Itchy has already won. He can see from how the wheel is rolling in its last slow spin that the ball may bounce with a few more sharp clicks, but is going to come to rest right on his number. Right on him. And the last thing he remembers is wiping a muddy streak of cinnamon from her cheek with a single finger, and her taking the finger into her mouth and holding it an instant against the sharpness of her teeth. And then he's pretty sure they left together. But not very sure. Not certain.

He's on the balcony. The light on the Aiguille de Midi is bright like the Pole Star. Something you can navigate by in this black, trackless world. Below him, two gendarmes are leading along a girl, wrapped in a blanket. She's walking on her own, but one of the gendarmes has an arm around her. Lending her support and holding the blanket in place. You couldn't really say for sure it was a girl, except that she's short so you assume so, and the hair that pokes from out of the tartan rug is feathered, brown and feathered. But Itchy's long gone now, far enough away on his booze journey to sleep, to sleep without dreams. He backs into the shadow as one of the gendarmes looks up, instinctively feels a need to hide. And then he goes inside, into the balm of his duvet. Sleeps.

It is 5 a.m. when Itchy is woken by his mobile phone, playing 'Dig Your Own Hole'. He wakes with a suddenness that scares him and a dread realisation, like a parent's, that for someone to phone him at this time of night it must be important. And that things as important as that are invariably bad things. So he pushes his mobile hard to his ear, as if its tightness there will hold the things that may be said in that little airlock a while longer. As if by stopping the words reaching the world he will be able to stop their meaning also. And a voice says simply: 'Remember the game!' and then laughs, and the phone goes dead. And Itchy thinks, 'Shit,' because they're on to him again, and he was doing so well.

Oh! that the Desert were my dwelling-place,
With one fair Spirit for my minister,
That I might all forget the human race,
And, hating no one, love but only her!

Byron, Childe Harold's Pilgrimage

December 25th, 3.37 p.m.

It's a white Christmas. Too white to ski. The wind is blowing the snow into waltzes out on the balcony, where the walls whirl it in on itself. The falling flakes are as big as silver coins. Snowmen, tumbling unassembled, like the toys when Itchy was growing up.

It used to be Airfix planes for Christmas, in brittle grey, with a pristine tube of sniff-proof glue and a squat pot of khaki paint. Then Zoids – spiders and crabs that walked ponderously, buzzing like glass-trapped wasps, and then broke. Lego was the king of junior DIY, though, the toy with the capacity to be remade a thousand times, that was itself remade: as pirates; knights; spacemen; BMX bandits; cowboys; cavalry; stuntmen; commandos; robots; Robin Hoods; musketeers; dinosaurs; deep-sea divers; Davy Crocketts; crocodile hunters; time travellers; ninjas; skateboarders; Phileas Foggs – charting the trends in the rest of the toy market like a chronicler. Now they do Lego Harry Potter and Lego *Star Wars*.

Star Wars itself and Action Man, both died away for a decade or more, have only just re-emerged; as if to claim the children of those who loved them first – but really to reclaim the fathers. When Itchy sees the figures in the supermarkets he is transfixed. Action Man's dependable, chiselled face, cropped hair, short straight scar, and the memories they stand in for, make Itchy long to have a child of his own. Something he can love more than himself. Something to shake him out of this nihilist world of self-indulgence. A child might mean more than the eternal life of his genes, it might yet mean salvation.

They didn't buy toys from Carrefour, though, Itchy, Sean and Aussie Mark. They bought a case of champagne substitute, at ninety cents a bottle. They bought a chicken as big as a turkey, because the real turkeys had all gone. They bought vodka and gin and apple juice and tonic. And vegetables. French vegetables are misshapen, but consistently so, old fashioned looking. They are gnarled and dirty, dappled in their colouring, but they taste a thousand times better than the uniform hydroponics clones churned out back home. They bought snowman's nose carrots and a cabbage and potatoes, lots of potatoes. Under duress from Aussie Mark they also bought sprouts. Aussie Mark grew up with barbecues for Christmas, doesn't realise that sprouts are not an aspect of the British experience to be lovingly recreated away from the parental table.

The chicken is yellow, like the Lego men, corn fed, or maybe fed with a dye. Its skin is flecked with tiny bumps, where feathers used to be, like shaved testicles. They have striped its salted and buttered back with Parma ham in place of bacon, which is too much of a delicacy to find.

'So you reckon we need to put foil over it?' says Sean.

'Yeah, to keep the moisture in,' Itchy responds.

'But we don't want it moist, bro,' Aussie Mark now, 'we want its skin to go crispy.'

'Trust me,' Itchy says, ripping a sheet from the light-sabre roll in front of him.

Aussie Mark laughs. 'Trust me, he's saying, the man who considers putting mayo on his ham baguette to be the height of culinary excellence. I haven't even seen you near the oven yet, bro.'

'All right, we'll ask Suzi when she gets here. But we need to get this thing cooking now, it's going to take hours as it is.'

'Hey, what's the similarity between an oven and a woman?' Sean asks, eyebrows raised in expectation of his own punchline. 'You've got to get them both warmed up before you can put the meat in.'

Itchy allows himself a chuckle, even though he's heard the joke before, and sets about putting the sheet of foil across the chicken; trying to get it to lie loosely over the bird's broad back, the way his mum does it.

Sean pops the ninety-cent champagne, the plastic cork ricochets, rubber bullet, around the room. Foam from the phallic bottle spurts over Sean's hand like a solo orgasm. That's why champagne is supposed to be an aphrodisiac, Itchy thinks. Human beings are pathetically two dimensional.

Suzi is looking great, when she and Daniel arrive, her brown hair in ringlets like chocolate money. She's carrying two more bottles of wine, which are blatantly three steps up from the stuff the guys bought. Daniel, behind, is carrying the small plug-in oven from their apartment, only a block away, the flex trailing over his shoulder like a dog lead. He sets it on the cracked-tile counter, which would be a breakfast bar if such things had been invented when it was made.

Itchy all but shoehorned the chicken into their own small oven. Aussie Mark had to agree in the end that the foil thing was a good idea, because the top of the bird was pretty much pressed against the ceiling element. Itchy carries on peeling potatoes now, after kissing Suzi hello. She smells of onion and raw meat, and produces a little figure – like a voodoo doll – of sausage and sage. She makes him dance along the counter until one of his legs falls off.

'It's the rapist,' she says, pressing the leg back into place, then rolling a tiny sausage-meat penis, almost absent-mindedly, 'we're going to cook him alive.'

Everyone knows about the rapist now, the creature that preys in the carpark, floors beneath their feet. At least the locals and the workers know; unimportant things are never revealed to the tourists. Things like avalanches and crevasse deaths and cliff falls and helicopter crashes and spines shattered on sliding chairlifts. And now rapes. There have been three attacks already, the latest barely a week ago. One British girl, one Swedish, one French; a beast with cosmopolitan tastes, or a plain opportunist.

Itchy finishes the potatoes, which lie plump and pale on a bed of their own peelings next to Suzi's sausage-meat rapist, but they are too fat and happy to be victims and look more like his over-pampered harem. While they are sliced in half, and once again for the larger lumps, the chicken is taken out of the oven and the foil lifted to allow the stuffing-man to be pushed inside. The bird takes him in its gaping hole with contemptuous ease, and a half-onion slab is slotted in place in the cave mouth to block escape.

The other oven is heated while the potatoes boil up and Suzi and Daniel get involved with a glass of the champagne substitute each.

'Merry Christmas,' Daniel says, and looks into each person's eyes as he chinks, in unshammed sincerity.

Daniel is selfless to a degree incomprehensible to Itchy: his classes have been snowed off today, but instead of being delighted that for once he doesn't have to work on Christmas Day, he is sad for the clients who have missed one of their six ski days per year.

When Daniel kisses Suzi Merry Christmas, though, they kiss with soft, barely parted lips, like a prelude to a first smooch, not like a long-comfortable couple, and even Itchy can tell that there is nowhere in the world Daniel would rather be than by her side.

When Itchy and Sean go out to the balcony to get in the plastic table and chairs it's still snowing hard, as if feathers have been thrown in the air. The wolf-man trapped in a bantam factory farm. Or a pillow fight in a girls' school. Late night. Squealing. Bare thighed.

The picnic table is wiped dry with one of Sean's T-shirts, and put at the end of the real table to create dining space for five. Aussie Mark clears the empty green bottles from the sideboard, not enough for many verses of a child's song, but sufficient so that they are all a little unsteady as the final preparations for dinner are made.

Suzi stirs the gravy, truffle-dark and oil-slicked with puddles of chicken fat. The granules are imported; Oxo cubes sell for more than lumps of hash in some expat communities and are invariably harder to get hold of.

A schoolboy Itchy was once sold a lump of welders' wax in place of hash – a heat conductor – he put blisters on his fingers and thumb like popping paper trying to burn it to crumble.

Sean carves the Christmas chicken surprisingly well.

'You make a good daddy,' Suzi says, smiling over her shoulder at his efforts, while she continues to stir.

Really Sean makes the worst daddy: Itchy is the oldest; Aussie Mark the biggest; Daniel the most sensible; Sean has no qualifications for the role at all, Itchy thinks, except that he is the only one to actually have a kid.

Sean has apparently never seen his daughter, which is a source of curiously scant remorse. She is the family of another boy now, no doubt made a man by the experience, and Sean has no claim to her but his genes, nothing to gain from an attempt at contact but debts, and so leaves well alone.

He gets a spoon and starts to stick it into where the bird's vital organs must once have been safely caged, freeing the onion from what is now just a bony tent.

Suzi says, 'Let me, I want to get the rapist out,' and she skips on the spot clapping her hands, deliberately malcoordinatedly, like a little girl.

She upends the carcass and the stuffing man pours out with the last of the juices, like a parody of birth and death by an experimental Czech puppet theatre on eighties Channel 4. He lies there, bleached by the heat, in a pool of blood, arms and legs splayed.

Suzi sniggers as she executes him, beheaded with a spoon. 'Be afraid, boys,' she says, 'be very afraid.'

Aussie Mark and Daniel do the wishbone, Sean does the commentary.

'Here they are, the two contenders for the title, pinkie fingers poised for battle. In the red corner, all the way from Australia, raised by dingoes but kicked out of the pack for having no table manners: Mountainous Maaark the Maraauuder. And in the blue corner, weighing in at twelve and a half stone...less than his opponent. From some unknown but opulent suburb in the Home Counties, I give you: Danieeel the Daandyyy. Now I want a good clean fight from both of you, no twisting, no ear biting. Grip the bone tight in your little finger, and when I give the signal, commence pulling. May the winner be granted their wish.'

It slips out of his finger at the first try, but at the second Daniel takes it: Aussie Mark's side snapped clean in two. Daniel holds aloft the broken bone that is the vestige of the competition and his prize and says:

'I wish for powder, powder over my head, and on my day off too.'

Suzi says that you're not supposed to tell anyone your wish or it won't come true, or worse it will, but turned, like a bet with the devil.

But Daniel just grins, and kisses her forehead and keeps holding up the two-thirds of a wishbone, like it's the World Cup.

Suzi seems a bit peeved that he's not taking her seriously.

'That's not how we do it in my family,' she says, and she says it with just a hint that somehow her family is self-evidently better than Daniel's. That if her family has a way of doing things that is different, then the fault must lie with those, like him, who differ from it.

And Itchy sees a chink in her armour. Or a spot left by the holder's thumb and index finger that wasn't coated by the invulnerability potion she was dipped in. The pride of a tragic heroine. Something someone like him could use as an in, an entry, if he didn't like her too much to fuck up a happy life, if Daniel wasn't his friend.

The chicken is the nicest Itchy has ever tasted, except for a barbecue he had on a beach one time. The wine that Daniel and Suzi brought round is delicious, it has a Southern-belle, farmyardy taste, wholesome but sexy, like Daisy Duke. At least that's what Sean says, doing an impression of a TV wine buff. The roast potatoes are underwhelming, possibly a bit too much oil was used, or they might have needed to cook for a bit longer to crisp up. The veg, well, the veg is veg, it's not supposed to be the main event, and isn't, but it's still damn good.

'All in all, that was a pretty fucking fierce meal,' Aussie Mark says, mopping up his gravy with a rag of yesterday's baguette, 'now what's for dinner?'

Itchy knows what Mark means; the food seems to have rushed past him. He tries to recreate the chicken's tang, salivating as if this will refresh some mental palate. He fails, so he runs two fingers through the last smears of gravy on his plate instead and licks them, leaving behind tracks like a skier's.

'Isn't it weird to be sitting here in the aftermath of Christmas dinner, when there's a monster that might be stalking underneath us?' Suzi says.

'He won't be stalking on Christmas Day,' Itchy says, head tilting, but eyes not moving from his plate, 'even monsters have friends.'

'I reckon he is,' says Aussie Mark, 'I reckon he's just hiding out down there in wait for a Christmas present in new Christmas knickers.'

'It's not funny, you know,' Suzi says. 'It's really quite frightening for us girls. I've got friends who won't go out at night on their own now.'

'So let's go down and look for him,' says Sean, 'work off a bit of dinner. We always used to go for a Christmas walk in my house, amazing who you'd bump into…'

'I know: Hide and seek in the garages,' Aussie Mark interrupts excitedly. 'Suzi and Daniel can seek together – we hide, first circle only, though, or it'll go on for weeks – loser does all the washing up.'

'No washing up ever again for anyone who finds the rapist!' says Sean.

The game is afoot. Suzi and Daniel have been given head-torches, Cyclops beams for peering into the murkiest recesses. The boys have one minute's head start. They bang into each other, charging down the spiral lighthouse stairway into the carpark basement. Aussie Mark and Sean have pocketed a couple of beers each. Itchy has a three-quarters-full bottle of vodka. Aussie Mark, the first to the door, slams it open with a bang that reverberates around the still, grey caverns of the carpark. There is no movement in them but the flicker of the strip lights that haven't yet died. The boys are paused, on the threshold of this other world. Heads turning this way and that, looking for a clue as to which direction the best hiding place will lie. Sean and Aussie Mark explode off simultaneously to left and right, away into the gloom, leaving Itchy alone.

Being Christmas week, this first part of the carpark is full; there are any number of hiding places behind bonnets, or under the floors of four-by-fours. Itchy considers briefly clinging to the spare wheel of a Suzuki that is backed against the wall. With his feet off the ground he would be immune to searchlight sweeps under the cars. But he doubts whether he could stay hanging on for too long, and in any case would be unable to swig from his vodka. He lifts the lid of one of the large, wheeled vault-bins, but though there is space for two or three of him inside, the smell makes him gag. It is putrid, a stink of disease and rottenness. Plague.

With maybe only twenty seconds left to hide Itchy is still standing in the centre of a bay, as blatant as a breeze-block in the fridge. Staring at a sign in five languages, which explains that the management company takes no responsibility – superfluously, since you only have to look around to see that.

Something draws him to the grating: he walks there almost without thought, as if a blacked-out memory makes him head for that darkest patch of shadow, or as if mesmerised by an Alpine Rasputin into doing his evil bidding. The grating groans with rust and disapproval as Itchy lifts it. He has to crouch to get into the cramp crawlspace behind. He is in a tiny low cupboard of a room, maybe originally intended as storage space, but clearly unused in years, or ever. Maybe it's an aberration of the architect: a vestigial tail; an appendix; a God-shaped gap in the psyche.

Through the iron grate Itchy can see quite a lot of the carpark. But it looks rather as he imagines flies see the world: numerous tiny segments that must be pieced together to get the real image. Itchy leans back against the wall and draws his knees up to his chest like a frightened child, but finds that he is quite comfortable in this spot, in this new lair. He is pleased with its discovery, not only as a hiding-hole in which he is sure he will not be found, but as a little place he can call his own. A rare gift in a world of small shared spaces. Somewhere he might come and think, to be alone. It is almost like coming home, to sit in this new den. In fact, he feels as if he could easily have been here before. He takes a swig of vodka and watches his weightless, floating breath dance with the motes of dust he has stirred up in the beams of faint divided lights that come through the gaps in the grate. The whole carpark is layered with dust, not the sort you get in places rarely cleaned, but a special white powder that forms in places that have never been cleaned, and never will be. It is like the concrete's own attempt to mop up the oil slicks and the sick and the melt that drips from the undersides of cars and the rusty dribbles from the *Blade Runner* pipes that wind serpentine about the ceilings, divided, rejoining, patched, spray-painted, insulation hanging open like slashed bellies.

Soon Itchy sees the head-torches of Suzi and Daniel, waving as they walk. Suzi's silhouette is trim and well formed. The differences between the two of them are framed by the sections of the grille, like diagrams: her hips gently rounded; his straight and narrow, thin by comparison to the square that contains his shoulders; the gentle jut of her breasts, when she turns side-on to look behind the very Suzuki that Itchy had briefly considered as his refuge; the slide of her thighs down from her bubble of a bum.

When did you begin to hate them so much? Itchy asks the rapist, who he finds he can feel, here behind the grating, in this little bit of limbo. When did it stop being enough to admire and marvel at the ways they were made? When did it start not to be enough just to fuck them? When did you have to start hurting them as well? Did your looks go? Did your scars begin to show? Because there are places, there are women, good-looking women, who will sleep with you. For money, yes, which is perhaps still hate, but less hurtful, less cruel than what you are doing.

Suzi calls out, 'I can see you,' but it is a trick, a child's trick that will not work on Itchy or the others, if they can even hear. But he loves her for it. He loves her for still believing that such a thing might work, or for not believing but still trying. Itchy loves them all, because they are all beautiful Don Quixotes – still ready to ride out for romance, still eager to believe in a world that doesn't exist. And he wishes that world did exist. He wishes that there was one special person waiting for him out there. He wishes that he could be content with her, to never want another, to grow old gracefully in her arms. But he is not willing to go along – to pretend it's true, when it's not.

Itchy knows he's not really a man: he's just a pig-dog that for some reason looks like one. But the thing is that no man looks anything like the little figures in the top hats that you see on top of wedding cakes – that some women see all around them.

Daniel and Suzi move on, beams barely flashing across Itchy's rusted trellis. They walk hand in hand under the low ceilings, feet crunching over scrabble-squares of broken glass; not looking back, because that's the rule of the Underworld, and because they think they can go forwards with each other for ever.

*

Aussie Mark was found first, too big to be easily hidden. But he has long since finished the washing up by the time Itchy returns to the flat; hours after the other four finally departed the carpark, shouting that the game was over, telling him that he had won. Even after the last of the vodka was gone, Itchy lingered in his cage. And when he eventually comes back to the others – who are watching a DVD of *The Great Escape*, for old time's sake – he is happy to slurringly announce that this has been his best Christmas ever.

**Sheffield University
Department of English Literature**
Course: Romantic Period Literature
Tutor: Dr Ragworth

The following extract, reproduced with permission from *Stanzas, Scars and Scandals – A Dramatic History of the Life of Lord Byron* by H. J. Ragworth, is required reading and will form the basis of a discussion in next week's tutorial on the historical events surrounding the summer at Villa Diodati.

Dark Summer

The carriage is identical to the exiled Emperor Napoleon's travelling carriage. Aside from a crest in gold, it is black and grey, drab, but the summit of specification and technology, drawn by a team of four fast duns. If this is not Bonaparte's coach, and that seems impossible in these days, then it must have been hand made to order at vast cost by an admirer of his, a deeply deviant and contrarian position, and a man either immensely wealthy, or careless of debt.

It is mud spattered from a long journey through Europe, where its very presence has thrust two fingers at the lately reinstated French king, the only monarch more corpulent, regressive and worthless than England's own regent. The Revolution that juddered across the globe is over with Waterloo, the reactionary status quo resurrected, an age of hope finally ended. Perhaps traces of the blooded soil of Waterloo are even now caked upon the coach's underbelly, because the travellers had stopped to take in those fields of still-recent slaughter. They had galloped across the churned plain where fifteen thousand fellow Britains had fallen.

Like Napoleon, the man inside the carriage – Lord Byron – is now an exile; but he has not been marooned on an island, rather driven from one. In the third canto of his great poem, *Childe Harold's Pilgrimage*, Byron will intimate that this flight is a glorious self-imposed emigration. It isn't. The poet faced a very real and urgent need to escape, with every chance of mob violence in pursuit of him and barely ahead of the bailiffs at every stage. He has spiralled as far as aristocracy can, slid almost to outlaw. His crimes, exposed in gossip not law courts, still sufficient that he might be attacked, in England, practically with impunity. His few friends left feared his assassination if he remained.

The poet's great creations, Childe Harold, Don Juan, Manfred, the Corsair, all are, or will be, dark and brooding figures, like Byron himself. Heroes condemned to 'Cain's unresting doom' for some unrevealed but unforgivable long past Stygian crime. Dissolute and damned protagonists, whom the public linked entirely with the character of the poet himself; but in a romantic manner at first, which temporarily forgave such intimations of depravity. The eponymous hero of *Childe Harold's Pilgrimage* – the poem suggested – though jaded from carnal delights, might yet be saved by a pure woman; and the beauties of London had queued to throw their 'purity' at his creator.

All dark cursed heroes still to come, in poem, novel and film, will have a tang of this creator about them, a whiff of Lord George Noel Gordon Byron. His own crimes, once whispered, are now writ large: incest and bisexuality; sodomy, with men and women, a peccadillo punished by hanging in enlightened England; perhaps even pederasty, though such things are harder to judge, since there is no age of consent for boys. Byron's heroes owe much to Milton's Satan, and Byron himself has fallen from being the most beloved angel of society to one cast out in shame and sin, as forcibly as the lord of shadow spat from the heavens.

Like Bonaparte – that squat Corsican, long England's devil, now also deposed – Byron is of the Jacobin age, born a year before the Bastille fell. Like the young Napoleon, the young Byron has championed freedom: his maiden speech in the House of Lords was to protest the rights of the squalid poor, the Nottinghamshire frame-breakers. In vain, since the act was passed, their leaders were hanged and left to rot in municipal gibbets. Byron wreaked revenge in the bedchamber: a very public cuckolding of his opponent in the motion; whose wife all but lost her brittle sanity in love to the poet.

But the glories of the French Revolution led to bloodbaths too. The guillotine's thirst was slaked, not just with the people's enemies, but also their first leaders. The hero-soldier, Napoleon the democrat, champion of Liberty, became dictator; and now the *ancien régime* is returned. The world has turned full circle. And the poet, snatched from obscurity – who woke to find himself famous – is shunned and alone, barely four years later, heavily armed and fearful.

Not completely alone, though. In the dark carriage are two others: Byron's faithful retainer, Fletcher, and a newly acquired physician, himself laden with literary ambition, saturnine good looks and a martyred manner, Dr Polidori.

Even in the triple gloom of night, a covered carriage and adversity, Byron's eyes are as coruscating and razored as the blade of the swordstick he carries, hidden in the cane that helps him walk. He has been lame from birth – one foot withered like a cloven hoof – and limps to a degree that he bears with deep humiliation, fiercely hubristic as he is. But, though he might sometimes rest his hand upon the door frame as he crosses the threshold, ladies have been known to faint when Lord Byron enters a room.

Profound as Hamlet, proud as Faust, marked like Cain, Byron is a man of the age. An age of satanic mills and postillions with shrapnel-loaded blunderbusses. An age of protest, scandal and war. Volcanic eruptions have blackened the skies this year, a portent perhaps, or merely geology; but this season will see storms not experienced in Europe in recorded history, mists and fogs unknown.

It will be a dark summer.

The coach stops at Geneva at one of the many Hôtel d'Angleterres now sprung up in the region, catering for the fashion of Grand Tours. A fashion that Byron himself has helped to promote in his verses. Travel weary and troubled, Byron enters his age as a hundred in the hotel register.

Staying at this same establishment, beneath the eye of Mont Blanc, one Percy Bysshe Shelley. Son of a Member of Parliament and grandson of a baron, Shelley was expelled from Oxford for his fervent promotion of atheism. Of late he has spent time in Ireland, trying to fuel revolt's embers there, against the absentee landlords and brutal British rule. Yet he is still only twenty-four, four years younger even than Byron.

Like Byron, Shelley is handsome to the point of girlishness, though more pale and delicate in frame, apologetically tall. Like Byron he is a poet; but, thus far, a gulf behind in acclaim. Like Byron he sleeps with loaded pistols in his bed. Like Byron he practises a form of vegetarianism, though that name will not appear for many decades yet. Shelley avoids animal flesh from morality; for Byron it is vanity – the fear of returning to the fat of his youth – and when he lapses, he can fall upon a joint of lamb like a thunderbolt, as readily as he has upon the chambermaids en route.

Shelley is the more radical, in religion and politics, but there is a great deal of similarity in view between the poets on these issues too. Though Byron is certain only that *he* will never see heaven, while Shelley publicly asserts that no one will.

Both men despise war and its wastes. Shelley is a pacifist, which rubs forcefully against his penchant for firearms and republicanism and indeed his nature: at Eton, he was known as 'Mad Shelley' for his violent outbursts.

Byron is also, more famously, dubbed 'mad', along with 'bad', and 'dangerous to know'; he practises hard at fencing, pistols and boxing, and is not averse to fighting and duelling at all. Which is fortunate, for one with such tastes as he has: for other people's wives and sons and his own half-sister.

There are more connections: both men have left behind a wife in England, with child and despair; wives they treated worse than anything else they may have done or will do. But sins like these are more common for young aristocrats and far more easily forgiven, in a society led by men who treat all women little better.

Shelley eloped with his first wife when she was only sixteen, but at heart he is an advocate of free love, not marriage. He frequently exhorted her to sleep with his friends and, leading by example, himself has slept with hers.

He has left her now, and left the country, travels with two more ladies, if at seventeen and eighteen they are ready to be called that: the stepsisters Claire Clairmont and Mary Godwin.

Mary has pedigree: fruit of a feminist writer and an anarchist publisher. Soon she will be Mary Shelley – the poet, advocate of freedom, enchained once more – the name under which she will publish her novel. She is pixie pretty, slim and quick as a Sicilian stiletto, dangerously clever.

Claire – her stepsister – has had a brief fling with Byron shortly before he fled London. She is now pregnant, though perhaps even she doesn't know it yet. And no one will ever be certain which of the poets, Shelley or Byron, was the father.

Friendship between these two men is as inevitable as dusk. But strangely the twain – so entangled; in the same profession; of such similar views, age and lineage; who moved in the same circles – have never met, until now, far from home, by a lake as wide as the Styx, under the shadow of the jagged Alps.

Byron rents a balustraded mansion – the Villa Diodati, where Milton himself once stayed. He fills it with a menagerie of half-tame creatures: eight enormous dogs; three monkeys; five cats; squirrels; rabbits; raptors.

The Shelley party – who Claire dubs the 'tribe of Otaheite philosophers', after the promiscuous islanders – spend much of the summer there too.

Where such debauched reputations collide, infamy is sure to follow, and the Villa Diodati is watched from hotels across the lake, through telescopes hired to tourists for the purpose.

Chamonix and Mont Blanc, with its glittering spires of ice, lie not forty miles behind them. Over the summer, all of them will spend time there. Shelley will leave a trail of scorn in his wake, signing his profession in hotel registers as *atheist, philanthropist, revolutionary*. Words that stink of blood, damnation and treason, to the other, more civilised, English travellers forced to read them, sometimes in orderly queues. For his onward destination, he will mark only *l'enfer* – hell.

Byron is more outraged when he hears a woman describe

Chamonix as 'so rural' – as if it were Highgate, or Hampstead, or Brompton, or Hayes – 'rural!' – in the midst of gargantuan rocks, dense pines, torrents, glaciers, and summits of eternal snow – 'rural!'

On all of the group, the valley has a staggering effect. Mary will set part of her novel in Chamonix: the bitter, threat-laden argument in which her misformed creature demands to be given a mate; the crux of all the death and woe that follow. And the endless crevasses and glass-cliff seracs she sees there inspire her denouement, at the North Pole.

Shelley, so confronted and broken sighted by the monstrosity of terrain, comes as close to a religious experience as such a hardened non-believer can. Already taking laudanum for his nervous attacks, he is literally overwhelmed by his own fragility before the enormity of such forces of nature. But scenes that for some inspire fear of God, for Shelley can prove only that there is no such thing. The towered certainty of death within the ravaged peaks is final evidence that there is no single intellect governing the world. His thoughts provoke perhaps his greatest work, elementally entitled: *Mont Blanc*.

The inevitable friendship of the poets sidelines Dr Polidori. Something they do not help by their treatment of him. For all their republican pretensions, the aristocrats look down on John Polidori, a tradesman, a mere physician – though he is the youngest man ever to graduate from Edinburgh in medicine, still only twenty-one. Perhaps what is harder, they mock his literary work; they inform him that his writing is laughable. Polidori is not a man who takes words lightly.

Nor should he; he is from a line of men of letters. Italian émigrés; revolutionaries whom the poets would probably support, if they gave Polidori the courtesy of listening. If he survives long enough, Polidori will see his nephew, Dante Gabriel Rossetti, achieve worldwide fame, and his niece Christina Rossetti likewise.

But Pollydolly, as the poets mockingly call him, lives in ways likely to shorten his time on earth. He sprains his ankle, goaded into jumping from a balcony by Byron. And a later incident enrages him so much that the doctor, eyes fired with hatred, challenges Shelley to a duel. Only Byron steps in, with a glacial application to fight in place of the pacifist, and Polidori has to back down, further humiliated and isolated. Not only is Byron his employer, but a duel with the lord would likely end in a death, and not that of Byron.

Polidori vents his rage on the Genevans instead, Lilliputian watchmakers, wealthily self-absorbed in the locked gates of their new republic, freed from Napoleon with other men's blood, the epitome of all despicable.

A warrant is issued for the doctor's arrest after various drunken incidents and a physical attack on a local chemist.

So Polidori doesn't accompany the two poets when they spend some days sailing around the vast lake, anti-clockwise, widdershins. Visiting the house of Gibbon, tracing enlightened Rousseau's steps, peering in horror at the columned dungeon recesses and lonely hangman's beam of Château Chillon.

A tempest explodes on their little craft one night, still far from the shaled harbour to which they head. Storms have characterised this so-called summer, but this one is as fierce as Jehovah. Wind-driven lake waves smash over the deck. Struggling against such forces, their boatman breaks the rudder. It seems certain they will be swamped. Lame Byron is a mythically strong swimmer – he has swum the same Hellespont as made Leander famous – even in such cruel water as this, he thinks the shore well within his reach. Shelley cannot swim at all; humiliated, he will not have his friend's life risked for him in this new duel. He grasps hard the iron rings of an anvil locker and expresses a fatalist and firm decision to go down with the boat.

It is no one's night to die. Somehow, rudderless, they stay afloat and skulk into port, like Coleridge's ship of curse and ghosts. An impoverished goitrous and wretched crowd has gathered to witness the landing in such weather, as if it were a medieval miracle.

The sheer insufferable black of this summer spurs Byron to write his bleakest poem, indeed one of the bleakest poems in the English language: 'Darkness'. A tale of the world engulfed in the void of a godless universe, of suffering and relentless soul-swallowing futility.

In the storms that continue to oppress, even the large villa becomes claustrophobic. A mood of despondent neurosis and superstition takes over, and something else, something discarnate. They begin to read each other terror tales by flickering candlelight and vivid lightning bursts. German *Fantasmagoriana* and English Gothic.

After Byron reads from Coleridge's 'Christabel', of a snake-skinned seductress, Shelley, shrieking and clutching his head, flees the room, convinced that he had seen eyes staring into him from the breasts of Mary.

Byron frequently fornicates with Claire, though he doesn't much care for her. She is too plain and too common for his tastes, but she is young, and she is there. Claire writes that she would ten times prefer to be his male friend than his mistress, a sign of a deeper platonic love perhaps – or more probably that she was aware of his tendency to tire sooner of his female lovers than his male.

When the company tires of their Teutonic ghost tales, it is proposed that each of them should write their own Gothic short, of entanglement with the ghastly and supernatural.

Four tales were told. Claire never produced a story. Mary's was eventually to be expanded into her masterpiece, a novel that affected the world: *Frankenstein, the Modern Prometheus*. A story of Geneva and Chamonix, of relentless pursuit and living hell.

And what of the other three tales, the works of Polidori, Byron and Shelley? They were told, on the original dark and stormy night, but little more than that is known. Polidori made some claims to have written down the stories himself, and also alluded to the fact that an intellectual matriarch who lived nearby may have somehow procured each teller's notes. There is occasional speculation that Claire Clairmont, publisher's daughter, who did not tell a tale, perhaps had the foresight to jot down those of the others. The truth is, they have never emerged, so must, like a mariner who does not voyage home, eventually be presumed lost.

Pinnacles of snow, intolerably bright, part of the chain connected with Mont Blanc shone through the clouds at intervals on high. I never knew, I never imagined what mountains were before. The immensity of these aeriel summits excited, when they suddenly burst upon the sight, a sentiment of ecstatic wonder, not unallied to madness...One would think that Mont Blanc, like the god of the Stoics, was a vast animal, and the frozen blood forever circulated through his stony veins.

Shelley

January 1st, 12.18 p.m.

Itchy wakes to hear a toilet flushing against his ear, from the flat next door. And then, from upstairs, there are shrieks and groans and bangs from a madman, or idiot-boy adult; until he is soothed by a calm second party and the clatters and unintelligible cries cease. Noise is always a problem in big blocks, but the overhead nutter is peculiar to Josey's place, so Itchy knows where he is, before opening his eyes.

There was probably an inevitability about being in bed with Josey: New Year's Eve is too hectic to invest time in pulling strangers. He likes waking up with her anyway. He can cuddle Josey, there is a comfort in being with her that other people might find in a real relationship. They care about each other, he likes being with her, and fucking her and laughing with her, and certainly going out drinking with her. But whatever the other thing is that's necessary, it isn't there. He could never settle down with her, less even than he could with anyone else. And to pretend he might would be false to them both. But Josey doesn't need him to pretend that anyway. She kisses him good morning like a mother – which is some fucked-up Oedipal shit, considering what that mouth has been doing in the night – and springs out of bed naked to make some coffee. Showing him the place where her name is tattooed over a butt beginning to lose its battle with gravity.

Itchy has slept with well over two hundred women. Which even to him sounds like quite a lot, said quickly; but it's not really. He discarded his virginity at fifteen and is now fast approaching thirty; two hundred is barely more than one a month. Though of course it didn't usually work like that. Sometimes he'd go out with a girl he found special, even believed himself to love, and manage to remain faithful for a little while. Life could slip by in a relatively contented way. Other times he's scored three or four in a week, though he couldn't seem to beat that. Not that he did keep score, nothing so childish. Nothing premeditated. The count itself is only an educated guess. An estimate reached during a night of drink-deprived insomnia; when clarity replaced the usual angry-drumming agony of sleeplessness and for entertainment he tried to recall every clinched kiss of his life.

Women's mouths taste metallic when they're turned on, Itchy thinks, really turned on, like they are the first time. Coppery. In books it's blood that tastes coppery. Blood can taste of different things, though: pain; fear; revenge; black pudding. Copper is the taste of women. You can smell it too, but it smells a bit different, more like solder – metallic but also live – maybe because copper doesn't smell. That's only Itchy's experience, but it is quite wide. He never set out to sleep with a lot of people, though, that's just how it happened. It's an occupational hazard, in some ways, the repetitive stress risk of a resort worker.

It started before that, of course, before Cham; though even in his youth Itchy knew he was nothing special. He's not one of those guys who reckon they can't tell what's attractive either. Macho men always say they can't spot good looks: 'I dunno, he's a bloke, inne', or similarly dumb platitudes.

Marty, his best mate at uni, always maintained that was bullshit: 'Of course they can tell, how would they not be able to tell? It's just a matter of proportion – some things fit, some are less appropriate. Wait until a good-looking guy starts talking to their girlfriend and see how quickly they develop a sense of another man's attractiveness.'

Even what little Itchy once saw in himself is dwindling, though. His cheeks are now a little too podgy to be described as 'chiselled'. His hair, though still there, has been losing seats as slowly and certainly as Conservatism, through about the same years.

Girls say it's in his smile, but probably it's not even that – it's just desire. Everyone and maybe even everything wants to be desired. When you have a genuine hunger for someone they can feel that, and Itchy has a generous hunger. He finds something in almost every girl and every woman that he can desire. To the point that he actually finds it quite hard to communicate with those few he sees nothing in at all.

It's not a straight looks thing either, it's more often something from the inside. And what he can see in them, they see reflected in him. Itchy is like a mirror – but not a straight one that shows the blackheads and golfball skin of cellulite – some kind of tricksy fairground gizmo, that shows only what you want to see.

That's why they like him, and maybe partly that's why he

likes them. Because he likes to be desired too, everyone does. And everyone likes to do things they're good at. Itchy is good at pulling, because they sense that he likes them, which makes them like him, which makes him like them more, which makes him even better at pulling, so he likes to do it more. It's a circle. Not exactly a vicious circle. Not vicious like a pitbull anyway. More like an old, incontinent basset hound: slightly pathetic; always unsatisfied; weary; sad; and condemned to live out in the cold.

Josey has got a magazine rack in her toilet and, sitting there, comfortable enough with her not to care for how long, Itchy flicks idly through some of them. *More*s mostly, with their 'positions of the month', and more sex than the last night of a Club 18–30 holiday. One of the mags has a self-help quiz in it: 'Are you an alcoholic', and Itchy starts to do it. He scores quite highly on the first questions, but these things are always full of shit, and he's too hung over to be bothered to finish it.

Itchy and Josey eat a lunchtime breakfast of bacon and eggs, with fried baguette. The bacon was presumably brought from home, because it's proper British bacon, from Denmark. The French have never got the hang of it, despite the refined congregations of pork products in their delicatessens.

Itchy is reclothed in the booze-stained detritus of last night, Josey is in a vest top that makes her nipples stand out and pink velour lounging trousers – no one calls them 'tracksuits' or 'jogging bottoms' any more, because no one who wears them does track or goes jogging. In fact they are the sort of trousers that the über-fat sport more than anyone else, for whom elasticated waistbands are the only comfort left, food apart. Josey looks good in them, sexy, like a chav-slut; though she's anything but underclass.

For Itchy, the only ways of giving meaning to today are going to be to start drinking again or to go skiing. Either of these will blanket life's pointlessness, like a court-bound paedophile under a policeman's coat. He hasn't skied with Josey yet this season, so they decide to hit Grands Montets together.

Itchy mops yolk and cureful bacon fat from his plate, while he watches Josey get ready. The apartment is tiny, even by Cham Sud standards, but she has it to herself. There is a photo frame that shows a large grinning family on a lawn as green as billiards and cricket. Itchy's own home life was fractured by a bitter divorce, which left him unwilling to side fully with either parent, and such pictures are conspicuously absent from his flat. But then, there is no such clutter from Sean or Aussie Mark either. There just isn't sufficient room to allow memories a physical form in their shared studio. Objects must be chosen for their function, not for what they represent. Sentimentality requires space.

There's a light dusting of snow on the ground, only enough to stop pizza sticking to the pan, but it might translate into powder up high. Josey kicks it about with her board-boots as she traverses the Cham Sud square and then does a funny trot to catch up with Itchy again. He's carrying her flower-graphicked deck, on which she's painted the words 'all guts, no nuts'.

She stops him as they're about to enter the flat and says, 'Itchy, you're a better person than you think you are,' and then she kisses him.

Aussie Mark is sitting in his boxers, on the sofa that doubles as Itchy's bed; watching TV, although he's flicking through the channels faster than he would be able to take it in, even if he did speak French. He jigs his knee up and down whenever he's not flicking channel, always moving.

'Sean come back last night?' Itchy asks.

'Dunno, bro, I was drunker than an Abo on dole day. Don't remember getting back myself.'

Josey punches Mark on the arm, for his racism presumably, and dances away out of his reach.

'You guys going up the hill?' Aussie Mark asks.

'Dur!' says Josey, in her full snowboarding kit, and she tries to punch Mark again.

But he grabs her and pulls her down on to his lap and starts to rub his knuckle in her hair, as Itchy's seen people do to little brothers.

'Stop, not fair, I'm a girl,' Josey shrieks, and then as soon as Mark lets her go, she punches him again and skips off to the other side of the room, laughing.

Itchy and Mark haul themselves into their kit, debating between them how many layers they need.

Mark says he feels too drunk still to drive, and more to the point, might want to get battered again before the end of the day, so they're waiting for the bus at the main Cham Sud stop. There are a scattered few tourists waiting there as well, glum with a missed morning on the hill. They have only six days of this pleasure to reinvigorate themselves for another year of work. Six days in the sunshine and the snow, before disappearing underground like jaded fugitives, into tube trains and offices. By midway through the week, like this, they are already anxiously aware that the time is getting away from them.

If Itchy had only a week's holiday, he would never come to Cham; it's too much hassle to get on the mountain, much better to go to Tignes or Val Thorens or one of the other concrete-monstrosity, purpose-built ski-factories, where you step out of the ugly door of some Bauhaus-inspired abortion and on to the slopes. Chamonix is a glorious place to live, but a hard place for a holiday.

When it finally comes, the bus swoops into the station at

speed, and Itchy is almost overcome by the urge to throw himself in front of it. He is not, as Keats said, *half in love with easeful death*, but half in love with violent exploding death. Itchy is scared of the approach of buses and trains and even large cars because the rumble and the rush of wind, which approach like an avalanche, make him long to mingle with them. He is terrified and exhilarated by the fact that he might just leap in front. And he knows that this is selfish because doubtless his family and friends will be upset and also the driver will probably need counselling and people will be delayed getting on to the mountain, but this all seems insignificant next to his knowledge of what it will be like not to exist. To go from being to not being in a single flesh-rending second.

But of course Itchy doesn't jump in front of the bus; his existence shows that he never does. He climbs on board with the others and it is sufficiently empty that for once they all get a seat.

There is noticeably more snow lying on the road as the bus slews its way up towards Argentière and even more beneath the cable car to the mid-station, trees still and coated like a snapshot from a foam party. The promise of powder and lack of a queue for the lift convinces them that it will be worth going to the very top. You have to pay five euros per trip for the Grands Montets cable car, in addition to the lift pass, which costs over six hundred euros for the season; the only resort in the world Itchy is aware of where such an arbitrary extra charge is applied. The mountains of Cham are big business – for all their stark beauty and hushed spirituality, it's still all about the money.

There is something very different about the summit of Grands Montets, though, which almost justifies the separate charge. It is the mountain's mountain. If mountains had Oscars, it would win every year. In Europe only the Meije in La Grave, the Matterhorn in Zermatt and the Aiguille de Midi, down the road in Cham, can compare to the Aiguille Verte – the vert. The commencement and conjoin of three monstrous glaciers. This is serious free-ride terrain; there are a couple of token black pistes to tempt the punters, but they are never bashed, so become fields of moguls as big as tank traps, which the unwary will take all day to descend.

It is the untamed glaciers that the aficionados and the addicts come to ride. A vastness like an ancient desert; ruffled by a child's hand and tilted for his sport by malicious Allah. Glittering ice towers with ghost and ogre faces, urged from the depths by compression forces that would make crêpe paper of blue whales. Seracs that may stand like sentinels for years – in wait – to collapse in an avalanche-spewing instant, while you are beneath them. There are holes in the glaciers too: crevasses and fissures; bergschrund cracks, where the ice wrenches from rock – dangerous hidden deeps, like the parts of people masked in their blackouts. There are places it is better not to know about; otherwise you couldn't keep sliding over the surfaces so blithely.

The cable car docks. The regulars have been door-hanging last on, first off, and surge out to get to the steps, before the dawdling punters come: with eye-level, erratic ski-tips, jabbing poles and unstable, slip-prone feet. The guys make it to the steps among the first, where they are strafed by the spindrift that sweeps along the ridge. The steps are hard-edged metal – two hundred metres, ice and snow coated – have probably claimed as many victims themselves as the runs of some other resorts. Chamonix makes no condescension to comfort. Go hard or go home.

Itchy had forgotten how good Josey was; she had skied since she was a kid, but switched to boarding her first season. She keeps up with Mark without seeming to strain, as they all plummet down the front face, on the Glacier de Pendant. The wind has cut the snow into tiny terraces, laid it heavy, but still light enough to blast through on slopes as steep as these.

'Yeah, bro,' Aussie Mark shouts, when they stop on the rock ridge, 'powder is the stuff they make cocaine out of!'

Itchy laughs, but wonders whether there isn't an edge of truth in the comment. Only in powder or in Class As can nearness to death feel so blissful. There are risks inherent in powder days – risks that they acknowledge and try to minimise with transceivers and shovels and avalanche probes. And there are risks that they celebrate: choice of line; steepness of slope; depth of snow; height of drop. The pleasure is so great that sometimes you can't bear the thought of returning to life without it.

Old Doc told him this Chamonix fable, one Derapage evening, about a time when the powder came so thick and fast every night, but every day was ruthless blue sunshine, and the snow was so fathomless that locals were riding stuff that had never been accessible before. Soon people were skiing anywhere, not caring about the route, in the delicious drunkenness of adrenalin, and because it didn't really matter whether they survived or not – some hoped they wouldn't – because the powder was never going to be this good again.

But Itchy's will to live is stronger than he imagines. On the next run down, wide out on the Combe de Cordier, the Argentière glacier this time, Itchy finds himself rapidly plunging into the ground. This is more than deeper snow. He is tumbling into nothing. Stops with a winding slam. Hardly able to see for the snow still falling around him and on top of him. Supported for the moment in purgatory. Held in the ice between who knows what depths and the heaven he was in an instant earlier. The only thing he knows, the only thing in his head, is that he must live.

Every part of him aches to struggle and flail against the bullet-proof blue-black walls of the crevasse that has swallowed him.

But Itchy knows he should stay as still as he can; the last thing he wants to do is to disturb the snow ledge, which is, so far, holding his weight. Sometimes the right thing to do is also the hardest: when there's an intruder in your house, you should turn off the lights, knowledge of layout is your advantage, but then there will be an intruder in the dark. Itchy manages to keep still only by biting his lip until it bleeds.

He's not wearing a climbing harness. For some reason, though he would never consider going up the Aiguille de Midi without one, like most others, Itchy doesn't bother when he's on Grands Montets. An unwritten distinction of nearness to safety that the mountains don't adhere to. But neither Mark nor Josey has a rope with them, so Itchy's harness would be only twelve ounces more weight on the probably brittle bridge.

He's shivering from the icy bloodstream of the mountain and the fear of sinking into its circulation farther still. Frightened that even his body's shuddering might shake down his fragile perch. There are people, many people, in these *aiguilles* and their glaciers who are never found, not even in their grandchildren's lifetimes. People who will only ever be a shred and tatter of flesh and bone spat out like the refuse of an owl's prey on the final tongues of these ice dragons. Itchy is very sure he doesn't want to be one of them.

'Help,' he shouts, '*aidez-moi, m'aidez, m'aidez*,' supposing, without his usual language satisfaction, that the international Mayday cry must come from bad French.

The snow shifts noticeably beneath him. Perhaps just compacting under his weight. Or getting ready to drop away completely. In Itchy's mind he can picture a black gash the depth of the glacier, until rock. And him sprawled, skis still on, half seated, on a ledge as flimsy as a palm-frond tiger trap.

'Itchy!' Aussie Mark shouts.

'Over here.'

'I know, bro, I saw you vanish. Hang on in there, I'm trying to make my way over lying down. Josey's got the pisties on her mobile.'

Eventually Mark's face comes over the edge of Itchy's pit, knocking more loose snow down on to him as it appears.

'Ah, that's not so bad,' Mark says, 'I thought you'd be deeper,' but his face, ashen and carved with worry, belies the hearty smile. 'Are you injured?'

'Don't think so, no pain. I'm trying not to move in case this drops.'

'I reckon I could reach an arm down to hold your ski pole, if you held it up.'

Itchy feels like laughing with the madness of the suggestion. 'You'd never pull me out, mate, it couldn't work. The basket would come off first anyway.'

'Just to support you a bit until the pisties get here, I mean, or just in case, like.'

Itchy holds up a pole, trying not to move the rest of him, and Mark can just reach it with one arm, his chest on the edge of the crevasse, weight presumably on a jammed-in board to make sure he doesn't fall in himself.

It is kind of ridiculous, because Itchy knows that if the floor beneath him gave way, there is nothing Mark could do. Strong as he is, he could never hold Itchy's weight like this, not for long enough for rescue to arrive, and he certainly couldn't haul him out. But even so, this link to his friend and the world outside the crevasse pitfall makes Itchy feel safer and stronger. And Mark keeps him talking like a pro, more words than you get out of the big man in a week, usually.

The pisteurs arrive quickly, and their rescue is textbook: a harness lowered to Itchy to clip under his arms, and he is hauled out by the team from secured belay positions. The ground beneath Itchy doesn't even tremble as he leaves it. By rights it should drop away dramatically at the final moment, to show the yawning chasm that might have swallowed him. But the ledge stays exactly in place, except for the imprints of where Itchy was so recently imprisoned.

The sky has never looked so blue. And Itchy holds his friends to him in a group hug, the like of which he's only ever done on the football pitch before.

'Happy New Year,' Aussie Mark says.

A little still she strove, and much repented,
And whispering 'I will ne'er consent' – consented.

Byron, Don Juan

January 4th, 8.51 p.m.

Itchy has a friend who works in the City. Who has money. Whose Christmas bonus, even in a period of relative failure, is invariably more than the sum of what Itchy earns in the entire year and his debts added together. This friend is married now, has a baby and another child. A boy, who is old enough to be able to say 'Itchy', but is not yet old enough to think that Itchy is rather a strange name for someone to have.

This friend is faithful to his wife. He doesn't pursue the few women in his office, even though they sometimes quite openly show that they would like to sleep with him. He doesn't get blowjobs from the young waitresses who serve him at plush restaurants; where he always tips after the first course to ensure good service, because tipping at the end has always seemed meaningless to him, when surely the point of a tip is to buy someone's willingness, in the same way as a wage. Neither does he sleep with the girls at his gym, who must be rich kids because it is an expensive gym, and whose breasts still poke forcefully into Lycra tops; who haven't suckled two children. He certainly doesn't have affairs with the wives and partners of friends or colleagues; because, even when he was young, he understood that there is a worse betrayal than of your significant other and that is of a friend. He doesn't make amorous advances to female rivals, even if it might help to clinch a deal. He doesn't chat up the girl who washes his full-options Range Rover and his limited-series Italian roadster at the weekends; who has said before, with a prolonged look and a top soaked with soapy water, that she could come another day if that would be more convenient. He doesn't linger with the hostess at the end of parties his wife has been unable to attend. He doesn't time his jogging to coincide with the routine of the redhead from the sleek-chrome flats opposite. He doesn't flirt with nurses, schoolgirls or policewomen, and he wouldn't even if he had occasion to come across them more than once in a blue moon. He doesn't let relationships with his secretaries cross lines of strict professionalism. He doesn't meet up with old flames. He doesn't send drinks to other tables. He doesn't loiter by groups of topless beach babes on holiday. He doesn't date. He doesn't cheat. He doesn't make exceptions.

He does fuck whores, though.

Not often, just sometimes on business trips. He doesn't regard this as a betrayal, because it is just a transaction, just an easing of tension – and he has a stressful job. There is no emotional investment. No need to feign interest, or worse: to be interested. It is all safe, latex wrapped and insured against the possibility of his wife ever finding out. There are no bunny-boilers on the books of the oldest profession. The girls are well versed in not leaving marks. And he doesn't use streetwalkers, of the sort scrutinised by the police and patronised by foppish, floppy-haired, British movie stars. The girls are invariably far more accomplished actors, and will always do him the courtesy of simulating things that may not actually be happening. Unless he has specifically instructed them not to bother. Which sometimes he does, since he doesn't see why he should both pay for sex and retain even the slightest worry about his partner's pleasure. It's just a posh wank to him. Usually, though not exclusively, when he's far from home, or else when protocol demands. It's a boys' club as well, you see, a business that goes with the contracts and the big bonuses. A part of the paraphernalia, which ensures that, however much fuss they kick up and however often they sue, women will never get equal status. Because they can never be as culpable. They can't enter this world of mutual understanding that what goes on tour stays on the tour bus. That careless talk costs wives.

He has no guilt, this friend of Itchy's, because this seems the kindest way to let off steam. Something that doesn't affect his happy and stable marriage. As for the prostitutes, they are well paid. And it's an easy way to make a living, after all. Devoid of the prematurely greying, ulcer-giving, head-pounding stress that he is accustomed to. It would never ever occur to him that what he is doing is taking sex from women under duress. Not duress from him, but from rent and bills and probably kids and usually drugs and often the men who treated them so badly that they got to this place to begin with. And that taking sex from someone under duress is rape. And that he is therefore a rapist. That would never ever occur to him. But then he is a busy man. And in any case, that is only one way of looking at it.

But that's how Daniel sees it: sex with a prostitute is second-degree rape, he says. Itchy is not sure how they got on to this discussion – except that rape seems to be the preoccupation of everyone in Chamonix now – but it is one of the most animated discussions they've ever had.

'OK,' says Sean, 'so what if you shag a girl and you don't ask her if you can, but she doesn't protest or anything?'

'Then that's not rape, bro, of course it's not,' says Aussie Mark.

'But what if she says afterwards that it was? Then it becomes a point-of-view thing.' Sean has stood up from his stool in his enthusiasm. 'What if she says she didn't agree to fuck you, and you have to admit that she never actually said the words, does that make it rape? Because that's just fucking stupid. But if not, then you're saying that you, like, automatically have right of way, until you get a red light, which is also stupid. Or are you saying that permission is a gut feeling that you get from other signals, which eventually takes you back to the courtrooms in the seventies: where women were assumed to have been "asking for it" if they were wearing a short skirt, or going to a club that was known as a scrubber hangout. Or worse, you could get to some Islamic shit where they reckon blokes can't even be expected to restrain themselves unless all women wear full-on ninja suits.'

Itchy colours the cubes of ice in his glass with Ricard, which turns an uninviting but magnetic grey-green when he adds a splash of water. The cubes crack and click as they split. The bar's surface and pumps are already polished like a crime scene, and there are no other customers but his three friends, so he has no choice but to listen to the growing debate.

'Letting you kiss her and letting you undress her and not protesting at any stage are different from wearing a short skirt, though.'

'Yes, but it's a blurred line, that's the thing. Some colleges in the States say students need to make a contract to have sex beforehand, because they've had so many date-rape cases.'

'It would kind of kill the moment,' Daniel says, 'but I can see some logic to it.' He takes a sip from his half of lager.

'Funny how everyone drinks halves in France,' Itchy says, motioning to the drink and using the gap in conversation to try and turn the topic. 'You'd be laughed out of the pub at home. But it's more civilised, I reckon, means people are less wary of buying big rounds and get bought back quicker. And the drink stays fresh to the bottom.'

'Maybe,' Sean says, but turns back to Daniel. 'But this is the biggie: the contracts don't count if either or both parties are drunk. Bang! How often does anyone pull a sober bird?'

Aussie Mark whistles through his teeth, like a mechanic in amazement that a single female has made it into his safe hands in the death trap she's been driving.

'And what about before a girl has the legal right to consent to sex, if she's underage?' says Sean, warming to the topic further.

'If she's underage then that is statutory rape, because she's not considered by society to be mature enough to make that decision,' says Daniel, quite firmly.

'But in America that age is eighteen, in Sweden it's fifteen, in Japan it's fourteen, in India it's twelve. These are random numbers, there isn't a *right* age.'

'Hang on there, bro. In India you can probably get *married* at twelve, but you have sex with a twelve-year-old and you'd better get ready to marry her, or else you're likely to be lynched and will definitely fuck up her life.'

'OK, then, what if a girl says no, but you can tell she doesn't mean it?' Sean leaves it hanging in the air, waiting for Daniel's inevitable rebuttal.

Daniel is silent, though. He takes a sip of his beer, straightens his back on his stool and looks quizzically at Sean, as if he has never seen him before. And Itchy gets the feeling that this idea is so alien to Daniel's world that he doesn't really get the concept.

But Itchy can remember a time in a lift, right at the start of the season, with a girl he had to pull there by the hand. A girl who had told him 'no' quite forcefully as he kissed her neck, and who had probably believed she meant it at that moment. But who was on her knees five minutes later, after he had stopped the lift on deserted floor 5 and held it there with a strip of duct tape over the button – an old trick for getting a bit of privacy. A girl who couldn't get enough of him. Who played with her heavy breasts for him, unprompted, and rubbed her fingers between her legs as she sucked him. Who told him she 'loved cock', which by her actions she clearly did, though he could tell she loved saying it even more.

And he has to agree with Daniel, when he finally says, almost wearily, as if tired of explaining to a child why it cannot play with the blender, that even if she does want it, even if it's clear she wanted it from what she does later, if you go against her wishes, at the moment she says 'no', then at that moment it is rape. Even if what Daniel says is logical and correct, Itchy knows it is also not quite true, or not always true. But that the opposing argument has no argument at all. It is just something you feel, against all evidence, like religious faith. But Itchy can't get involved with the discussion, not only because his side is impossible to argue, as Sean is now discovering, but because, though he may be innocent in the lift incident, Itchy remains guilty of graver crimes.

Suzi comes in, bringing with her a smile like an upturned rainbow. She is with some of the guys from her work: Chamois – the Chamonix Chalet Specialists. They are having a staff night out to keep spirits high, no doubt Suzi's idea. The first couple of weeks are the hardest on the chalet staff: when they don't know the ropes and the routines, but have the highest-paying, most demanding guests. A lot of companies get big drop-out rates in January. The female chalet hosts cluster around Suzi, their line manager, like she's Brown Owl.

Daniel kisses Suzi hello, but then returns to his stool by Sean and Aussie Mark, seeming happy to share her with the world.

One of the hosts, Vince, greets Itchy with a high-five, perhaps contrived to let the others know what good friends they are; perhaps just because he's a dick.

Vince has done seasons before: La Plagne; Les Deux Alpes – seems disappointed with Chamonix, disappointed perhaps with how hard it is to break in, disappointed with the anonymity, the lack of status. It's not like other resorts here, workers don't stand out in Cham, locals have been here for years, the *real* locals for generations. It is obvious that Vince doesn't like blending in, even without the fact that he wears sunglasses inside, as if fame were the bane of his existence.

He's a social smoker, Vince, for which read cigarette skank. Itchy's seen him at it, weaselly gaze following hands as they go for packets. Monitoring everyone in the room who has fags and how many they have left. Knowing just when to draw the line. How many it is acceptable to take from each person. Itchy suspects he looks at other people's women the same way: feeling who's ripe; sensing arguments and ill feeling between couples; gauging when to pounce. Vince is coast-Cornish, the blood of the wreckers flows through his veins.

'So how's it hanging, Itchy?' he says.

He has a scar on his lip that Itchy assumes came from talking when he should have been listening, but may equally have come from being caught with someone else's bird.

'Yeah, good, thanks. You?'

'You know, pretty cruisey.' Vince leans in conspiratorially, but then speaks louder than ever. 'Pulled a darling last week.'

A couple of Vince's co-workers come over and hang to the side of him; they are just kids really, eighteen, nineteen. From the way they look at him it's pretty clear they think Vince is the man. Their clothes are new-looking versions of what he wears, skater clothes. A lot of reinvention goes on in ski resorts, a lot of shamming, but these guys don't even know who they are yet.

They're not skaters, though, you can tell skaters from the ollie-scuffs on their trainers.

'She was one of my guests as well. I actually shagged her while her husband was out skiing. And he tipped me at the end of the holiday. What a sucker, eh!'

Itchy looks over at Suzi, who raises her eyebrows, but is unconcerned. Vince obviously does a good enough job that she is willing to overlook his failings. Maybe she likes him. Itchy doesn't.

He says, 'Good skills,' though, tries to muster a genuine-looking smile. The problem with being an accomplished barman is that you have to let everyone believe they are your friend. Itchy sometimes wonders whether that makes him a fake as well. Or does it just go with the job? Is it like a lawyer's obligation to do his best for his client, however obvious their guilt? At least people like the barman, everyone hates lawyers.

Suzi wants shots for all the hosts, so Itchy makes a show of it – gets out the metre rack and gives them flatliners: sambuca, tequila, Tabasco. The Tabasco is dripped in like blood, then settles between the two spirits in a horizontal layer; a straight line, like the bad news on a heart-rate monitor from which the drink gets its name.

A lot of the hosts are coughing and grimacing with the burn of Tabasco, having downed it too slowly. Vince takes his shades off after he's done his shot and huffs on the lenses, unsubtly showing how cool his breath still is. But he looks like a geeky kid at school polishing his spectacles. Vince is about as cool as the other side of an insomniac's pillow.

When Itchy is walking home, alone but for a bottle of Stella – floor mopped, fridges stocked, grilles and taps washed – he stops to look over the bridge at the River Arve, by the side of

La Terrasse. Faint white lights reflect in the flow like shards of broken mirrors, centuries of bad luck. The Terrasse was built at the turn of the last century, art nouveau, sinuous organic swirls like nowhere else in the Alps. But even its elegance is as nothing to the river. The water is black with the night and lonely secrets, cold with the meltwater of a billion tons of snow and ice. There may be drops within the Arve tonight that fell as flakes the year that Byron and Shelley ambled through this valley, drops that have frozen and compacted into glacier, and then wended their way so slowly down the steep sides that generations have grown and died looking up at them, without them seeming to move at all. But now they rush, liquid at last, and on their way to the heat of the Mediterranean. Carrying with them particles churned from the mountainsides by forces so gigantic they are hard to comprehend. The bite of a shark twenty miles long might be a start, but it isn't really even a bite, just the passing of a gargantuan belly. It is all about gravity in the mountains. The snow that blankets. The glaciers that shape. The force that generates the skier's speed. What must be fought against to climb. And, thanks to gravity, though fortitude often fails him when he tries to get any higher, Itchy knows that he will always have sufficient strength to fall.

The Last Summer

THE SKY WAS beautiful the day that Marty killed himself. Little fluffy clouds, like the tune that had been pounding the night before. There was a wild boar with a pelican's pouch under its jaw, ready to devour the sun. A poodle's head, seen from above, which could also be a womb in cross-section, Marty said. Pinocchio. A praying mantis, with a crown. A pagoda. A skull, or a partially eaten lump of cheese. A turtle with great wings on either side of its shell. An hourglass. A dog rolled half on its back, cautiously willing to accept a stranger's tickle. That *Thunderbirds* machine that had the tank tracks and the drill on the front for burrowing. A Viking longboat, less one member left flailing in its wake. The skeleton of a dinosaur, or else a chicken faintly drawn. And all of them, even in what was only a slight wind, were willing at a moment's notice to change into something entirely new.

They were both reclined on sunloungers made of the white picket fences of American dreams. Lounge lizards on sunloungers, Marty had said, and Itchy came to suspect that it had long been his own ambition to be a lounge lizard. There was something very alluring about it, suavely degenerate – cocktails, cheap suits,

Muzak tinkling softly in the background – and cool: there was always air con in the bars where the lounge lizards roamed.

It was baking up on the roof; a sun as bright and high as in a child's painting shot laser blasts at them. It was only his shades and heavily iced pints of Bloody Mary that stopped Itchy dissolving into a puddle on the floor like the witch in *The Wizard of Oz*.

The floor of the rooftop was paved with beige, but then almost everything was bleached beige or white in Tenerife. The tiles were cracked, almost to a one, but still whole, hairline cobwebs, like on expensive vases, that for some reason didn't crumble.

All around them the cicadas clicked like printing presses or primary school percussion sections. A noise that changed the more you listened to it, and became the only noise in the world, even though there was a strimmer going somewhere down below and in the distance a man in a bright orange boiler suit was driving a sit-on lawnmower – looking like a James Bond villain in one of the little buggies they use to get about in underground lairs.

There were shells embedded in the concrete of the low wall, not deliberately put there to prettify, but present in the way the sea seemed to permeate everything on the island. Even the air, so thickly salted and so hot it made breathing a strain – though it was also a pleasure, condensed with the essence of foreignness.

It was the last day of their holiday, a cheap deal that had become not very cheap at all, once they went out every night, but had been far and away the best time of their lives. Exactly what Itchy needed to utterly block out the thing they still hadn't talked about.

Marty smoked a cigarette that was white all the way down, without the faux-leather filter demarcation of the cigarettes that Itchy was used to seeing. The fags were so cheap that he had seriously considered taking up the habit, if only to save money, but in the end he seemed to have squeezed in sufficient vice anyway. He watched the ash tumble down slow-motioned from the cigarette and into the dark-haired and newly tanned folds of Marty's stomach.

When they arrived they were white of course, though not as white as the beer-bellied British lads they had played football with on the beach that first day – even with Itchy and Marty onside, gently punished by lean, sand-skilled local youths, some still with the muscled pots of childhood.

Helicopter gunship dragonflies swooped in loose formation over Itchy's reclined head; he could almost hear 'The Ride of the Valkyrie', like in *Apocalypse Now*, while he watched them hover. Only one day, he remembers thinking at them, you'll be dead by tonight.

Insects were everywhere over there, a land of things that ran and jumped away from your feet as you walked the jungle trail to the beach. The path worn smooth by flip-flopped feet, earth baked and scorched by the sun anywhere it was unshaded, cracked like the back of an old man's hand. Swaying sabre blades of African grass growing high on either side.

But that day they had decided to stay up on the rooftop garden, which it seemed strange to think of as a garden, since it was almost devoid of green. Except for a weed, like a chartreuse starfish, that flowered out from between a gap in the tiles; growing in who knows what speck of blown sand or dust. Things had to be tough to survive out there.

Itchy and Marty had won a fight the previous night, as much as anyone wins such things. They had sent two fellow drunks running anyway, and were themselves mostly uninjured, except for bleeding knuckles, and reasonably sure they were in the right.

The door to the stairs down from the roof garden to their apartment was braced with wood, like a Mexican jail in a John

Wayne film. It was all like a film that day – so clear, so precise – and Itchy had the feeling that he was the main character in the whole world and no one else really existed once they left the frame of his story.

Rorschach blots of algae were spread across the door-wood's surface, patchy, like penicillin. In the shape of a snail, England, a snake that was also the River Thames, and a mandrake root – though Itchy was not entirely sure what mandrake roots looked like.

It was a happy land, Tenerife, despite security guards with Maglites as big as cavemen's clubs. Where even the statue of an ancient inhabitant showed stoical acceptance of the hordes that ended the evenings sprawled at his feet. Where policemen were only there to be toyed with and outrun, as if Itchy and Marty were football hooligans – which, in fact, appeared to be the hobby of choice of many of the new friends they'd made.

One new friend had invited them to stay all summer. Said there was money to be made in traveller's-cheque fraud by fresh-faced, middle-class youngsters like them. All they had to do was practise signatures by poolsides and take a few trips to unwalled bureau de change windows.

'If you've got a moped with the engine running there's no chance of being caught, but no one gives a toss anyway,' he had said. 'It doesn't come out of their economy, see.' He spoke in broad Scouse, which made the gap in his smile look even more like Jimmy Tarbuck's, but they had declined his offer.

It was a land of wind that made a golden rushing through the trees and a crunch of grass that grew on sand, quite unlike the cushioning soil back home. The sand was everywhere, in fact, in their beers, in their hair and even inside the girls they'd fucked.

Itchy had tried to picture one of them, who he had quite liked. But he could only remember the baize cloth under his hands, of a snooker table by the side of a swimming pool, and the moonlight reflecting off the metal corner protectors, and the black ball – nodding as the table rocked minutely – which had been all that was left to pot, except her.

Highways that shimmered with heat haze, like in road movies. Red rust stains like old blood that seeped from unseen metal innards through the pores in too quickly constructed concrete buildings. A new beach towel with a picture of a smiling shark. Snide swim shorts, not by Ralph Lauren. Trees moving in the breeze like bad dancers. A brochure, for a trip they hadn't gone on, which had said that the volcanic Peak of Tenerife had once been thought to be the highest mountain in the world, though it was really nothing of the kind. These were the things he could remember.

A throaty Barry White bird sang with a beat as repetitive as any they had heard in the clubs that week, and a feather rippled in a cobweb, cluttered with old lunches, like an anemone speeded up for a David Attenborough voice-over. A beetle, brown and round like a chocolate button, scuttled over and then invisibilised against a stack of sea-smoothed black pebbles set against the bottom of the rooftop wall, put there by a child no doubt, and piled like a miniature cairn. A lizard, lithe and staccato, bolted in bursts for a hole that looked too small for something half its size. There was so much life up there that day.

And Itchy realised that what he had to do was to stay in these places for ever. To remain in these lands where everything was great. Which most people only visit but where some, like the kebab man, Gary, could make a life. But Itchy wasn't really one for the heat. And he didn't overly care for the sea. And he certainly didn't want to make kebabs.

There was a big terracotta pot in the corner with different holes all around the sides of it that plants could trail out of, though they were empty. It looked like the log in which the young Peter

Duncan, the *Blue Peter* presenter, is forced to put his hand in *Flash Gordon*, and is bitten by the poisonous thing. Red leaves, like Rolling Stones tongues, blown there on trade winds, were heaped at its feet. Sticks like savoury snacks. Blocks of marble with spots as if a shotgun had been fired into them. Brown shale gravel like the bacon bits in the salad buffet. A spider that for some reason was ignoring the trail of ants that walked right past it, waiting for a different prey. The sweat that formed on Itchy's brow, for once the cooling elixir that nature had designed and not an irritant. A pigeon, feathers slick with rainbows of petrol, that stumbled along on toeless gnarls of feet, then took off, suddenly graceful in the air. Soaring past a wisp of white plastic bag in the wind, which swirled like milk in a Cadbury's advert, or the beginnings of a thought.

Itchy had noticed all these things, all the minutiae happening around the wall, before he noticed that Marty was now standing on top of it. And then, amid the drum-roll of the cicadas, he no longer was.

So Itchy's holiday was unfortunately extended, his passport retained until the autopsy was done.

The reports concluded death by misadventure: Marty had in his bloodstream high levels of LSD and MDMA and enough alcohol to put him twenty times over the drink-drive limit. But the authorities were, in any case, not unused to young British males falling from the sky.

Itchy cooperated with the police as far as he could, for his own sake and Marty's, but could only really tell them that a guy, in the bar named after the footballer famed for being clean cut and liking crisps, had sold them the drugs. That the acid tabs were called Black Dragons and the Es were Teddy Bears. And that he didn't know why Marty had done it.

Itchy will wonder for the rest of his life why Marty did it. He likes to think his friend just didn't want to go back. That he had decided life had reached its peak that day and it could only be downhill from then on, could never be as good again. And Itchy will have to conclude that, if this was the case, he was probably right. Other times he thinks it was because of her. Because of Tina. Because a new term might make it impossible to keep forgetting.

Itchy would never go back to Sheffield either. When he returned to England a letter was waiting for him. A letter that informed him he had another holiday to go on. He had won the writing competition, first, second and third. And his prize was to be sent to another of the places where everything is great, that most people only get to visit. He found Cham.

And bending my steps towards the near Alpine valleys, sought in the magnificence, the eternity of such scenes, to forget myself and my ephemeral, because human, sorrows. My wanderings were directed towards the valley of Chamounix.

Mary Shelley, Frankenstein

January 10th, 9.17 a.m.

A gorilla must have attacked the apartment. It has eaten all the food, drunk all the booze, wrecked the place, punched Itchy in the head, shat in his mouth and then left in the night. There is still a faint, peanut-smelling mustiness.

Itchy has woken, not just with a vicious hangover, but also the early morning awareness that there is something he has got to do, and that he is probably already running late for it. After a moment he remembers he is supposed to be meeting Wendy at Brevent for 9.30.

Aussie Mark is sleeping contentedly, but still twitching occasionally; his snore is like the raspy asthmatic breath of a bulldog. Sean has his duvet pulled firmly over his head to shield him from the world, and especially the daylight streaming through a gap in the eighties orange curtains. At least if he goes now, Itchy thinks, he can leave them to sort out the carnage of the flat. The sink is full to overflowing with plates and pans, most with something pasted on to them that will require a steam-stripper to remove. Empty bottles, cans, pizza boxes and, for some reason, a lot of silly-string litter the room.

To save time Itchy tries to put both his legs in his baggy Billabong pants at once and topples over into a pile of dirty underwear, fortunately his own.

He leaves the flat, ski boots clomping on the corridor floor, feeling crap, but whistling. The truth is that Itchy enjoys hangovers, he likes the light-headedness and the lingering tingle of the invulnerability he had when he was drunk. And he likes knowing that the pain is temporary, he can look forward to that first beer at lunchtime, or maybe a cheeky *vin chaud* before that; alcohol is the only poison that is its own antidote. For Itchy, thinking clearly is to be feared far more than a hangover.

The sky is mulched with grey, washing gloom over Itchy's walk to the bus stop. There's a huge euro-bloater on the pavement ahead of him; Austrian or German maybe, but most likely Dutch – the Dutch are the new Germans anyway. This one's an absolute pie shop, in a purple all-in-one, with a silver freeride helmet perched, seemingly precariously, on the top of his head – though, like a shiny tin can at the fairground, it would probably be a lot harder to knock off than it appears. The backs of his undone, white, rear-entry boots flap as he walks, like camp hands. He carries two sets of skis on his shoulders, his own and his wife's, and he swings them about as he talks to her, careless of the people around him who have to duck or move aside into the road as the skis come at them.

His wife has his poles – in the manner all such women employ when holding their partner's poles, which is to say that they have them by the handle, because that's where you're supposed to hold them, isn't it? – even though this makes them far too long and means they have to lift their arms ridiculously high in the air, like a toddler asking for a carry.

She looks even more like a child beside the bulbous hulk of her husband. And Itchy can't help but imagine them fucking: this tiny peroxide blonde thing, whose muff-hair no doubt matches the fur trim on her shiny gold parka, being squashed breathless as she is shafted by her enormous, bearded beau.

There are a lot of people at the bus stop for Brevent, which is a good sign, as it means one should be along shortly. He hopes Wendy will still be waiting.

Wendy is a friend from seasons past. She had popped into the bar last night to let Itchy know she was out for the week, and he had agreed to meet her for a ski. Unfortunately the quiet night had afterwards developed into something large; Itchy can resist anything but temptation.

Wendy is an Alpine legend – like the dragons and the cave trolls and the Dahu, with its two short legs and two long for walking round the mountain slopes. She is talked about by people who have never seen her, mentioned on training courses, is more famous than all but a handful of the top freeriders.

Wendy once fixed a coach that broke down on the twenty-one tight hairpin bends that lead up to Alpe d'Huez. She tottered along the aisle in her high heels, walked down the steps, careful to hold her leather miniskirt against her muscled bum as she descended, flung open the engine canopy, fixed the fucker, and returned to her seat amid cheers and applause from the other guests.

In Val Thorens, when the singer in the après-ski band at the Frog and Roastbeef was struck down with food poisoning, Wendy took over for the week, and the Frog took its best takings of the season.

In Val d'Isère a sneering roisterer, with a coiffed fringe, upturned collar and a scarf that let the cognoscenti know which school he had gone to, asked whether she was a man or a woman.

Wendy had replied that she was more of a woman than he would ever shag and more of a man than he would ever be, and proved it, by kissing him and then knocking him spark out.

In Les Arcs she saved the life of a high mountain guide.

In Megève she collared a car thief.

Some say that in Andorra she has been given the keys of the city.

He spots her right away when he has clambered off the bus at the base of the Brevent mountain. She's wearing a shrimp-pink jacket, the colour of the sweet, not the crustacean. Itchy wonders why they don't seem to make them any more, because everyone loved shrimps – maybe they were carcinogenic?

'Itchiee,' she says, in her strong Geordie accent. 'I thought you weren't going to make it. Hawey, let's get in the queue.'

Wendy has a scar from a life-saving operation that made her decide life was too short not to live exactly how she wanted. She likes to make tea as strong and sweet as treacle.

The Brevent lift is probably the most efficient in the valley, despite hanging from antiquated and visibly crumbling concrete pillars, and they are soon heading up the steep sides with a cabin to themselves. One of the benefits of skiing with Wendy is that you often get a cabin to yourself.

With her mittens off, her fingers are big, workman's hands, reliable looking, with pink-painted nails, and covered in enough rings to hang a set of curtains.

Itchy tells her about going down the crevasse the other week, as a *choucas* – a chough – swoops by the window, black and silent as a stealth bomber. Choughs and crows are pretty much all the birds you see in Cham, all the corvidae are tough. It disappears as they head into the cloud; just wisps at first, like smoke from burnt evidence; before becoming a mask of white that covers everything, and makes Itchy wish he hadn't come. Skiing in a whiteout is no fun, dangerous and strictly for punters. But then Wendy is a punter, of sorts, and he agreed to ski with her.

The grim day is only a temperature inversion, though. They burst through the clouds, which lie as a layer across the valley like the baileys in a B-52, and out into flamboyant blue on the other side.

At the top they stop for a while to take it in. This must be the first time that Wendy has been up a mountain in nine months at least and she stands in awe, skis hugged against the ample breast shapes beneath her quilted jacket. The French call the mist formation *la mer de nuage* – the sea of cloud – and that is exactly how it appears from above. A gently choppy swath of white water which extends across the valley, leaving Mont Blanc and the Midi on the other side of the valley jutting out of the waves like steeply peaked desert islands, or icebergs edging inevitably into the path of a passenger liner. The *mer de nuage* is one of the most beautiful sights the mountains guard for those who come to worship them. The clouds look strong enough to step upon and they isolate the chosen few on high, in a world of forgiving sun, vivid skies and glistening snow; while the masses below are screened off by grey and gloom.

Wendy almost skips up the steps to the cable car, which will take them to the top spire of Brevent itself – cold turret of a Byronic mage. Her legs are broad and dense with strength. Itchy's own legs are skinny, to his eternal disappointment, to him look wasted, like a famine victim's, and no matter how much sport he plays never seem to grow significantly. He used to blame this fact for why no football club ever took him on at trials, reckoned he was prejudged for his apparent frailty. The truth is, he has come to realise, he just wasn't good enough. The world doesn't reward also-rans, especially in football.

Wendy must be very good at what she does. To be a woman in a man's environment you have to be twice as good. To be a transvestite you have to be three times as good. To be a transvestite who works as a diesel mechanic in a mining town you probably have to be ten times as good, and as hard as a brick-badger.

They take in the view again at the top. It is awesome – in the original sense, of something inspiring respect and trepidation, not in the gnarly Pupsi-Max way. The sea of clouds extends in every direction for hundreds of miles, as far as the eye can follow it, broken only by the massive shark's teeth of the Chamonix *aiguilles*.

The vastness of the mountains makes Itchy confront agoraphobia far more than vertigo. They make him face the fact that he instinctively wants to hide in a little hole with five sides covered, like the animal he evolved from. The brevity and utter irrelevancy of human existence is explicit here, among gargantuan peaks formed billions of years ago. But the feeling is also curiously liberating: as if realising you are nothing is the first step to becoming something. Itchy might have become a Buddhist monk, except that would ask too much of him. To give up sex, booze and meat is a high price for Nirvana.

At the first bend of the trail they cut off the piste and begin a rollercoaster of steep drops and uphill trudges, following the line of the ridge. The faster you allow yourself to go down, the less far there is to walk up the other side, but fear of going over the ridge is always present. Wendy is heavier and has more guts than Itchy, but he is the better skier and they travel one behind the other; not really chatting, but passing occasional remarks in a way that is more significant than small talk. A path to follow has been long beaten down since the last snowfall, and countless cups have been pressed into either side of it from the passing of ski poles, but they are the only people they can see.

Itchy pauses sometimes, to take a deep breath of icy-cold air and appreciate the high-mountain solitude. He knows he is a lush and a loser, by society's definitions, but who can say whether he is squandering life or showing his gratitude for it? People who talk about the 'real world' fail to understand that this is the realest world there is: to be alone, or with chosen friends, at the top of a snow-covered peak and to know that in a moment this hermit's tranquillity will change into reckless exhilaration. How can a man-made office in a man-made city be more real than that?

And in minutes they are there, busting through the snow down the Pente d'Hôtel. Utterly alone, on a face as wide with possibility as a dream. Wendy on old 210s, crazy, almost antique, Plake-straight skis, jumping tight turns, but at surprising speed. Itchy, on his *zeitgeist* technology, oil-painting-beautiful Factions; slashing his way in Zorro arcs, scaring himself awake. Aware of what it meant to be alive in his ancestral past. Not exactly fear, but a sudden and sure awareness of what's going on. The proximity of danger. The knowledge that at any moment he could be called upon to react. And that if he fails that test he might die. And that if he succeeds he might die anyway. But that probably he will just ski down, grinning like a dolphin that's fucking while it swims.

Twice more they lap the Hôtel face before they take a breather at the Restaurant Panoramique. A cup of tea for Wendy, a G&T for Itchy, and for both of them a view that runs from Switzerland, through France and Italy, and back to Switzerland again. The gin goes down with a glow, slipping into the permachol in Itchy's system – the part of him that never really sobers up.

'So do you fancy doing karaoke with us tonight?' Wendy says.

Itchy knows that the 'us' is a Northern us. Wendy is on holiday on her own, and in the aftermath of only one drink karaoke already seems like an all right idea. It's his night off, and after a power nap he'll be wanting to go out.

'Where is it?' he says. 'I didn't even know we had karaoke here.'

'Don't worry, I'll keep you right, tourist,' Wendy says with a lipstick grin. 'I saw a poster, it's on at Elevation.'

Elevation 1904 is not, as the name suggests, seven hundred metres higher than the rest of Chamonix town. It was previously called Café 1904, because of the date it was founded. When new owners took it over, they wanted to keep something of the name, but also to pep it up a bit. They're good guys; they look after the locals and the workers, and treat everyone as a friend, in the way that Itchy tries to, when he's behind the bar. But they seem to do it with more feeling than he can muster; maybe because it's their own business, maybe they're just better people.

Itchy agrees to meet Wendy there later, and since it is lunchtime now, they decide to stay on the restaurant terrace, gleaming with sunshine and holidaymakers, and get something to eat. Itchy orders a half-carafe of house rosé, which is chilled enough to kill its bite of cheapness. They both get *tartiflette* to eat, the regional speciality. Like most regional specialities, it is peasant food, what the people had to make do with before the tourist money started pouring in. It is crammed with calories, gooey cheese oozing between pork lumps and potatoes. It solidifies in your stomach, takes about a week to fully digest – just right for tramping through the mountains with a herd of goats, or a gun, or a set of skis.

And yet a little tumult, now and then, is an agreeable quickener of sensation.

Byron

January 10th, 9.06 p.m.

Wendy is at the bar already when Itchy arrives, at just gone nine, and fights his way through to her. She's drinking bubbly. It's ladies' night in Elevation, which means that for five euros they can drink all the 'champagne' they like, and Wendy is more than enough of a lady to qualify. It also means the bar would be packed, even without the karaoke. Mostly with men hoping to cop off with one of the ladies inebriated on cheap champagne. At bad times in Chamonix the male–female ratio can allegedly get as much as six to one. It doesn't bother Itchy, though, just makes life more challenging.

The guy who's running the karaoke starts things off by doing a number himself. He's got hair the grey of the slush in the streets and he croons out an Elvis song, a bit too enthusiastic with his hand gestures for how bad he is. It's all a bit like Itchy imagines Butlins to be.

Two podgy punter chicks get up next, to do a rendition of 'I Will Survive'. It's dire, and one of their tops keeps riding up, exposing a belly bloated and white like the soft underside of a bottom-feeding fish. They squawk like feedback when the tune goes higher. And get offended when the compère suggests they're sisters – neither wanting to think that they look like the other.

Itchy sips his drinks, alternating between a demi and a pastis. A few people are staring at him, sitting beside Wendy, but he's not embarrassed. In some ways, Itchy knows, he cares too much about what other people think of him, but he has always been proud of his friends. More so even than he is of his family, because friends have chosen to like him. He thinks about Marty and salutes him silently before he next takes a drink of his beer. And then he raises his glass again and gives a protective nod to a bloke who is looking suspiciously at Wendy.

One of the gratifying things about Elevation is it actually has quite a lot of French customers; they are pretty rare in most of the bars Itchy frequents. A big group of Frenchies are sat at the tables down by the front of the karaoke set-up. Slung over a chair there is an ESF jacket, the red of steak tartar, and Itchy recognises one or two of them as ski instructors, so they probably all are. A couple of the girls look quite tidy from behind, but Itchy knows he would have no chance of getting in there when they're out in a big group like this. And, although he doesn't like to think he's prejudiced, Itchy doesn't much go for French birds anyway. There's something about their unconditioned hair, the smallness of their faces, something slightly wiry, slightly stoaty about them. Although he can see how other people fancy them it just doesn't work for him. It's rather like looking at an attractive man – he can see that all the elements are there, the things that someone would find sexy, but that someone isn't Itchy. Besides, French birds require a lot of effort, they almost never put out when you first meet them – unless they're on holiday. Everyone fucks on holiday.

British chicks, on the other hand, are now renowned the world over for being easy – even among the Swedish, the Dutch and the Aussies, the nations we think of as easy – it's good that we're being recognised on the world stage once more.

A girl with big freckles, like finger-paint marks, and a laugh like a child's toy machine gun, gets up and does 'If You Don't Know Me by Now'. She is followed by a middle-aged guy, who sings something by Eric Clapton. He has a nose riddled with burst blood vessels, tributes to a life spent boozing, sending a sliver of disgust into Itchy, which it takes a swig of Ricard to ease.

The walls in Elevation are filled with old clocks, ticking lives away, unheard in the din of karaoke.

Wendy is ploughing her way through the champagne, wig bouncing as she sings along to the songs. She knows all the words.

'Are you not going to do one?' Itchy shouts in her ear.

'I've got me name down for two,' she says, 'Burre's not called us up yet.'

A bobfoc – Body off *Baywatch*, Face off *Crimewatch* – does an old Kylie song, dancing well to it; Itchy has noticed that bison with good bods tend to dance well: they have to lure from a distance.

Wendy is not finally called up for another hour, but she's like a hand-held nuclear device on stage. She does 'Great Balls of Fire' and has the whole room singing and stamping along. People are cheering and thrashing their heads. The karaoke man sees he's on to a winner and keeps her onstage for 'Feel Like a Woman'. She does the chorus with a throaty growl and works the front row like a cabaret star – the Frenchies down there love it and start dancing, and that gets half the room up on the tables. She has a presence, Wendy, something you can't teach or fake, star quality. A Geordie transvestite is never going to make it in Hollywood, but she can rock a bar in Chamonix. She does another song before she is clapped back to her stool next to Itchy. And one of the owners presents her with a big blue cocktail, overflowing with crêpe-paper parasols, naked-lady stirrers and mini-sparklers, like a meagre bit of Las Vegas.

The karaoke is drawing to a close, and most people have sensibly realised that they can't follow Wendy. The ones who try are the worst of the lot, warblers and no-hopers. Itchy is ready to call it a night and is putting his coat on when the girl gets up.

She's with the French party at the front, the ski instructors, stands at the microphone as if in front of a firing squad, her arms straight down at her sides. She wears a one-sleeved top the cold blue of mountain ice, tight over her breasts; a scar traces the line of her collarbone on the bare side. Her hair is dark like teak, hanging straggly as if she's just climbed out of the sea. Her eyebrows rise to a point exactly in their centres, like officer's stripes. The eyes themselves are black as chess pieces, show a quickness, but are big in her face like a baby's. Even if her lips were as thin as autumn leaves Itchy would be smitten, but they aren't, they are full and inviting, and when she parts them the room fills with the most beautiful voice he has ever heard.

'*Non, rien de rien*,' she sings, not with the croak of Piaf, but with a voice pure and unwavering as a little girl's, '*non, je ne regrette rien*.'

She doesn't look as though she could have anything to regret. Itchy has never seen a face so unsullied by sin. She must be twenty-three or four but her skin is pale and immaculate, there are no lines on her but the shadow that falls between the end of her top and her taut belly and that pale pink scar across her shoulder.

'*Ni le bien qu'on m'a fait, ni le mal…*' Her eyes are closed now, as in sleep or easeful death. She is too beautiful to be a sparrow, even a little one; she is a nightingale at the least. A *rossignol* in French, same as the skis.

'*Non, rien de rien, non, je ne regrette rien.*' Itchy wishes he could say the same; his life is a trail of regrets, all leading to the same place, like Roman roads.

Every eye in the room is aimed at her now, though her own are still closed. Itchy himself is cemented, as if it were Medusa he stares at rather than a nightingale, his coat still half shrugged on to his shoulder.

The karaoke man must have a feel for finale in his routine, because he switches on a spotlight that shoots out beams from behind her like the tails of comets.

'*Avec mes souvenirs j'ai allumé le feu,*' she sings, '*Mes chagrins, mes plaisirs,*' her hands rising to beckon an invisible lover, her lower lip tremulous but her voice still proud.

As she starts the final verse, as she is about to tell Itchy one more time how little she regrets, the karaoke man triggers a smoke machine. The billows are still tumbling about at her feet, like a tribe of tabby cats, when she hits the crescendo. But at the point at which Itchy presumes Piaf would be amplified, the nightingale slows and sings more softly than ever.

'*Aujourd'hui, ça commence avec toi,*' and she opens her eyes, dreamily, with a hushed smile on her mouth, like one who wakes to find that what she wished for came true.

And of course it is by chance rather than design – since he is standing up, still poised to move in the centre of the room – but she is looking right at Itchy as she sings that final line. Their eyes have met across a smoky room, and for an instant Itchy thinks he might believe in love at first sight. But she steps down into the hugs of her friends, and he pulls on the rest of his coat, and the sense of that possibility vanishes with the last of the dry ice on stage, which is equally insubstantial.

Itchy clasps Wendy's hand like a mate then kisses her cheek like a lady, and walks away into the night, resisting the urge to take one more look at the nightingale.

He crawls behind the grating in the carpark, into his hole. It is well stocked now; half-empty bottles, looted from the bar, line the short wall: crème de menthe, Drambuie, cheap house whisky – shit that Doc never notices. Itchy likes the smell of the booze even more than the scents of petrol, oil and old stone that surround him in the garage. He pours some whisky into the Drambuie to make himself a flagon of Rusty Nail. He brought an old rug down last week, to sit on, to stop the cold of this place seeping too deep into his bones. It's a tartan blanket, such as old people take on picnics and babies cuddle scraps of, but Itchy just sits on it and sips his drink. Listens to the murmurs of pipes and generators. Like the midnight gurgles of a stranger's house to a small child, they make him glad of his blanket.

Shadows dance around the garage through the grille, from sputtering strip lights that project the inequalities of vehicle lines into Gothic gargoyles. There is a painting on one of the walls opposite him, outside his den, in an empty bay between cars, a dark space like a missing memory. It is not the usual graffiti of phalluses and primeval, territory-marking tags; it looks like the silhouette of a young girl, head tilted sorrowfully. All black, like the imprint left by a person's shape after a nuclear bomb has gone off. The figure is too big and too elaborate to have been done with a stencil, too intricate to have been done with an aerosol. Somebody has taken the time to paint it on by hand. Someone with an eye for female form, evidently, because it is perfect. Not perfect like the girl in the bar, the nightingale, but the perfect capture of a moment, of a feeling. It echoes the sadness that Itchy feels down here, the melancholy that he bounces off the walls like the Cooler King in *The Great Escape* bouncing his baseball.

Itchy is still not entirely sure why he comes down here. Whether it is to lie in wait for the rapist, or to try to feel what it is like to be him, to touch his world. To understand what it would be like to revel in the sensations that are instead destroying Itchy. What would it be like to be as free as that, to care so little about anyone else that you could take exactly what you want from them? Does the rapist fool himself that he sees some attraction in their eyes, does he think they want him, or manage to let himself believe they do, or does he just not care, are they no more to him than discarded accoutrements of pleasure? Like the beer cans and the bottles that are heaped beside Itchy in his hermit's lair.

Entry Number: 232
Narrator: Dr Polidori
Entry Title: The Butcher's Shoulder

3rd prize! £100 Book Voucher and a signed copy of Stanzas, Scars and Scandals.

Mont Blanc is generally held to be saddle-like in shape, though there are those who say it looks rather more like a joint of meat. Indeed, in the Savoy dialect it was once equivalated to *L'Epaule de Boeuf* - the Shoulder of Beef, or *L'Epaule du Boucher* - the Butcher's Shoulder.

Before travellers brought this love of the mountains, high places were feared; it used to be held in common conviction that dragons lived at the peaks and that demons inhabited the rest and maybe they did, for it is sure that old other one has no liking for exposure and light, but mountains have also an excess of dark valleys, deep caves and cracks that may well reach to hell itself. As for the dragons, a number of rigorous scientific journals have cited their existence among the summits. And dragon stones, which the adventurer must cut from the forehead of the sleeping beast, are offered on the market even today, said to cure ailments as diverse as dysentery, gout and consumption and may even out-efficacise Mercury in the treatment of those distempers one hazards in harlotry. A boon indeed, for Quick Silver, as I am certain you gentlemen know well, can be a hard salvation.

There can scarcely be doubt but that it was Wordsworth and other still contemporary - if out of favour among this company - English poets, who helped first found this modern love of rugged scenery. But before such uncommonly blessed men of leisure felt a calling to invent new ways to dispose of their leisure time. Before this peace at last descended upon Europe and the tours could recommence.

Before the thermometer and the barometer were invented, before the microscope and the telescope were in common usage, before Horace-Bénédict de Saussure wrote *Voyages dans les Alpes* and Thomas Burnet wrote *The Sacred Theory of the Earth* and Jean-Baptiste Lamarck wrote *Philosophie Zoologique*, but still not so long ago as you might suppose, there lived a butcher in the village of Chamouny. Of course one lives there still, indeed I can promise this to be the case, having seen his premises, but he is not the same man that I talk about now. For my story is of the coat-tails of the seventeenth century, when France was last ruled by a king, and a Sun King at that.

The butcher I reference was a man named Jean-Paul. Jean-Paul Gris to give him his full name, which was not something anyone was much accustomed to doing in so small a place as then was Chamouny.

Had this butcher been a count or a lord there is little doubt but that he would have been adored and fawned over by all who met him, but being less in rank, he was no less. He had a structure to his face that spoke of breeding, and he had a certain grace of movement, unencumbered as a mountain ram, and arms as strong as any; no doubt from hours spent rending meat from bone, which all flesh clings to till the last.

Jean-Paul was much pursued by female hunters, less prone to modesty in mountain haunts even than in the withdrawing rooms of London. Yet he was not married, excepting perhaps to his work, for he worked hard. And diligence and duty being much respected in such communities and Jean-Paul being also the possessor of a brooding charm, he was held in general esteem. He lived in stead of wife with his sister, his constant attendant, also his ward; the senior Gris having passed from this world – via Chamouny's much trod other exit – while the girl was yet in childhood. It was said by the villagers that he mistook his sister for a princess, since the succession of hopeful suitors who came to her were rejected out of hand, as if it were he held out hope for a prince. But her nature was sweet and her visage most agreeable and she should indeed have had a husband worthy of her, though the butcher himself was perhaps the worthiest in Chamouny at that time.

The butcher was a thoroughly noteworthy man, but perhaps his greatest singularity was that he never could resist a wager, and being of immense size and strength, but also of a rare if uneducated mind, there were few enough wagers that he had not the wit nor force to win.

He had once a bet with a chamois hunter, a fellow thick of thigh and firm of foot who felt himself the better of any through dense trails. But Jean-Paul it was who emerged first through the forests that were chosen as the race course, and claimed the man's barely weaned Tarentaise calf as his own. And also the naming of the woods themselves, which are known as the Bois du Boucher to this day. Whereupon the hunter bet him, for the calf's return or match, that Jean-Paul would not be able to lift it up still in six months' time. A foolish bid for Jean-Paul to take, the onlookers said, and his sister chided him like a wife, but Jean-Paul was as shrewd as a slipknot and he had an idea of how he might proceed.

He kept the calf behind the shop and fed it little enough to keep it the gypsy's end of healthy, though scarcely fatted, and he lifted the beast twice a day every day and thrice on the Sabbath. And sure as God curst Cain, when the allotted time had expired, the butcher's muscles had grown at the rate of the bovine and he was able still to lift it clear off the floor and was stronger than ever besides.

On another occasion a caravan rode into Chamouny who could be nothing but bandits, stocked as they were with munitions and blades. And their leader had a look as fierce as Tamburlaine, a nose as hooked as a Turk and a falchion as curved as his nose. They demanded food and wine from those who could scarce afford it, for in those days Chamouny was a place more wretched by far even than today, and they made neither attempt nor offer of recompense, but only demands for more. Well, soon enough the strangers were uproarious and bode no good for anyone's rest.

I believe the village mayor was hiding, or perhaps there was none, but the watchman was long gone, for he had at least the presentiment to watch for trouble. Instead a deputation came to the butcher Jean-Paul, who had a natural authority in matters, and was a man, as I may have mentioned, who could never resist a challenge.

Bandits are well known to wrestle and Jean-Paul it was said could pull a bull to the floor as Hercules himself once did, though for Jean-Paul it was to cut its throat and not to let it loose upon a Thracian palace. And so he had a mind that if he beat the brigand chief or his champion in a battle of pitted strength, the blackguard band might be induced to move along and take their trouble to Martigni, or to hide out in the mountain cols as the Saracens did of yore.

But by the time his scheme was laid and Jean-Paul had paced his way down to the tartars, they were already to a man beset by the blade of Bacchus. For there's nothing, I have often said myself, calms the spirit more than religious faith or wine; and the bandits, being less than blessed with one, were all the more inclined towards indulgence in the other.

Jean-Paul may have taken this to be advantage, since though the drunken man is more apt to propose a fight, he is rarely as good in its execution. But the bandits were armed beyond the teeth and past gullet with musketry and even while engaged in revelry had the air of those well prepared to loose a volley.

The bandit laird had his head swathed in a big kerchief over eyes as chill as death and less forgiving. At his one hand lay his ready curtalaxe, a flintlock and a dirk, at the other a pewter goblet overbrimming with eau de vie.

Jean-Paul hailed the chief and sat beside him at the table, requisitioned by the throng from some shack, and drew such looks from the other brigands that they alone might have slain one less blessed with fortitude than he.

'*Mon cher monsieur*,' said the butcher, in commencing his conversation, 'it seems to me your welcome wearies in this place, perhaps I could persuade you to move on a while, that another village might enjoy your company.'

The laird stared like a snake, coiled until the instant of its strike, but instead of lashing with fist or armament, he broke into laughter.

'Have you money to pay us, to move our feast, or maids to tempt us away with? For we are only settled here a couple of days and it is hardly our custom to hurry.'

'I'll offer you only a wager, at wrestling or drinking or the sport of your choosing and the winner will be the one to remain,' said Jean-Paul, quite confirmed that at any contest he'd win, for he was known as a man who could drink as well and that is one race in which a lead is less than beneficial.

But the footpad said, 'Knives, then,' and stuck his own dark blade in the trestle, 'and the rules are to death or mercy, but know thee I have none of the last.'

'Then if you choose the sport, I choose the spot, and we fight in front of my butchery,' said Jean-Paul, and he walked home to his shop with the brigands and villagers behind, as if he was the leader of the raggedest army in the land, like a captain of Boney's on retreat from Russia.

As he stripped off his coat, to his apron and shirt, the butcher's sister clung to his arm and kissed his brown locks and begged him not to do this thing. But the wager was set, and Jean-Paul was not a man who could spurn a wager, even to the death.

He took the largest of his hooked blades, which he knew to be the keenest in the rack. For it was the knife he used for killing swine and Jean-Paul was anything but a cruel man. Then he walked outside and chose his ground, a piece of long-subdued and level dirt beneath the large canvas awning which kept his shop front in the shade from the heavy summer sun, the same place where he had strived and enjoyed such meagre frivolities as he allowed himself and held his sister's hand, as if her paramour.

The cateran faced him with a smirk of one already exulted in victory and looked at the sister as he played with his blade, with the manner of one well versed in fighting and killing and facing death, for not only the virtuous are brave. But Jean-Paul cut the awning ropes as his opening blow, for neither are low means the preserve of the wicked, and the bandit was swathed in canvas, wrapped like a babe in swaddling and just as helpless. The cur was swiftly dispatched with a fist to his head and grateful perhaps to have been spared when he might have been murdered. As he came to, the bandit was true to his word and took his clan with him away from Chamouny. To end their journey no doubt at the end of a rope or up the twenty-four final steps of Madame Guillotine.

One more tale I have, about the butcher Jean-Paul, before the final story I would tell tonight. At this time, the always massy glaciers, those oceans of ice, threatened to engulf the very village of Chamouny, because of the rate they augmented. Their glassy tongues reached even to the valley floor and the inmates of that place, at least those the most prone to the stories of dragons and demons, were sure that some fiendish malediction was reaching into their land.

It was decided, by a council of the commoners, for such was the forthright way decisions were taken, that a petition must be made to the Bishop of Geneva, the most powerful churchman of the area, to exorcise the glaciers before they expunged the populace.

This sentiment drew only rare mirth from Jean-Paul, for he was not a believer in such spirits and hobgoblins. And since he knew as much of the mountains as any man then alive, so was he well placed to say if there were devils in the crevices. The butcher made plain his view that such things are in the nature of the mountains, that glaciers ebb and flow like the frozen seas they are and that the bishop's ministrations could be only as efficacious as Canute's attempts to rule the tide.

Cautious with his means as with his sister, Jean-Paul did not contribute to the fund the bishop demanded for his ministrations. Nor did he doff his cap when that man and his minions rode into town, for Jean-Paul maintained that if one donkey was sufficient for Christ himself, he could see no reason why a bishop required a cavalcade.

With a glaring eye this pride was marked by the man who held himself as God's Aristocrat and the bishop declared that they who shared not in the cost or the spirit of the undertaking would neither benefit from the exorcism. Let the butcher protect himself from what forces lurked in the entangled forests and frozen wastes.

The task performed, the glaciers did indeed recede, but since the process took many years it was hard even for the fiercest yea-sayers to be sure the money was well spent.

Jean-Paul did not care about the bishop's curse, for he feared nothing either in the underwood or on the peaks. The butcher was a conqueror and admirer of craggy beauty long before such things came into the fashion. He could climb through fatigues and fears of sorts that would bend another man, and he had conquered many of the mountains around the vale of Chamouny to see those fiercest views.

Though not of course Mont Blanc, for this was long before Dr Paccard and sturdy Balmat first made their glorious attempt upon that mount. Indeed Saussure, who would one day post a purse as their bounty, was not even a homunculus in his mother's belly when Jean-Paul lived and strode. Such a feat was deemed impossible back then; the butcher had climbed higher than any of the crystal prospectors or chamois hunters and even he had not assailed beyond the last outposts of rock that broached the glacier's domain, between its swollen grasping fingers.

One June day a beggar came to Chamouny, a queer choice of destination for a half-starved wanderer with a leather cowl and a tallow-face, as if exposed more commonly to dark than day. Yet though he looked as thin as death, the beggar asked nothing of anyone save for who was the best climber in the parts. Bedraggled greedy crows, the vagabond's vultures, eyeing from above, followed his progress to the butcher's shop, where Jean-Paul was at work of course. The great man of a small village, who knew neither science nor fear; barred by God from his true sweetheart, and as fond of a wager as Old Nick himself.

This resolute wretch encountered Jean-Paul and hazarded him two louis against the best shoulder of meat in his shop, or else his sister's elopement, that he couldn't climb to the top of Mont Corbeau and back by sundown the next day. Jean-Paul asked to see the sum, to show that it existed, and the beggar drew two gold coins from his cloaks and laid them on the counter as carefully as on a dead man's eyes.

Mont Corbeau means Mount Buttress or Mount Raven, but I prefer the former interpretation, for it is that peak which sits well below Mont Blanc, the last of the mounts of rock, splitting the tumbling piles of ice like a ship's prow in Arctic seas. Though he had never been up there, Jean-Paul surmised it an easy enough ascent and without a cloud in the sky the morrow promised to be mild. Besides, the bet was not one he reckoned he couldn't pay, for his sister would never be given in marriage to another, but he could afford the stake in meat without fear of beggaring them both. So Jean-Paul spat on his palm and shook the ancient hand of the vagrant, which he would have sworn was as cold as the stone of the mountain itself.

When the butcher set off at dawn, Mont Blanc wore its hat of cloud, a sure sign that ill weather will come fast, and little grey epaulettes sat about its shoulders. The remainder of the sky was dry and clear as a linen shroud, but the wind bowled along the valley like chainshot and Jean-Paul's heart was heavier than his feet as he fought to get up the mountain fast before the heavens broke.

He passed through sounds of spuming waterfalls and forests dense and a clearing glen where a goatherd tended his flock, solitary and stoical. And making such strong progress was he that Jean-Paul stopped and talked to the man while he ate the provisions he had brought and shared some fortifying wine. They watched the man's old black billy, named Satan for its eerie look, which had borne the bell and led the herd through five years, since before Jean-Paul's sister had much more than a trace of woman about her little figure. But that afternoon it was challenged and submitted to a younger bearded rake and fled off into the forests to die alone, with the sudden knowledge that its time was passed.

'*Tempus fugit*,' saith the preacher, but he mistakes, for time does not fly, it wastes, it dwindles and shuffles and twiddles into nothing, '*Tempus fidgit*' is a truer phrase. And the butcher looked up to see that he had squandered a precious portion of the day, though he was rested and well victalled. So on he climbed beyond all track and sound of shepherds, through places where the chamois hunters trod not, leaving behind the canopy foliage. Through desolation he passed, groves of pine trees, leafless, broken branched, mighty trunks snapped like twigs to a child, bared of bark and cracked and tumbled, from force of avalanche, but on he climbed. Through narrow defiles and torrent beds and growling billows of waterfalls that misted like the tail of the pale-ridden pale horse, yet on he climbed. And all the while angry clouds thickened in the sky; wicked peaks, crenellated like Gothic spires, piercing them through.

Jean-Paul clambered from cliff to crag through scraggy patches of snow that lay between, shivering in his thickest leather coat, for the sun was as masked as the executioner of a king. And at last he reached the summit that he sought and waved the sheet of red upon its peak to signal his success to one lone telescope below; a hue still unimbued back then with pride of revolution and sorrow of its blood. Yet as he waved, the clouds poured out the sky's wrath, thunder broke upon his ear and lightning slashed the gloom. First graupel, then snow, fell as thickly as in deep December's chill, and the butcher saw the depth of his undoing.

The beggar was awaiting the assignation when Jean-Paul stumbled back into Chamouny, scarred from falls and fighting branches in the dark and long after night had fallen. The snow lay grumous enough upon the streets that two sets of footprints could be followed through the village, the heavy tread of Jean-Paul, of course, and beside them the small light steps of his conductor tripped, erratic and spirited, as if in scurry or dance. So gaily moving and so nimble that they hardly seemed to leave a print at all; and what marks were made were more like those of stilts or hoofs than feet.

In the morning, when the villagers came, the shop was dressed with blood even by the standard of a butcher's. The eyes, on the hook-racked hares, bulging and terrified, looked like gazes of love set against the expression on Jean-Paul's face, which was as white as a skull and still as the snow-caked street. His sobbing sister clutched him like a wife, but her tears could not undo the harm of what she had seen through the shop's keyhole.

The butcher's hand and arm sat beside him on the counter, next to a missing sheet of greased paper. And, neater than he could have done it himself, the best shoulder of meat in the shop, some would say in the whole valley, the butcher's own right side, had been cut away.

Which is why - though Mont Blanc may look rather more like a saddle, in shape - the old Chamouniards, in black jest and from respect, call it the Butcher's Shoulder.

I never will live in England if I can avoid it, why must remain secret, but the farther I proceed the less I regret quitting it.

Byron

January 19th, 6 a.m.

Six in the morning is a time of day that Itchy prefers to see from the other side – going to bed, not getting up. But Snow Spirit Holidays, who Sean works for, have lost two staff members in the past week and Itchy has been offered dumb money to rep a coach to Geneva and back.

The dark Cham Sud square is expectantly quiet, like the still before a dawn-break duel. The snow has melted and refrozen repeatedly over the last weeks to form a crust beneath Itchy's trainers which excretes the same effortless blue as the sickle moon.

The bushes, in what might be a flower bed by design, are scrawny and bedraggled beneath ice clusters that choke them like shrink-wrap. And in their midst, which he has never before noticed, is a stone pillar. Itchy takes a moment to look at it, his breath solidifying in the freezing air. It is an old water fountain, on closer inspection, probably predates the rest of the square by a century, maybe more – Itchy is no expert. It is weird how it has been left poking up like one of Obelix's menhirs, when everything else around is made of concrete from the seventies and eighties. The stone is flecked with black spots like a diseased lung and there is a wound in its side, where presumably a spout used to protrude. The basin beneath, once pooled with water, is filled with more shrubs and weeds, competing for whatever scant and frozen soil is within it.

Itchy meets the coach at the rendezvous at the main Cham Sud bus stop. It is half an hour late, as they always are, but he has shuffled and stamped himself warm like a pro, wiping a running nose on the borrowed uniform fleece.

The driver has eyes that wander independently of one another and sparkle with life's hilarity, and an early morning cheer that is more than slightly irritating. He erupts into a gravelly giggle when Itchy mounts the coach, his quivering grunts shaking the thinning grey hair that stands from his head like Einstein's. Beneath his gaping, gummy grin, a dribble-smeared beard the same colour and length flows down, as if one clump or the other were an escapee. He looks as though he should have been retired or institutionalised years ago. Probably he was, but is dragged back into service on winter Saturdays, when there is hardly a spare coach driver in the region.

Snow Spirit is at the upper end of the market, so the pick-ups are all hotels: several of which have been attending to the needs of British tourists for more than a hundred years. There is something infinitely more servile about being a rep than there is working in a bar; Itchy feels as if the guests harbour expectations that he will bow, when they step out of the three- and four-star residences, built in an era when England had a king as mad as the driver.

Itchy has done plenty of early morning transfers in his time and knows that the guests want to be left alone to doze, so he keeps his departure talk to a minimum. Just the usual junk about how long the journey will take and to let him know if they feel sick. The driver turns his radio on to 'Bad French Folk FM', playing their special early morning wake-up mix, the moment Itchy has finished.

They take the main road out of town, the original road, which has now been made into the dual carriageway down; the suspended road only takes you up. There are other ways in and out of Chamonix, though. There is the tunnel bored straight through Mont Blanc to Italy, which amazingly cost not a single life in the making but claimed thirty-nine in the fire after which it has only just reopened. There is the back way, the old trade route into Switzerland, a sly winding road through national park and insular villages. There are train tracks, and passes, and ski touring routes that drop you into Courmayeur, Trient and even Zermatt, if you have the stamina. Chamonix is the conjoin of three countries and there is innate power at crossroads. Originally part of the Duchy of Savoy, but in independent spirit closer to its Swiss neighbours, Chamonix voted to become part of France, has been occupied by Italy and Germany; and now, by creeping purchase, some locals fear it may yet fall to Britain.

The nose of the coach is low, as if it's snorting the white lines from the tarmac. They have no cat's-eyes in France, and there are no streetlights on the road; it is only those pale lines that the driver's agley eyes have to go on in the black.

The music and the vibrating window, which his head is resting on, keep him awake, but Itchy has his eyes closed, pretending to be asleep as deterrent against any of the guests speaking to him. Through his eyelids he can feel day coming, while his thoughts twist about. About Marty, who he seems to have been thinking of a lot recently, and about Tina, who he has never thought about enough to make amends, but who increasingly occupies his dreams. The end of the season will be the ten-year anniversary.

When they stop at a motorway toll, Itchy jerks and opens

his eyes as if he has just woken. Not really sure why the acting is necessary, but feeling himself doing it anyway – like the exaggerated gesture of looking at his watch or slapping his head he would make before turning around on a road to walk back the other way. As if it is important to communicate to the people around him what he is doing and why he is doing it. Recently he has started to feel himself doing such things more than ever. Felt himself posing, as if people in the supermarket are aware of how coolly he pushes the trolley or how carefully he selects his ham. Though he knows they aren't really, knows it's just a charade, and no one cares about him but his few good friends and the sub-nuclear family he hardly sees.

There is a breakdown by the side of the road, steam pouring from an engine that has been stressed beyond its limits. The car's owner is alone and no one is helping him. The old mad coach driver laughs as they speed past.

It's the first time Itchy has been out of the resort for two months and he drinks in the landscape through the soiled windows. There is currently no snow at this low altitude, but he still sees the terrain in terms of skiing: bumps that could be jumped off; rock drops; slopes to straight-line, or cut-in carves. He looks at everything with the same eyes colonial explorers must have, in terms of what they could do with it, how it could be conquered and owned.

And what he notices most about England now, when he goes back each summer, is how flat everything is. Very level, very secure, sturdy even – but flat. It no longer feels like the kind of place where he wants to live, even in the imagination.

There's a brittle wooden cross nailed to a tree by the motorway's side, with a bunch of weather-battered flowers beneath it. Unconsciously Itchy scratches his cuticles, where somehow or other he has got traces of black paint.

*

The driver tries to engage Itchy in conversation, once the guests are dropped at the departures point and he has parked up. But the flight they are taking back to Chamonix is not due for several hours and Itchy has no wish to be trapped talking small in French with a senile chauffeur for that time, so he rapidly makes his excuses and slopes off into the main terminal building.

Geneva airport: signs for bespoke watches and financial services; tanned trophy wives with lip-line tattoos; shops for jewellery, gadgetry, silk, leather; Swiss obsessive–compulsive disorder, toilets you can't even use because they're always being cleaned; people kissing; à la carte restaurants; croissanteries and juice bars; no junk food; taxi drivers waving bits of old cardboard box with important names on; joy tears; pilots, dapper and overpaid in naval blazers; old folk who will never see each other again waving nobly; warnings to watch for suspicious packages; sulking jailbait rich girls; Toblerones; tour ops; empty multi-faith spiritual sanctuaries; full smoking rooms.

Groups of British holiday reps are hanging out in company cliques near the arrivals area, full of chat and bullshit. The Oakleys on their heads have the new plastic smell of freshly unpacked geometry sets, the stuff that everyone thinks they need for secondary school but will never use. There is no sign of any uniform from Snow Spirit, but Itchy would rather avoid them anyway, he's too tired to hear stories of epic adventures and guest disasters. He heads for one of the bars instead, gets a vodka and coke, for the caffeine. Reads a newspaper supplement that someone has left on the real-marble counter top. Faint Arabic music is playing, tinny and prayer-like, which makes him think of veiled dancers and plane hijackers.

The monitor flickers periodically with refreshed arrival time predictions, but the flight Itchy is waiting for has not even reached the bottom of the board yet. He scrapes up his change, in shiny silver coins – Swiss francs even though he paid in euros – and leaves a sip in the bottom of his glass, so the barman knows he's not an alcoholic.

Outside the bar is the cockpit of an old plane. A little boy, dark and serious, is sitting in the pilot's seat, making noises of take-off. Itchy watches, until he notices the mother, watching him watching. Everyone is a potential abductor now, he supposes. He smiles at her in a way that he hopes says that he is a nice guy, just enjoying the charm of childhood, but she doesn't smile back.

There are free Internet terminals in the main arrivals area. Itchy waits until one of them is available. The guy who goes is wearing Diesel jeans, but he's old, like sixty, and Itchy doesn't get why the man would spend over a hundred and fifty quid on a pair of jeans he's still going to look sixty in.

Itchy checks his Hotmail; there is nothing but spam, mostly for software to stop spam. On Google, he types in her name, hoping to see that she is happy, or at least coping, at least still alive, but finds no such consolation. Her name is too common, though she was a princess, and search engines spit out 11,899 possibilities. Everything from Australian estate agents and American gymnasts to a lonely wretch of a woman with her own cross-stitch website, but nothing he can link to her.

A cluster of African migrants stand – presumably waiting for the contact who found them work – surrounding their nylon-frond shopping-bag luggage. They are being eyed warily by the Portuguese cleaners, who got to Switzerland first.

The Alps themselves were formed when the African plate first collided with the European. And they are still rising higher, as Africa continues to force its way northward; not just on planes, like these fortunate few, or in teetering dinghies and suffocating cargo-hold containers, but in the entirety of the continent.

The flight Itchy is waiting for has appeared on the bottom of a monitor, next time he looks. BA 6274, in bold yellow letters, like on teletext. BA stands for Bad Attitude, at least it did for BA Baracus, who was famously afraid of flying.

'I ain't goin' on no plane, fool,' Itchy says; the impression is lame and half hearted, but only he is around to hear it.

There is still an hour to strangle before the flight lands. Itchy mooches around a big *tabac* and newsagent's, thinking he can get rid of the Swiss coins that are valueless in Cham. But they are of similar worth in the shop, where even a can of Fanta is beyond their purchasing power. He watches an exceptionally short guy trying to survey the porn on the top row of the magazine rack. Obviously wanting to make his mind up in advance, so that he only has to make one clutch at the shelf – which he probably can't reach except by straining and standing on the newspapers at the bottom. But the slash of cover left to the world, under the mostly greyed-out cellophane wrap, is as small and discreet as the eye slot in a Muslim woman's hijab and leaves him little to go on.

Short Man averts his gaze when a lady with a beige dog in a matching handbag stands next to him. He pretends he was looking all along at the lads' mags – which would themselves have been porn twenty years ago – trying translated copies of *FHM* in one hand and *Arena* in the other, as if he's at a fruit-stall and his final decision will rest on weight or firmness beneath the finger. Just as Itchy suspected, though, as soon as the lady has moved off, Short Man steps up on to a pile of *Figaro*s and snatches something from the top shelf.

Curious now, Itchy marks the spot on the pile behind, and moves over to see what it was that Short Man bought. It is nothing particularly depraved, looks soft if anything, it's called *Dix-Huit*, and the visible strip is of a pretty young blonde face gazing wistfully at the camera.

Such looks go past the lens and into the reader, though. They confirm what men half suspect, and the stories invariably verify: that they all want it. Her availability is assured by longing eyes and urgent nakedness; but she is more beautiful than most men should dare hope to be with. Even Itchy – who is among the fortunate few to have glutted on girls in his time – feels a pang, confronted with this confusion of promise and the unobtainable.

Hard porn is something different, the women are normal looking, even plain looking, and their gaze is rarely directed at the reader. They do not want it: they are getting it, often from more than one person. You are even more superfluous to their world than to the real one. Hard porn explains that you can't have everything you desire from life. That sometimes you have to be content with watching other people. Hard porn is indeed 'adult' material – soft porn breeds spoilt kids, maybe rapists.

Itchy is wearing his best welcome smile when the thirty-three guests finally come through, long after the plane is down, pasty faced and piled with luggage, exhausted and angry. Their skis have been left off the flight, almost to a pair, despite paying twenty pounds extra each for the privilege of ski carriage. Itchy is faced with their wrath since he is the company's representative, even though the flight is not a charter, so there is nothing he or Snow Spirit Holidays could have done about it.

'The good news is,' he says, when he's gathered the guests together, 'that in situations like this, where the airline has deliberately offloaded equipment, probably because the flight was dangerously overweight, your skis should be coming on a later flight. They haven't been lost, so the carrier will endeavour to get them to you this evening. And of course your ski carriage will be refunded.'

The other good news, he thinks to himself, is that he will not be on the scene by the time their equipment probably doesn't arrive this evening.

'So we've got your guarantee that our skis will get here tonight?' asks a belligerent bearded guy; he looks as if he Morris dances and talks as if his tongue is too fat for his mouth, like that TV chef.

'Obviously I cannot firmly promise you that, because it is not something that I have any personal control over, but that is what would usually happen in this situation.'

Itchy finds himself slipping into rep speak; reps always seem to use overly formal language, like baby lawyers. Maybe, like lawyers, it separates them from genuinely caring about their clients. 'Sorry, sorry, sorry – money, money, money,' is all reps are ever really saying.

'*That is what usually happens in this situation*,' a woman mimics him, 'so this happens every week, does it? How can you not know there's going to be skis on a ski flight?'

'What if the skis aren't there in the morning?' Beardy says. 'Are you going to pay for ski hire?'

The crowd around him is beginning to get mob-like, and Itchy knows from experience that they will pacify better sitting down and split up.

'If you've all filled in lost baggage forms through in the arrivals area, then there isn't really anything more we can do here. So probably the best thing is if we go and get on the coach and start towards Chamonix and I can answer any further questions as I come round to see you individually on the journey.'

'Oh, yeah,' Beardy says, 'we can't give you your skis, but we still want to come round and sell you a lift pass! Why don't you get a proper job?' and he stares at Itchy as if he actually wants an answer.

In other circumstances Itchy might answer him too. He might

say: yes, I could get a 'proper job', as you call it. I'm not work shy; you have to work hard to live like this. I just don't want to turn round in twenty-five years' time, when I'm your age and braced for my decline, with nothing to show but a half-paid-off house in some nonentity suburb of a city that I don't even like. Occasionally fucking a pleasant enough wife, and probably someone else's as well, because nothing seems to ease the constant soul-drenching monotony, or help me face the aching realisation that my life is not what I chose, just what I ended up doing. Mostly, though, you should just be happy I don't want a 'proper job', because if I did, I might want yours!

But to say that in front of the crowd would not only be letting Sean down, it would be tantamount to suicide, so Itchy just smiles politely at Beardy and asks the most angry woman if he can carry her case – which she would like to decline, but is not stupid enough to do, so is forced to choke 'Thank you' instead – and he leads them all out to the coach, like the Pied Piper of Croydon.

Darkling I listen; and for many a time
I have been half in love with easeful Death,
Called him soft names in many a mused rhyme,
To take into the air my quiet breath;
Now more than ever seems it rich to die,
To cease upon the midnight with no pain,
While thou art pouring forth thy soul abroad
In such an ecstasy!

Keats, 'Ode to a Nightingale'

January 25th, 12.23 p.m.

Part of the pleasure of life in a ski resort is its simplicity. It removes all need for motivation or reasoning. If you have a day off – you go skiing. If you want to meet friends – you go skiing. Any time you are not involved in something else – you go skiing. There is never any need for deliberation. Unless the weather is really bad.

Today, though, Itchy feels like he has been tricked. He got the bus up to Argentière on his own, thinking he would bump into someone he knows up on the mountain, or ring around the usual suspects if he didn't. But the light turned flat and mist closed in so much he could hardly see. He did one trip up the Bochard lift and then the home run to the bottom, and he has no intention of going up again.

It seems a waste to turn around and go straight back into

Chamonix, so he walks to the Office Bar. The bar is garish on the main street of the ancient village – purple-painted, with film posters on the walls – it is a centaur or a satyr, half one thing and half another, looks as though it would prefer to be in a city centre somewhere. Of course, it is Brit owned.

It is also empty, so Itchy leaves after downing one demi, out of politeness. His skis are still locked on the rack outside, so he thinks he'll go on up the street to Super U and get some deodorant and a couple of other things he needs. Then see if the Office is looking more fun yet or go home.

Super U is closed, which should be obvious, but Itchy will always be exiled by French opening hours. He will never get used to convenience stores being shut for precisely the period it would be most convenient to use them. He stares in through the window, as if the shop might open up just for him, if he could catch someone's eye, but it is as empty as a graveyard.

There is a real graveyard out behind Super U, and having nothing better to do, Itchy thinks that he'll go and have a nose around it. It is walled and gated, but the iron gates are open. Outside them is a woodcarver's cabin, adorned with carved crows, goats, and faces bleached skeletal by time and wind. Logs are piled as high as fortifications and whole uprooted trees are stacked, with their roots held up to heaven like desperate fingers. The weathercock on the church spire wavers before the cloud-covered sky.

Inside the walls the graveyard is compact, like an anti-Tardis. There is another person in it, tidying some flowers, so Itchy sets off the opposite way around the path. The same names crop up again and again: Ravanel; Charlet; Ducroz; Simond; Devouassoux; Bellin; Grivel. They are the names of streets and peaks and shops and climbing equipment. They are the names of heroes. Few of them died of old age by the look of the dates on the gravestones. The stones themselves are either hewn into the form of tusky mountains or are odd-shaped lumps of rock, left as they fell. Other graves are marked by simple wooden crosses, like something thrown together by a comrade. Where cause of death is given, it is invariably the name of a mountain, not an illness. Though there are also those who died *Pour La Patrie Par La Montagne*, men who fought to free themselves at the end of the German occupation; the Col du Midi was the site of the highest battle of the Second World War. And there are others who fell, not from cliff faces, but sunk in water and despair, in trenches in Belgium, the flattest land they must ever have seen.

Itchy has one friend who committed suicide, one who died in an avalanche, one of an overdose and one in a car wreck. Natural causes seem a most unnatural way to go somehow, to him. But since death is life's only certitude, maybe all ways are ultimately natural. Death is probably the only natural act humanity still owns. Death and sex.

As he continues round the graveyard, Itchy sees Ravanel née Devouassoux; Devouassoux née Ravanel; Ducroz née Ravanel; Ravanel née Ducroz; Devouassoux née Bellin; Bellin née Charlet; Charlet née Ravanel and Ravanel née Charlet. Until it is clear that all these great names must be linked. All the family trees, of the founding fathers of Alpinism, as tangled as a food web. But here it doesn't smack of inbreeding – it's more like pedigree.

At least these people left their line. Without descendants there is only descent. Itchy has nothing to hope for after he is gone and nothing to live for now, except for hedonism and the possibility of powder.

He went to Jim Morrison's grave in Paris, when he travelled back from Cham one year. Couldn't see what the fuss was about. It was just a load of stoned hippies leaving spliff butts and beer cans – because that's what Jim would have wanted, isn't it? – and desecrating other graves with spray-painted directions.

The graveyard in Argentière is different, it makes Itchy feel something for these lives, and for his own. Provokes a sadness for the waste, and a slight, self-indulgent envy of the dead.

The flowers on the graves, even some of the most ancient graves, are fresher than the flakes they lie on. Roses, like blood, are never redder than when they rest against snow.

The girl who was tidying a grave at the far end has finished by the time Itchy's path has led him round there. She is standing up now, one hand on a slim hip, looking at the headstone impassively; impossible to tell whether in sorrow, or admiration of her handiwork.

She is the nightingale, the girl from karaoke, impish beauty glowing rosy and red nosed from beneath a tufted wool bobble hat. She looks at Itchy when he approaches, the second time he has stared into those manga-large eyes, and her mouth dimples into a smile.

They swap *bonjours* as strangers, but hold each other's gaze briefly, as she moves to let him clomp by in his ski boots, feeling like an ape dancing with an elf. As he passes, she grabs his arm and raises a finger to her lips to silence him, which draws down her lower lip, shows him the pinkness inside, which would silence him even if he didn't know what the gesture meant. She points the way he has just come from; sitting on the wall now is a bird. Sleek in build and slick in a two-tone ska suit of feathers: black-and-white bars along its wings and back, ending in a bright yellow hat. It cocks its head at them and slowly hops along the wall, as if it wants their eyes to follow it. As if it still has to build up confidence in its obvious allure. A beautiful teenager, flirting – only half knowing what it does, but half suspecting that it may be irresistible.

'It's a three-toed woodpecker,' she whispers to him in English, which is just as well, since he has no idea what the French for woodpecker is, 'very rare.'

Her hand is still in the crook of his arm, and Itchy is keeping still more to avoid dislodging it than through fear of startling the bird. But it hops from the wall anyway, and flies off with a bobbing trajectory towards the Aiguille Verte – a peak that would be *the* big mountain in most ranges, but in Chamonix is only nestled in among its peers, like the greats in the graveyard.

The nightingale removes her fingers from Itchy's sleeve and ripples them, a mini Mexican wave, as she says, '*Adieu.*' Then she turns and walks away from him, moving with a feline liquidity, the furls of hair beneath her hat echoing the motion of the woodpecker's flight. Gore-Tex-wrapped shoulders, slightly too broad, yet perfect; sloping gently down to an outward-curved arse, simultaneously concealed and advertised in baggy jeans. Legs that move so gently, but are most likely hard as wood. As Itchy looks at all this, he feels as if the world has suddenly become bigger than he thought it was.

Only later will he realise that he should have had a look at the gravestone, to see what her surname is, or at least might be. Now he is only whistling to himself and trying out *adieu* in his head. It is not like *au revoir*, 'until next time', nor is it the 'see you soon' of *à bientôt*; there is no implicit recognition that you will ever meet again in *adieu*, which bothers him, but maybe it is a natural thing to say in a graveyard in Argentière: 'till God', you may be back tomorrow or you may never be back. Philosophy is compulsory at all French secondary schools; thirteen-year-olds study Sartre; they have a deeper perspective on life.

There is still no one Itchy knows in the Office Bar when he walks by, but he pops in anyway. And on a strange urge he has an Orangina and a bag of crisps instead of booze. Reads yesterday's

Times alone at a table while he eats and drinks. The crisps are Walkers, most of the Brit bars sell them, for at least twice the price of back home. When the packet is nearly empty, as often happens, Itchy pulls out a crisp that looks no different from any other, but turns out to sizzle in his mouth with salt-and-vinegariness, as if nearly all the bag's flavour has been absorbed by it. And it makes him think of the nightingale again, because that's the crisp that she would be.

While he's on his way to work later, back in Cham, with the sun safely tucked up in bed, he sees a woman walking along with a dog. She is looking at him determinedly, wanting to catch his eye, wondering whether she still has it. She does, in fact, she's early forties but still trim, still pretty, little lines around her questioning eyes the only clue. But he still feels sad for her, because she had to ask him, because the opinion of a stranger walking down the street mattered to her, and because one day the answer will be no, and then what will she do?

Her dog snarls as he passes; dogs don't like Itchy, though babies seem to. He can't help looking back at her, a hundred metres farther along the street, and when he does she is bending down, as if in a curtsy, but really to pick up her dog's poo – with a plastic bag that will not start to biodegrade until long after she is dust.

No one comes in for a while when Itchy has opened and set up the bar. Still thinking about the nightingale, he has a coffee with a mist of milk and two sugars. Then he re-creates imaginary matches of noughts and crosses – which is more fun than actually playing on your own. Really just doodling, but leaving the impression of a game. *The Game*, fuck, that means he's losing again – so he sends a text message out on group sender, to even the score. It just reads:

```
Remember The Game
suckers!
Hope u all well.
Itchy
```

The Game is something that Itchy and a few of his childhood friends have been playing for years. The object of The Game is not thinking about The Game. It's beautiful, because when you're doing well you're not even aware of it. You only know how you're doing when you're losing again, in which case the best thing you can do is to try to drag everyone else back down to your level. It could be a metaphor for life. Because life is at its best and its most enjoyable when it is at its least considered: when you start to think about how you are doing; whether you are progressing; where you are going; what you could have done; then you are no longer living in the moment, you are only regretting or planning and you can only console yourself if your situation is at least no worse than those around you. The Game isn't a metaphor for life, though. The Game is just a game.

Doc pops into the Derapage to work for a bit, although there isn't really enough for two to do. Itchy likes working with him, time goes quicker when he's there, which is not always the case when you're working with your boss. But Doc knows stuff, he's always got a story about something. You tell him where you went skiing today and he'll tell you about the time he got stuck out there for a night and had to sleep in a snow-hole. Not in the boorish, trying to outdo you way that you sometimes get with punters, he's just telling you something that happened to him.

There are a couple of guys in the bar who are obviously former season workers, they can't wait to get their jumpers off, so that everyone can see the staff T-shirts of yesteryear they have on underneath. Staff T-shirts are like rock tour T-shirts, only you get your own name on the back, among the names of friends who will fade even before the T-shirt. They're just a memento, but some people, like these guys, wear them as medals. True veterans don't need medals, you see the scars.

Sean once said that your first season is like that perfect point of drunkenness – where you are wittier, more confident, happier – before the bad bits kick in. But you can't stay at that point, with beer or winters. You either have to stop drinking, go home and sober up, or you have to keep drinking and take the bad with the good. Most people choose to go home and sober up, but when they come out for their one week's holiday a year, they like to pretend that they are still at that perfect point of drunkenness, that they never left it.

Sean comes in later, with Daniel and Aussie Mark. Itchy feels very dimly jealous that the guys are spending more time with each other than any of them do with him, but he isn't really cut out to be jealous, even of his mates: Itchy doesn't need company as much as others seem to.

Aussie Mark is drumming his fingers on the bar, as usual, the boy can't sit still. Sean is on his mobile, affecting to give a fuck about some Billy's problem; he motions to Itchy with his free hand that he'd like a pint. Daniel smiles and claps Itchy on the shoulder, in the way that he does that persuades people he's one of the good guys, which he is, which is probably why it works. Daniel's hair is starting to get quite long now and he's grown a goatee, which makes him look a bit like Jesus. Or like they say Jesus looked, as if anyone knows.

Itchy pours himself a demi to drink with them; Doc doesn't mind so long as you don't take the piss. He knows a lot of the workers only come in to see Itchy, he's not daft.

Doc gets a phone call from his daughter anyway, bright love appearing on his wrinkled, wintered features, and he disappears off to meet her.

'Don't wait up for me, *chérie*,' he says, blowing Itchy a kiss as he leaves.

'There's been another one,' Sean tells Itchy later, lowering his voice so the punters can't hear; his tone says that he means another rape.

Itchy knew this anyway for some reason, maybe because he noticed that another painted figure had appeared in the carpark last night, another slim silhouette with head lowered in shame and sadness. Maybe because he is getting closer to the rapist now, he is beginning to feel the monster's thoughts when he's in his lair.

The continued crimes are separating the workers from the holidaymakers more than ever. A few reps, like Sean, are warning guests not to walk back alone and particularly not to go through the carpark alone, but the majority of guests are left in blissful ignorance; taking not even the basic precautions that they would at home, in the cotton-woolled suburbs of St Albans or Stockholm.

The latest victim is another English girl, Sean says, but no one knows much more. The tourist board must be pressurising the gendarmerie to keep the details quiet. Otherwise there should be a description at least by now, an artist's impression, a photofit, something to go on, but there is nothing at all.

The guys stay in after closing, pretending to help clear up for a free drink each. Daniel is the only one who is much use. Aussie Mark is too pissed and Sean just moves the mess about with his mopping.

'How's Suzi?' Itchy asks Daniel, while they wipe down tables. 'I haven't seen her in a while.'

'She's good, she's Suzi, just working hard. She goes out with the staff from her chalets a lot, to bond with them.'

'You should tell her to take it a bit less seriously, man,' Itchy says, 'it's not like she'll get a bonus.'

'She's just a perfectionist. But she's good, don't worry, there's no problem.'

Itchy wasn't worried, just making conversation, but he's noticed before that Daniel always reads people as more caring and thoughtful than they really are.

They all leave the Derapage together, Itchy and Sean taking slugs from a bottle of white wine that would be sour by tomorrow night. They swing down the street to walk home along the Arve, a decision made organically, as if the same gravity that draws the river is pulling them down beside it.

There is a row of flags that hangs out over the dark torrent; almost every country in Europe is represented. Almost. There is no Union Jack. Brits have a bad reputation in Chamonix, some of which is deserved. But it probably wasn't a spiteful decision not to raise their banner. More likely it's for safety's sake: because, even with the rows of downward-pointing, evil-looking spikes, Brits inebriated on alcohol and atmosphere would try to climb out and get the Union Jack. Either it would go missing, or, more likely, they would fall into the flow, only kept from freezing by the rapidity of its movement, and be lucky if they drowned before hypothermia or the rocks took them.

There is a huge and beautiful, but derelict, building by the edge of the square, probably once a hotel; the shutters on its iron wrought balconies have been closed for so long they are rotting into each other in their pairs. Such urban decay doesn't belong in

Chamonix at all, let alone two steps from the casino, in the town centre. Itchy always looks at it slightly regretfully as he walks by. Tonight Vince is alone in the alley to its side, beneath the street sign which reads 'Chemin du Folly'. He doesn't see the guys come round, silent for once where they have been hypnotised by the jostling waters. His back is to them and he has an aerosol in his right hand. The ball bearing in it rattling as he makes the universal wanker sign. He is poised to spray when Daniel says:

'What the hell do you think you're doing?'

Vince looks around, and grins as if he has seen old friends. 'Hey, boys,' he says, 'just a bit of tagging, thought I'd leave my mark on the town.'

'Tosser,' Daniel says, as he takes the can from him.

Vince looks as though he is going to offer Daniel out for a moment, he squares up his shoulders and squints. But Daniel is bigger and much fitter and it wouldn't be any kind of a fight, and seeming to realise this, Vince turns and starts walking away.

'Yeah, go home,' Daniel says. 'If you're lucky I won't tell Suzi about this, or you'll probably lose your job.'

When he's farther up the street, a safe distance away, Vince turns round and shouts: 'You want to worry about you and Suzi, not me!'

'What the fuck is that supposed to mean?' Daniel asks the boys, still weighing the spray can in his hand.

'Don't worry about it,' Sean says, 'he's just talking shit.'

'Yeah, that's humiliation talking, bro,' says Aussie Mark, 'that's not real, forget it.'

Itchy doesn't speak.

Second Semester

NICOLE AND PAPA, her wearing this Laura Ashley dress, which it looked as if she might pop out of at any moment. The Gold Blend couple, why didn't they just fuck, instead of all that tortured TV flirting? Liquid Gold, an account advocated by a rhyming Arthur Dailey. Midland, the Listening Bank. Sunday supplements, always with further revelations about the crisis in the royal marriage. *Now That's What I Call Music 19*. Aussie lagers: 'Think we've overdone it on the sherry, mate.' Kemps frozen yogurts. Harp, stays sharp to the bottom of the glass. Right Guard, double protection. You can tell when it's Shell. Swinton Insurance. The Colonel's Summer Combos. Levi's adverts still lingered, though the fashionable no longer wore the jeans. Those were the days, my friend.

Itchy walked around bald, below, for weeks of that second semester. Having discovered to his dismay and disgust that there was a colony of creatures living in his pants. Tiny waving crustaceans that would be cute if Marty was looking at them under a microscope, but were not when you were their host. So

Itchy applied the razor, thoroughly, like a Chippendale, leaving no hair beneath his neckline. And took mega-hot baths, with vinegar in, just because that seemed like the sort of thing that would help, and maybe it did. They disappeared anyway. Down the plughole, to nest instead with whatever alligators lurked in the Sheffield sewer system.

The girls he slept with in the weeks afterwards thought it very strange, he could tell. Though doubtless they would have all gone Brazilian by now; it's only indifference to personal etiquette or hoisting the hairy flag of feminism for girls not to shave or shape now, and guys are starting to follow. But back then, if they asked, Itchy just said his mates had done it for a joke, when he was passed out. Which was very believable, since his mates, the football team, were well known, and that was exactly the sort of thing they would do.

They called themselves the Regulators, after Billy the Kid's gang. Though it was never established who Billy was, and they were not even particularly interested in fighting. Not like the rugby team.

'So is she raped, or is she seduced?' the tutor asked, pacing at the front, finger raised to catch invisible hoops.

'We don't know,' someone said, not Itchy. Tina didn't do Victorian Literature and so Itchy rarely contributed, in fact had not even read the book.

'Correct,' said the tutor, who had a curious Captain Ahab-style beard and a bald head that would catch the sombre city daylight whenever he paced too near the window. 'We must presume this to have been Hardy's intention. But there are other factors; he's probably not being deliberately ambiguous, for its own sake, as some irritating writers are today. For many Victorian readers, sympathy for Tess would have evaporated if she had yielded to seduction – or, worse still, been a willing participant – so he has to leave the possibility that she was raped.'

The tutor continued, 'But, as modern readers, we can appreciate there may have been more subtle powers at play. She was trebly in debt to him: for her rescue; her job; the gift of a new horse for her family. And she was alone in the woods, the significantly named "Chase". These are forces of coercion, but not rape. She twice afterwards becomes Alec's lover, which could suggest she consented. Also, Hardy stresses the naturalness of the event through his language: "primeval yews", "roosting birds" and "hopping rabbits and hares". And later in the book, Tess thinks to herself how: "She had been made to break an accepted social law, but no law known to the environment in which she fancied herself such an anomaly." Ultimately, Hardy probably suggests that it doesn't much matter how the act took place – afterwards she is ruined. And in those days it was a maid's duty to keep herself out of situations where such a thing might occur. Because it was well documented that men could not control themselves.'

'But isn't Hardy saying that's not fair? That morally she was raped, if not legally?' A bloke saying it, perhaps with his own Tina somewhere in the class, his own reasons for appearing intelligent and well adjusted.

'Actually, recently some have suggested that even legally Hardy may have been giving clues. He was a justice of the peace and so presumably knew, in terms of Victorian law, precisely what constituted rape: if a woman was asleep, as Tess is just before the incident, then she was unable to consent and thus it was rape. But again we don't know if she is asleep by the time the act takes place. In an earlier draft, considered too immoral for publication, she was also given an elixir by her seducer. In English law of the time, if a woman was given alcohol and then put into a sexually compromising situation, it could also be considered rape. Might be something for some of you to ponder!'

There are titters of laughter at this, which the tutor's expression had beckoned; he considered this to be a joke, not a point for serious consideration.

Back in those days, there were still a few girls who arrived at university afflicted with virginity, and invariably this was cured with a regular application of alcohol. The wonder liquid – which can sterilise and anaesthetise the wounds it causes.

This was also the age when alcopops first appeared – Hooch, Two Dogs, Mad Dog – the forerunners for some reason obsessed with the canine. The press soon began to obsess with scare stories of the inevitable rise in teenage drunkenness. As if it was only the taste that prevented children everywhere from drinking on the way to school. As if cocktails had not been around for ever, and Baileys and Kahlúa. As if kids weren't more than willing to apply themselves in overcoming the unpleasantness of smoking, so as to reap its benefits of stink, shorter life and addiction. Cost, not taste, keeps kids from booze; which is why they don't drink alcopops and cocktails. Children drink cider, fortified wine and Special Brew, same as tramps. Women drink alcopops. And they are wise to do so: it is much harder to slip Rohypnol into a narrow-necked bottle than into a glass of wine.

The football team, the Regulators, went skiing once. Just to the dry slope. Sheffield laying claim to having the biggest ski slope in England at the time. A drab grey hill covered in egg-box hexagons and carpet offcuts. A strange sensation, sliding about on bits of brush, feet held rigid in stormtrooper boots. But Itchy took to it like a slug to slime. Stayed out there, skiing the same two hundred metres of plastic, even after all the rest had retired to the bar.

When he was a kid he'd had this recurring dream that he could fly. Only he'd never been able to get far from the ground, just flying along at head height, unless he really picked up speed, in which case he could rise a little farther. Accelerating down hills to evade his enemies. Enemies mostly unseen, but sometimes a thin spiky creature, as if it were made of thorn bushes. Itchy used to wish for this sensation when blowing out birthday candles: to fly! to fly! Which his mum had said was silly, because you should wish for something that might come true: like a new Action Man or even a dog. But, it seemed to Itchy, that was even sillier: why wish for something that might happen anyway? If wishes come true, why waste magic on the possible? And if they don't, then it doesn't matter. But Itchy began to realise on that dry ski slope that wishes can come true.

Tina remained his deepest wish, though. He wrote poems about her. Bad poems. Self-indulgent poems. Romantic in its modern, mindless sense – without any echoes of the *Romantics*, which he continued to study with her. Sitting unbearably close. Like to a fire: the part of him away from her too cold; the part that faced her too hot; the whole uncomfortable; unable to look away from the lure of the flames. Let the fire consume everything, just so long as it continues. Let the fucking house burn down. Burn it all. Live like a last crazed Bedouin pitched among incinerating oilfields.

Itchy thought he saw Tina's ethereal form out in a club one night. Her wearing a pale gown, like a temple vestal, better suited to another scene. Only the red ribbon in her hair breaking the nebulous white of her figure, as far from the other whirling shapes as the moon to fireflies. But when he reached the spot she was gone. And though he searched, he couldn't find her again through the bacchanal masses. His desperate questing eyes never alighted on her large innocent ones, nor her soft mobile lips, amidst all the human pollen.

Later he realised he must have been fooled from the start by the apparition. The nightclub where he thought he had seen her, the chain Chasers, was the last place Tina would have gone, more usually the haunt of townies and boob-flashing trash. There were no goddesses on those daises, only amateur pole dancers and the extinguished coals of cheap fags.

There was a kind of festival at the end of the academic year. A fair outside on the playing fields. A sunny summer's day with lifejacket-yellow inflatables and outside bars and games. Itchy and Marty fought on a jousting balance beam. Bashing each other with unwieldy rubber clubs. Evenly matched, but Marty emerging the victor.

'Survival of the fittest, motherfucker,' he'd said, hugging Itchy round the back one armed.

One of Itchy's end-of-year assessment comments had said that 'a charming smile and flashing eyes will not be sufficient to pass exams'. But he had anyway, in the event, all of them, not only the Romantics. He had survived.

The Regulators spent most of that last day together, the last time that they would be a team. Some would be leaving at the end of their final year. Some had failed their first years. Some would be dropped, when better players joined the uni. As it turned out, Itchy would not return anyway. And Marty would be dead.

Pleasure's a sin, and sometimes sin's a pleasure.

Byron, Don Juan

February 3rd, 7.26 p.m.

Football works for some; for others rugby; or war, which both sports have tried and failed to replace; the National Anthem; the Queen; democratic government; tradition; empire; language; liberalism; the NHS; the welfare state; the Beatles and/or the Stones; Shakespeare; Shelley; Lord George Noel Gordon Byron. All of these, no doubt, provoke passion in the kingdom's citizenry. But only one icon makes Itchy truly proud to be British: James Bond.

The first time he felt a stirring in his chest, anything akin to patriotism, was that scene in *The Spy Who Loved Me*: where you see 007 plummet over the four-thousand-foot cliff on skis, and you know he's dead meat this time, or at least you don't see how he can get out of it, short of some cinematic trickery. But then his chute opens into the glorious Union Jack and the music starts up – 'Nobody Does It Better' – and you think, 'Yeah, it's pretty cool to be British.' Though, of course, it is still better to be it somewhere other than Britain.

Itchy has made a videotape of all the ski sequences from the various Bond films. It's beginning to lose quality through over-watching, but the guys are watching it again. It starts of course with *The Spy Who Loved Me*: Roger Moore rustling some Russian bint on a pile of furs before a log fire; caveman, and yet suavely sophisticated, in a late seventies kind of a way. Then the ticker-tape watch, which is all he has on – technology on the edge of credulity at the time – sends out a message that England needs him and Moore is off in a blur of bright yellow all-in-one. The bad guys, in black neoprene, are in hot pursuit. But Roger outskis them, or at least a stunt double does, interspersed with close-up shots of Moore swaying in front of a moving movie backdrop. Bond spins about to shoot an adversary with an exploding dart from his ski pole, backflips over a kicker on the first ever pair of twin-tip skis – twenty years before they were commercially available – and disappears over that incomprehensible cliff and into cinematic history. What a film.

On Her Majesty's Secret Service is Itchy's favourite, though, a controversial choice among Bond fans. George Lazenby, apparently told by his agent not to do any more, for fear of being typecast, was barely ever to work again after turning down future productions. But, even aside from the fact that the film contains by far the most ski and snow sequences, Itchy argues it is the best.

'He's supposed to be a spy, right?' Itchy gains nodded assents from Sean and Aussie Mark. 'But *Her Maj* is the only film in which he adopts a disguise, one of the few in which he even assumes a different name.'

'But he's a wuss, he's weak,' Aussie Mark says; he prefers Connery, even though Lazenby was actually Australian.

'He's just human in it, he's not weak, he shows weakness: you see him scared for the only ever time; you see him in love for the only time, when he marries; and then heartbroken, after his wife is murdered; and he doesn't rely on gadgets, it's the closest to the books,' Itchy counters.

Sean, of course, favours Moore, style over content, the

womanising, wisecracking Bond. To try to sell on this point, Itchy points out that George Lazenby sleeps with an entire Swiss finishing school, which is more than any other film in the bird count.

'But he just doesn't have the class that Roger Moore does,' Sean says. 'Moore you believe slept with those women. Lazenby, it's just in the script.'

They watch the rest of the sequence: Bond on one ski better than the bad guys on two; Telly Savalas as Blofeld; Diana Rigg as Mrs 007, fresh from *The Avengers*; skiing over chalet rooftops; jumping snow-blowers; bezzing about in a big red Mercury Cougar convertible with ski-rack on the back; not getting buried in an avalanche that should have killed him – but then Bond is lucky, that's his most uniform characteristic, that's what all the Bonds have in common.

Itchy looks at his hands; an ex, more of a fling really, was into palmistry. She taught him where his luck lines and love lines and health and heart were. At least meant to be – Itchy doesn't have a heart line. She also taught him how to lick the shell off a pea, but that's another story. Your left hand is what you were born with, supposedly; your right is what you make for yourself. And Itchy has noticed recently that though the luck line on his left hand is long and well defined, on his right it is small and faint and he could almost swear it is shrinking by the day, but then who believes in that shit?

For Your Eyes Only, with the spike-tyred motorbikes, is next, the snow-school class tumbling down like dominoes when the chase goes past. A stuntman died during the filming of skiing down the bobsleigh track, tied by a wire to the sled. It is perhaps most notable as a film, though, for the fact that it is the only instance of Bond turning down the chance to bed a beautiful girl. Itchy can't believe 007 would really exclude her for her age, because seventeen is legal for England, and besides, he is licensed to kill, it seems unlikely he would be prosecuted for consensual sex with a minor. It is purely out of character, then, a nod to political correctness from the film-makers, when Bond is a blatantly misogynistic murderer. No one minded if in *Goldfinger* he slept with the mastermind's girl over a microphone, to no end, and knowing this would mean her death. But somehow, a middle-aged Moore shagging an eager seventeen-year-old would be too much for people to handle: much worse than unblinking and brutal killing of security guards and joking about it; or driving countless cars down crowded pavements.

Personally, Itchy is in favour of a degree of youth, and that world-wise seventeen-year-old would make it within his watershed. He likes birds with dimples between their back and their bum, where the flesh is still high. Birds whose bras are there to pad, not to support, and don't match their three for £10 La Senza G-strings. Birds whose only lines are the polite refusals their mothers once taught them; lines they never use anyway.

The ski sequence for *The World Is Not Enough* is supposedly in the Caucasus mountains, but actually filmed in Chamonix. The helicopter swoops past the sharp needles of the *aiguilles* that the guys could see out of the window, if it wasn't dark and they weren't watching them on telly. The chick who will turn out to be a baddy drops out of the helicopter with Pierce Brosnan – who nobody would vote for, but everyone agrees is better than Timothy Dalton – and they ski down the languid miles of the Argentière Glacier, past alluringly deadly seracs and crevasses, with a computer-generated oil pipeline running down the middle of it.

The whole film is a homage to *On Her Majesty's Secret Service*; the title is Bond's family motto, revealed by Lazenby when he posed as a genealogist, and the ski sequences in particular doff their fox-fur caps to Lazenby's film. But this time, when avalanched, Bond is equipped, with an inflatable protective bubble that comes out of his jacket.

He has been forearmed by Q for the final time; Desmond Llewelyn – the only actor to have appeared with all five 007s – would be dead before the film's UK release. Killed in a crash, while driving a fast car, alone. Llewelyn bows out with these words of advice to Bond:

'I've always tried to teach you two things. First, never let them see you bleed.'

'And the second?' Bond asks.

'Always have an escape plan.'

The only man to have played Q then descends into the floor at the pace of a lowered coffin. Such things are not coincidences.

Itchy twists the top off another beer; he always has an escape plan too.

The final film segment in his pastiche is the first film he ever watched at the cinema, forever tied to skittish excitement. Moore was by then showing his age and ready for replacement in the dynasty; 007 is the bastard son of Dorian Gray and Dr Who, doomed to battle evil and the void for all eternity.

'Do all the martinis and all the beautiful girls help to silence the cries?' he was asked in *The World Is Not Enough*.

They help. They must help. They help Itchy.

View to a Kill starts with Bond searching in the snow; he has in his hand a Barryvox transceiver, forerunner but technologically little different to the ones the guys wear when out riding. Another double-0 agent is buried, barely beneath the surface, in yet another avalanche, but the man doesn't have Bond's luck and he is dead. Moore shows little expression, because death goes with the territory and because of the enormous sunglasses he is wearing. The same rules still apply today: the more of your face they cover, the cooler you look.

The Russians chase him, never learning, but nearing the end at last of the cold war. When his ski is shot off, 007 hijacks a snowmobile. When that is blown up he takes its runner and, to the music of the Beach Boys, snowboards to safety. This was a time when snowboarding was more of a theory than a sport – the first occasion it had ever featured on a big screen.

Aussie Mark is whooping as Bond surfs over a lake; the commies foolishly trying to follow on skis all sink, instead of just shooting him. A Union Jack hatch opens in what looked like an iceberg. Sean stands up and salutes, Itchy just feels quietly proud. The rescue craft is piloted by a slim and stunning blonde, instead of a tattooed submariner-sergeant from Hull. But then Bond is lucky – we know that.

They're going to Hotel California. Burning paraffin in cut-off beer cans guides the way up the hill, torches like some primitive procession. A lot of fuel must have been used to get the fire burning up as well; the forests on either side are thick with fallen wood, but snow-covered and damp.

'It's a bit Pearl Harbor,' Sean says as they walk up.

'Eh?' says Aussie Mark, who must never have heard the old platitude.

'There's a nasty nip in the air.'

Hotel California looks like a Second World War relic too: a Herman pillbox or something. There were Nazis in Cham once, on the border with Switzerland, where resistance heroes and shot-down airmen might try to flee, but the shell that is called a hotel is really just an abandoned ski jump control tower. It's concrete and three storeys, glassless windows barred with iron, blossoming with smoke on the bottom floor, where the wood fire is. The bars with flames behind look like devils' mouths. The jump itself is long collapsed and vanished; only the building and the slope cleared through the trees in the mountainside remain. It may have been built for the first ever Winter Olympics, which were held in Chamonix in 1924, but probably not, and the crowd who are assembled are not the sort of people who would be able to answer that question.

A lot of them are from the mobile homes, converted vans and kombis from the park down below the hill. They're vannies, not pikeys. Itchy hates real pikeys, hates their horrible inbred faces, their cockiness, which they seem to base on the fact they think they've had a rougher ride than you. Hates the fact that it's true, and of him more than most. Hates himself for his prejudice. But if there's one thing he hates more than pikeys, it's posh people.

'Hi, chaps,' Crispin says, as they trudge up the last few yards towards Hotel California. Crispin's got a scar on his head, where a harp fell on him as a child, and rugby-boot-stud stamps on his hand.

Techno bangs from someone's cheap boom-box. Techno goes with vannies, and with parties by abandoned buildings in the woods.

Crispin gives the boys a beer each from a box of Super U own-brand. He's a shit-hot skier, his mother is half Norwegian, he's probably spent a month a year skiing since he could stand up. And he gave up a good job to come to the mountains, which you should respect. But somehow you don't. Because his unkempt hair, carefree stubble and scruffy hat look like a bad disguise as soon as he opens his mouth.

The fact is, though, that Itchy, Sean and most of the Brit seasonaires in Cham, probably even most of the vannies, are firmly middle class, burdened with their own guilty shares of encouragement, luck and opportunity. There is a mutual pretence that they are all free spirits, taking only what they need from the world. But that is always easier with the safety net of a family home you can bolt to for a while, if things don't work out. Maybe that's why Itchy sees people so visibly wince whenever Crispin speaks: he's breaking the rules, because you're not supposed to have to think about how fortunate you are in life, just about how fortunate you are to be in the mountains and how sensible you were to reject all the other lives you might have led. Crispin does sound dumb, though.

'So are you chaps going to be going up on the hill tomorrow?' he says.

Aussie Mark smiles, masking it behind his beer, but not spitefully; probably Crispin's accent sounds even posher to an Aussie.

'Yeah, I'll head up with you,' Itchy says, feeling like a rat suddenly for his thoughts. 'Let's do the Midi. I haven't been up there in ages.'

He leaves Crispin with a promise to meet in the morning and goes into the building, walking up outside steps to the second storey. People are sitting around the concrete floor, which is warmed by the fire beneath. A ginger chick is trying to scrape coke or speed into lines on a make-up mirror that isn't really big enough for the job. The first time Itchy ever saw coke racked up it was like magic, like watching a tuxedoed croupier at a casino: a professional, careful, sophisticated action. It is tawdry now, though. It's all tawdry now.

The chick pulls her hair up into one hand, like a temporary ponytail, while she snorts a line, revealing a neck that is long and pale, a vampire's wet dream. Itchy keeps looking at her – just long enough so that she notices and meets his eye, then he looks away again – but his interest is now logged.

He turns his gaze out of the window. The bars run horizontal on this floor, thick like cattle grids. Chamonix town is like a constellation; he doesn't remember ever having seen it from above, after dark, before. Its size is shown by the pinpricks of light from every apartment window, running from one side of the forest's frame to the other. It looks like a real town, which it is, he supposes. Cham has a McDonald's, a one-way system and a selection of beggars – what else do you need to qualify?

Aussie Mark comes up and stands beside him, passes Itchy another beer, but doesn't speak, joins him in looking down. Aussie Mark is one of the few people Itchy would like to have with him at a party or a disaster; he does strong and silent better than a campaigning George Bush. Without being a brainless prick.

The chick is dancing now; she glances at Itchy when her head flicks his way. But there is no chance of him joining her, not with techno playing, when the dance floor is a ten-square-metre section of a derelict tower. She's got a nice body, though, at least her lower half – her top is obscured in a puffer jacket. She's slim, but not too skinny – French birds sometimes overdo it on the coffee-and-cigarette-plan diet. She's not French, though; he'd say from Bristol, if he had to guess, but it would be a guess.

Itchy isn't a great one for dancing anyway. Sean can be quite keen; he likes it as a way of plucking himself from the crowd. He does a bouncing hip-hop step, which can, if he wants it to, lead into some on-the-floor b-boy manoeuvres; a little routine, which looks as though he is going for a backspin. Itchy happens to know that Sean can't really do a backspin, but in his routine's culmination Sean fails to do it in such a way as to create the impression that usually he succeeds. It's all a sham.

A cluster of wolf spiders hang together in a corner. Itchy had never given any thought to what spiders do in the winter. A skull, fox or maybe a young chamois hangs from a rusted hook, where presumably something more practical was once attached.

*

She's from Gloucester, not Bristol, but that's close enough for Itchy to feel smug. She's doing French at uni, just lucked out getting Chamonix for her placement abroad – didn't even ride before she came here – is a teaching assistant at one of the schools. Chamonix has several schools; maybe that makes it a town?

The walk to her apartment is long, right at the other end. She lets him feel enough of her on the way to show that he can expect the goods at destination, though. Kisses him with urgency, so he knows he's not just protecting her from the rapist. Saying periodically, 'I don't normally do this, you know,' like they all do, like they always do. Like they must get told to by *More* magazine: 'How to make a one-night stand feel special.'

It was MDMA powder, not coke or speed; she tips a small pile from the wrap of a Cantina flyer and stretches it out into four neat lines on the weary Formica table by her bed. Itchy sits Buddhist on the floor and does one with a ten-euro note, which he leaves furled by the side. She takes her coat off and hangs it from the door, pulls the cord from a towelling dressing gown that also dangles there and tosses it to Itchy. Who holds it blankly, head tilted.

She kneels down and pulls a powder line into each of her nostrils, dips two fingers into a glass of stagnating water, which sits on the table, and snorts that into her nose behind the drug. She is long since expert at twenty.

'Tie me up,' she says, pushing her hands up Itchy's chest and drawing his head down to hers, biting his lip.

It seems slightly spoilt to want to be tied up the first time, a way of getting out of doing any work. But her bluntness and the idea of doing this with a stranger reaches into a mind long inured to finding much in fucking still kinky. The MDMA has gone directly to Itchy's cock too.

He grips her wrists in one of his hands and draws them up towards the bedhead, ties them there with her still hunched on her knees. He pulls her top up, so that it uncovers her pale back and covers her head. Roughly undoes her bra.

Briefly he contemplates leaving her turkey-trussed, and going back to the party or out for a beer, just to teach her not to be so fucking naive. But his knots aren't so expert that she wouldn't be out of them in a couple of minutes.

She says, 'Squeeze them hard: try and hurt them,' when he reaches around to tease her nipples.

He remembers Sean's joke: 'Whip me! Whip me!' the masochist says.

And the sadist says...'No.'

He lifts her up on to the bed and draws her bra higher, so that it hides only her eyes. Her breasts almost disappear when she is on her back, but she has the pale pastel Hubba Bubba nipples that he hopes for on ginger girls, and standing out like the spikes of ski poles. He twists them hard enough to make him wince; but she only groans with joy.

She kicks her own shoes and socks off. Lifts her hips to help him with her jeans. Her pants are navy blue, like gym knickers, with one of the Mr Men on them; a cute little snail-trail in the gusset.

Her hair down there is cayenne pepper, cropped and shaved into one line, like a landing strip. Her lips are as puffy as crying eyes, little bubbles of expectation between them.

He goes down, and makes her come like that, half his hand submerged in her.

'Fuck me,' she says, through gritted teeth, 'for fuck's sake fuck me!'

Not for the first time, Itchy wonders when they got so dirty. Because they are definitely getting dirtier by the day. When did girls start to do stuff in the course of casual sex that he's sure would have made a prostitute blush twenty years ago? Chicks are noticeably filthier now than even a decade back when Itchy launched on to the scene. Than even five years ago, when a blowjob was still unguaranteed. Where can they go from here?

In the morning, she says that he doesn't have to take her number, but that if he takes it he has to call. And he nods as if he's listening and coming to a decision, but ultimately takes it just because that's easier, knowing that he near-certainly won't phone it.

And he nicks a stubby from her fridge, as he leaves, because he needs some breakfast if he's going to ski the Midi with Crispin. Most of Itchy's calories come from booze these days. They say it's bad for you, but it's all that keeps Itchy alive.

But sleep did not afford me respite from thought and misery; my dreams presented a thousand objects that scared me.

Mary Shelley, Frankenstein

February 8th, 8.50 a.m.

Itchy has a recurring dream. He's in a bar, even in his dreams he's in bars, but this one's in Ireland, which he knows just in the way that you know such things in dreams. There must be music playing, because people are dancing, but Itchy doesn't hear it. He's absorbed completely with watching a girl. She's like a pocket Venus, a perfect miniature, with queen-size eyes, gypsy-black hair and Porsche curves. She dances with her hands held together above her head, swaying her hips and showing the space of flesh where her napkin T-shirt doesn't meet her tight grey pants.

Every time she turns, her eyes meet his. Not so much 'come to bed' as 'fuck me now'. But he doesn't move and slowly she comes over to him, rubbing and writhing in front of him, until he is hard in both dream and reality. Then she takes his wrist and leads him out through a back door into a barrel-and-crate-stacked alley, where she forces him against the wall, surprisingly strong for her small frame. She kisses him purposefully, pushing her weighty breasts into his chest. But as suddenly as she started, she stops and steps back and laughs. And her beautiful eyes show nothing but hatred, sheer unabated disgust. He doesn't understand this until he senses the presences on either side of him. Big looming figures, one of whom presses something against his temple. And because it is a dream, Itchy can see it as well as feel it, and it is an ugly slate-coloured revolver, with a stubby, brutal barrel.

'Ha' you bin kissin' my girl, squaddy?' the figure with the gun asks in an Irish accent.

'Aye, he was shit as well,' the girl sneers.

And then Itchy understands that it was all a trap, that they're going to kill him and leave him in a ditch or a shallow grave in the woods, and that the best he can hope for is that he won't be tortured first. And he tries to persuade them that he's not a soldier, but they don't believe him, or else they don't fucking care. Then they smash his teeth in for talking at all.

Usually Itchy wakes up at that point, sometimes too scared to go back to sleep. Which is just as well, because they say that if you die in your dream then you will really die, and he is in no doubt that they are going to kill him. This morning he is still asleep after they have bundled him into a car and told him to keep staring at a painted spot on the floor, which he does, with the gallows-walker's despair, without any attempt to escape or fight back. He is still asleep after they have driven him out to a disused carpark, where they cable-tie his hands behind his back and push him to his knees and drench him in petrol from a battered khaki jerrycan. He is still asleep even as the girl flicks open a Zippo and lights it on her grey flannel leg. And though at this point he finally wakes, he does so panting with fear and to a bed wet from sweat and his own urine. Which is not a good way to start the day.

The state of Itchy's duvet and undersheet have necessitated a trip to the launderette, which was probably well overdue anyway. Vince is in there, with the two kids who he hangs around with most of the time; like the Fonz, trying to make himself look cooler against a background of dweebs.

Next to them, Itchy feels as cool as the sweat down the side of an iced glass, even though he has pissy sheets in the bin bag he carries. He nods to Vince and the kids and empties the sack directly into a free machine.

'Your mate went off on one the other night,' Vince says.

'Guess you shouldn't have been tagging walls, then, huh?' Itchy says, uncommittedly, not turning round.

'Yeah, well, no worries, hey? Doesn't have to affect our relationship, Itchy, I've got no beef with you.'

Itchy turns round and smiles, a smile that digs in at the edges, like too-tight ski boots. 'Sure thing,' he says, 'not going to affect us.'

He shakes the proffered hand, only because it must have taken a lot for Vince to make his little speech, but Itchy feels his eyes sparkle with the insincerity of a politician.

'Nice one. We're going to grab a demi while we wait,' Vince says, gesturing to the machine his clothes swirl round in. 'We'll be over the road if you fancy?'

'Bit early for me,' Itchy says; as if! 'I'll just sit and wait, I think.'

'Well, you know where we are, if you change your mind.'

Itchy gets powder from the age-creased ice-cream box that sits at the bottom of the detergent dispenser; alone now in the launderette, enjoying the smells of soap and heating cloth. The powder machine and the change machine are heavily scrawled upon by French marker pens, but none of the washers is, as if that would break the vandals' code of conduct.

He pours the powder into the slot on the top of his chosen washing machine; bright blue flecks stand out in the white gunk that clings to the sides from previous users. When his coins are inserted water washes the powder out of the plastic furrow before he has shut its lid, which gives him an idea. Taking a look behind him, Itchy lifts the slot lid on Vince's machine and unzips his jeans. On tiptoe he points his cock and pisses into the softener trough; he won't be the only one wearing clothes washed with his urine.

He sits down beside an orphaned sock, feeling juvenile and vindictive; disappointed with himself, more even than usual, he looks around for something to distract him from the feeling. He would quite like a beer or two, even with Vince, but can't go now.

The pine-panelled walls are studded with old staples; posters advertising tae kwon do lessons; cinema listings; motorbikes, cars and snowboards for sale; information wanted on a young Scottish guy who's gone missing – who will probably be spat out of the end of the Mer de Glace in two hundred years' time. Water spumes against the glass front of his machine, like a cruel sea on TV, waves a hundred feet high, but in scale.

Part of the *Herald Tribune*, a Yank newspaper, is lying on the scuffed tile floor. Itchy picks it up and reads any articles that interest him in the slightest; most of it is domestic US stuff that he couldn't care less about.

There's a story about a woman in Florida that grabs his interest, though; she has won a rape case, in the defendant's absence, because the man she married turned out to be a Cuban spy. Her lawyers have successfully argued that because her consent to sex was fraudulently obtained, it did not count. To pay the damages three recently hijacked Cuban planes, in American possession, are to be auctioned off and the profits given to her. The article's author, clearly left wing by US standards, is worried about the precedent set by this: that a sovereign country's airline can be held responsible for the actions of one of its citizens; and about the non-return of hijacked property. There is no comment about the precedent that a man who lies about himself pre-coitus can henceforth be considered guilty of rape.

Witching hour plus two. Itchy is down in the garage again, in his hole. Watching the dark caverns through his bug-eye grate. Swigging from a bottle of Genepi, which might just as well be meths, by the strength of its taste and by how little attention he is paying to it anyway.

His phone beeps. The Morse code which indicates a text message arriving. Dot dot dot, dash dash dash, dot dot dot. SOS. Save my soul. The message is a reply to the group sender Itchy sent a few minutes ago. To the guys he plays The Game with, saying that he didn't want to play any more, that he's had enough of it.

The reply text reads:

```
Request noted & refused.
U wud still b playing anyway.
Only death can end The Game.
& even that may not.
Remember The Game. Lol
```

While Itchy ponders the meaning of this, which is surely nothing, a girl walks into the carpark; crossing by the brightest parts; even in her new adult world of alcohol, still holding on to her childhood fear of shadows. It is a fear well founded in here, a fear that might save her. But Itchy knows it's not enough. She is blonde, pale skinned; trendy, in the offhand teenage way that money and style can never reclaim. She looks down at her feet just as she passes a black-paint silhouette of a girl also looking down. It becomes obvious to Itchy that she is next, that she will be the victim tonight. Unless he can stop it.

He eases out of his lair, silently, smoothly as a spider. Trickles after her through the gloom, so that she won't see him, so that he won't frighten her. He follows her, as she traverses through tunnels and concrete glades, keeping just out of sight, like a private dick, or a hunter.

She disappears round a corner; Itchy slows, to give her time to lead off before he follows. His trainers scrape through a pile of sticks and litter dropped from the streets above, through the bronchial shafts, intended but inadequate to circulate this stale air. The heap of detritus looks like the last exhausted attempt at nesting by a diseased ground bird, even in dying unable to resist its urges.

Itchy rounds a pillar with his back pressed tight against it, making himself as small as possible, taking advantage of the half-light to hide. He is so intent on keeping hidden from the girl that he doesn't notice he is watched by three men, until they have closed in on him.

'*Qu'est-ce que tu fait?*' one man asks.

'*Il suit la jeune fille*,' one of his two companions says.

'I'm only following to protect her,' Itchy tries to say, but his throat has clammed up with the cold and the shock of this sudden confrontation. He coughs to clear his throat, like someone about to make a speech, like a defence lawyer.

'*C'est lui*,' the biggest of them says; his hair is cropped close, military style. They all wear dumb jumpers, which look like unsolicited Christmas presents, and stink of booze even through Itchy's own stink.

'*Quoi?*'

'*C'est lui, il est le violeur.*'

Itchy is still pressed hard up to the pillar, so the first fist knocks his head back against it. It catches him right on the nose, with a pain that squeezes out sideways, blurring his eyes. Itchy can be quite handy in a fight, but not against three. He is taking more blows than he can possibly defend. Tirades of punches are landing. Winding him. Leaving him choking for breath, like a strung shark. One blow hits him in the forehead; so slow, he could have dodged it if he'd wanted. He doesn't know why it wasn't important enough to dodge. But every side of his face has been struck now anyway. His hands cover his eyes and he bends over as fists continue to blitzkrieg against his head and his back. Soon he is toppled into the pond-slime pool on the floor. Curled up and screaming silently, like a fetus being untimely wrenched from comfort into death.

'Enough,' one of them says, but the boots keep coming, slamming into Itchy's back, and legs.

'That's enough!' the voice says again. 'We'll take him to the gendarmes.'

Which doesn't thrill Itchy, but means at least that they are not off-duty police themselves – which he had momentarily feared, by their build and haircuts and taste for sudden brutal violence – because who is going to save you when you're being beaten by the police?

They pick him up by the arms and legs. He makes no attempt to struggle, because it's too late, like in his dream. He is damned and he might as well get it over with. His head lolls to one side, as if his neck is broken. It isn't. The pain in his legs and back tells him it isn't, but it still droops as they carry him. He can see rainbows of oil and sparkling cubes of glass on the floor. Lit by fractured strip lights. He spits blood from his mouth; it feels like there's glass in his mouth. Maybe that's why he can taste blood, he likes the taste of blood, always used to suck his cuts when he was little. He'll do that later; when someone stops this, he'll suck his cuts. He'll have some good scars from tonight. Some African tribes rub dirt in them, so they stand out for ever. There's plenty of dirt down here. Scars are good. Scars tell you that the dreams were real.

'He's too fucking heavy.'

'Alexandre's right, we're never going to carry him to the gendarmes.'

Itchy is dropped to the floor, arms and legs still held in the air.

'OK, two of us guard him while one of us gets the police.'

'Who's going to get them?'

'Not me, it's too far.'

'Not to the station, it'll be shut anyway, just go to the barracks.'

'They won't come if they're not on duty, no chance. Anyway, why me?'

'I'm not going because you two can't be trusted not to beat the shit out of him some more if I go. We'll be done for murder.'

'Who gives a shit if you murder a fucking English rapist?'

'The gendarmes!'

'Why doesn't one of us stay and two of us get the *flics*?'

'Yeah, right, and what if some friends of his come down? Or some other English who don't believe he's the rapist? You think they're going to believe you? Fuck that, I'm not staying on my own.'

'You go and get the *flics*, then.'

'Not on my own.'

And Itchy is thinking, through his busted agony, 'There is a solution to this, it's like the puzzle with the fox and the hen and the bag of grain, there is a way you can do it.'

'OK, let's stick him in a bin, put something heavy on it and then we'll all go.'

'*Tu as raison, Alexandre, bonne idée.*'

Itchy is carried a little farther and hoisted into the air, as if for the bumps, then dropped into a large vault-bin. The smell is beyond rank, beyond putrid; foul enough to shake him from his stupor, Satan's smelling salts. He begins to vomit even before the lid has been shut. He hears his captors laughing, and something being lifted on to the lid. Then there is silence, but for his own gagging reflexes and more vomit. Acid from his stomach full of Genepi, burning into the cuts around his lips and mouth.

As he moves to try and lift the lid, plastic sacks split underneath him, releasing further rancid stink and covering him in bin juice. He can't even lift the lid an inch. Whatever they have put on top is too heavy for him to shift from within. He wonders whether he should shout. It might be easy enough for a passer-by to slide the object off. But the chances of any passers-by are slim, and they might not release him anyway, and he feels too weak to shout.

Surely it will be all right when the gendarmes come? He must have alibis for when some of the rapes happened, mustn't he? He can't remember anything specific, though; any time when he was definitely somewhere else. There was a Scandie chick he was with that once – Sophia? – but he pretty much blacked out that night and he has no idea what happened, much less how to contact her in Sweden. He has to believe it will all be all right, though. People don't go down for crimes they haven't committed these days. Do they? But what if it's karma, what if this is all about a crime he has committed?

Waiting in the dark for fate to fuck him, Itchy feels like that guy in *GoodFellas*, trapped in the boot of a car, while his soon-to-be executioners have dinner at one of their mum's houses. All he can do is moan softly to himself, an awful helpless moan of the trapped. Rocking on his seat of sick and sour milk and uneaten pasta, hands on his shoulders, arms crossed over his chest.

He tries to pray but it is too late. He should have done it years earlier, should have asked for forgiveness when it would have meant something. His prayers in the black and stench of the bin are dried of meaning, just senseless sequences of sounds. He can't force belief into them. Against his will he grins at his own unrestrained hypocrisy for trying, the foxhole atheist. But the smile is a leer into the gulf within him. Into the colourless void that sits inside. It is the spoiler's smile. The smile of the drowning man that sees his enemy below him in the depths. But there is no enemy except himself. Beneath him nothing but bags of rotting waste. And only self-loathing is satisfied that he may finally get what he deserves.

The scrape on the tin roof of Itchy's prison as the object is dragged off is like a chisel down a blackboard, but magnified a thousand times, as if he is the chisel. It makes a heavy crack on the concrete floor by the bin's side. Itchy lifts his head and opens his eyes, ready to finally face the music. Thinking that maybe he should even admit to these crimes, to atone for his own. For a split second of pain-induced insanity, he even questions whether it wasn't him all along. But the bin lid doesn't lift. There are only footsteps running away.

When he lifts the lid himself, the garage is deserted. Whoever freed him has gone. He climbs out on to the chunk of cement-joined breeze blocks that had recently imprisoned him and hobbles back to his flat, battered legs stiff and shrieking at every step. Wondering who freed him, but sure he already knows. Only one other also lurks in the garages and might have watched events unfold. Only one other knows Itchy is innocent of those rapes. And only one other would profit from his escape – because a false scent has now been laid. Cheated of the chance to pay his debt to the world, Itchy finds himself instead indebted to the rapist.

Entry Number: 87
Narrator: Byron
Entry Title: The Sensuous Emir of Akhkanstan

I

Far in the East, in the lands of the Mussulmen, in the kingdom of Akhkanstan, there reigned an emir. A man tall of stature and thick of beard whose presence was at once magnificent and terrible; but this being a fitting figure for a ruler, he was the more revered by his people for it.

His was a kingdom of scarce conjecturable wealth, where shepherds sometimes stumbled upon rocks of gold pointing through the surface of the roads. Defended by armies as massy and as fierce as such riches could buy: black Ethiope mamelukes who could leap full three ranks of lined pike; elephant-riding Tunicians, descended direct from the warriors of mighty Carthage; Gyption bowmen; slingmen of Greece; hoplars of Persia; even companies of halberdier from Basel and Berne. Thus protected, Akhkanstan had known seven decades of peace with its neighbour states and since all profited from trade and alliances there was no reason to suppose that this would not continue to be the case.

Deprived of the dual guides of war and of a father's hand - since the erstwhile emir had died before the babe was yet a boy - as monarch, the emir led a life of indulgence and indolence, the like of which makes our own regent seem stoic.

He banqueted so vastly that his leftovers fed four strata of society before they reached the truly poor. And even when not dining, a troupe of slaves, trained to move with platters upon their backs, scuttled about him like crabs, laden with lion 'jewels' and humming-bird hearts and a superfluity of any other canapés for which the emir might feel caprice. For if ever the prince's whim was not instantly gratified the redound to the malfeasant was to find himself in agonies unimaginable for the flit remainder of their life.

The palace's vast vault torture chambers were Akhkanstan's most infamous and unconcealed secret, it being incumbent upon all the rulers of the Mussulmen to impress their populaces with fear of great pains and punishments. And the emir expressed his own considerable imaginative genius in the invention of ever more wondrous and neoteric means of exacting excruciation and eventual death. He had built great golden mechanicals to decollate, flagellate and harrow which set even his most callous and truculent torturers at an occasional tremble. But the emir was well versed by his mullahs that from seeds of terror, flowers of piety and peace can bloom.

Yet carnal pleasure was the emir's first religion and he indulged it with a zeal the envy of any spinning Dervise. Within his haram were ever troops of girls as beautiful as houris and no less trained in caresses, though always maidens, until their prince himself picked them from his flock.

So near were these dancing girls to the true heavenly state of good Mussulmen, that the emir, for japes, would sometimes have an unfavoured courtier lapsed into insensibility - by means of a few drops from a phial of dark liquor made from arachnid venoms, and orchids that he had bought at great expense for just this purpose - and bringing them around in the royal haram would have them so plied with succulence and sensuality that they would be quite convinced they had died and gone to the paradise of the faithful. Of course, when he had tired of watching the sport from one of his hidden galleries, the emir would have the courtier verily murdered, for tainting the sacrosanctity of his haram - and the concubines killed alike, for being tainted.

The only men allowed within the haram's high buttressed walls, carved from bone-white sandstone carted from the coast, were eunuchs, whose badge of office was also their loss and shame and posed no threat to usurp the emir's reign.

It being known that even a gelded horse might, from memory perhaps or simply the flowing of blood, still produce a stallion's rise, the emir had them castrated beyond the necessity of preventing a cuckoo clan, or prolonging the singing voice of a boy. So thoroughly de-manned his haram guards were that they were equipped with little pipes of hollowed rhino horn - a waggish crack on the aphrodisiac perhaps - with which to pass their water. These they sported about their waists, just as a fusilier might carry his powder flask, though with no chance themselves of firing.

The haram had another wing, unwindowed even by so much as a loophole, well separated by brawny castellations and accessed only from outside, for here the emir allowed the occupants to retain the contents of their codpieces. The dark-eyed, polished-skinned youths and boys within belied any claims that their sex was less fair and even that it was more worthy, for they existed only as another piece of this private paradise, a diversion with which to while away the emir's hours. What the Roman Church calls mortal sin, and the English state calls capital offence, the Mussulman knows to be a pleasurable alternative.

Through all his vice to Christian eyes, the emir was still a good Mohametian and broke none of the laws of his creed. Five times a day, when the shrills from Moorish minarets called his people to prayer, the emir alike stopped his occupation and obeyed from his palace upon his mat of silk and gold as surely as the basest beggar did upon the beaten earth streets.

II

It seemed as if nothing could be rotten in the emirate of Akhkanstan, not for its prince at least. Until, one day, lounged upon his chaise-langue throne, the emir was presented with a skull. It was the cranium only of an enemy, bejewelled and proffered upon a pillow of velvet plush. It had been fashioned into a goblet, for the emir was fond of drinking sherbets from his foes, a gift from a Wazir desirous of ascendancy, as such things had been given many times before. And yet the empty eyeholes, functionally plugged with silver to stop liquids sluicing out, stared into the emir. The row of top teeth, still attached, laughed at him. The bone, scrubbed white until it shone, shouted out to him: 'You too shall end like me.' And this was the moment the emir understood his own certain destruction. This was the instant he comprehended that all his puissance and desires must come to naught: he was mortal, as doomed as his enemy to end as a skull, and even that would one day disintegrate to powder and fragment. Between astonishment and grief, horror and detestation, he held his satin turbaned head in hands and wept.

From that instant, not tumbling dwarfs, nor the smoke of hookah, nor caresses of virgins, not even the pool – a previously favourite debauchery, in which he might swim with the voluptuous naked boys that he called his tadpoles – could rouse the emir from unquiet melancholic ennui. In all fornication he saw only death, every touch reminded him of the bones and sinews that lay beneath; his pool became to his blighted sight but a basin of floating gore.

He ceased to banquet, for all the food was already dead or dying; the raisin is but a grape decayed, and the grape is doomed to be a raisin. Even lambs ripped untimely from their bleating mothers before his listless eyes tasted already rotten to the emir.

He tried oysters, eaten live – though they were against his creed – but he felt them die within him and their deaths suggested his to come. He survived only by eating raw green vegetables, whose bland taste was near enough to purgatory in itself.

Hearing one night the revelry of his Swiss mercenaries, heated with wine, the emir determined to try alcohol and for a time it worked. Even for some weeks he was able to lose himself in the release of liquor, forbidden to his kind. He had brandy and Madeira brought from Spain and Portugal, and he declared his courtiers also must drink it, for he wished not to be damned alone, though already in his depressive drunken ruminations he had begun to suppose that Allah too must be dead.

When his emissaries returned with bottles of the finest French champagne, it was already almost too late. The first glass of the sweet bouled wine was the last occasion that beverage would divert the emir from his despair; by the end of the bottle even those dregs had become stale and lifeless, further intimations to the emir that he must die. That all his lascivious pleasures and power must end. That every day he was only drifting through the minutes until inevitable death.

The emir's once effervescent desire lapsed entirely into despondency. He was mired into the depths of melancholic reflection. Instead of comely catamites, perturbation and discontent became his most constant companions. He commanded all his viziers and councillors to his chambers to consult with them, yet none could conceive of a plan; for not all the riches in Akhkanstan could buy the emir an eternity.

Still the emir grieved and tormented himself with impotent fear of the black nothingness that awaited him. Which only brought that terror closer: his constitution, depleted by convulsion, could withstand no more, his senses gradually degraded and his limbs ceased animation.

He lay in torpor for three days, the blood almost turgid in his veins, his heart beating only as that of a mountain adder in winter, and his being as stiff and frozen. The viziers feared him at the point when soul and cadaver would diverge and, knowing their own fate if that occurred, and that of the kingdom without his heir declared from among his hundred sons, they called for physicians and for mullahs and for soothsayers.

The mullahs engaged in reading of the Koran, they praised Allah and the Prophet, and begged their assistance in recovering the health of the emir, humblest of servants, but all the wailings and prayers produced no effect upon the ailing prince.

The physicians for all their unctions and potions could

induce no improvement and all were too pusillanimous to suggest bloodletting from the royal veins.

When the soothsayers took their turn, they cast entrails upon the palace floor and measured the alignments of the planets and the composition of the excrement of camels and 'pards, yet they were of no avail either in aiding the emir, in his festering delirium, or in quieting his indisposition.

It was the emir's chief librarian, whose position gave him access to vaults that had been kept barricoed and sheet-shrouded for long centuries, who finally offered hope. And the emir sensed in this other the fruition of his own desires and felt his vigour returning to him even as they spoke.

For in the dusky obscurity of cellars lit only by his oil lamp's sullen rays, the librarian had unearthed a volume containing arcana deliberately obfuscated by the generations since their first finders, who should more wisely have taken such secrets to the worms. In the emir's own labyrinthine libraries had lain the tome containing the secrets he sought: truths on the bearers of life perpetual; that race known to the Hellenics as *Broucolokas*, and the Romany as *Vardoulacha*, but called *Vroucolocha* in the East. The pages revealed the patriarch of this clan, the primogeniture who had power to pass his gift on to others: that being which could bestow eternal life; the one chance of man to dispel his own mortality. Not only who he was, but exactly when and where to find him: at the Pool of Mount Pilatus, on the celebration of the prophet Isa's crucifixion.

III

So preparations were laid in place for a great journey. The

emir had a mighty caravan assembled, and chose from his forces and favourites those who would accompany it. While over the long weeks the logistics were made ready, the librarian told the emir where they were to go and the history of the one they were to hunt.

He had been a Roman procurator, the emir was enlightened, documented in the Western tradition for his part in the death of the Nazarene, a man regarded as prophet also by the emir's people, though vastly surpassed by Mohamet. This procurator, a man named Pontius Pilate, was so cruel and wicked a governor that eventually even the tyrant Tiberius Caesar tired of his excesses and ordered his death. Pilate had no wish to suffer a torturous execution, so took his own life; some said, also in regret at Isa's crucifixion. The Emperor Tiberius, furious that his command was cheated, had Pilate's body weighed down with rocks and flung into the Tiber.

But over the following weeks Rome was plagued by the most ferocious tempests it had ever known, and a vicious rash of sanguinary murders alongside. It was declared that the cadaver must be moved, to placate its evil spirit.

In punitive spite against the discontented Gauls, the corpse was brought to Vienne and thrown there into the Rhone, and yet again the most disastrous weather and horrendous bloodshed wreaked itself upon the region. Alerted as to the cause of this plague of ills, the people of Vienne found the procurator's remains, still queerly intact, and moved them to Lake Genève. Only for a verisimilitude of the evils to occur to another town: bodies appearing daily, drained of blood and life-force, as if a colony of leeches had been a-work, and thunder's peal and the momentary brilliancy of forked lightning were all that broke the unvarying immensity of black skies, which should have been in the content of summer.

And so, a group of brave and sturdy men moved Pilate once more, this time up to the mountain that still bears his name. There they cast his carcass into a lake, where it remains; in winter frozen solid, and too far from inhabitation for the procurator to hunt in the summer months, when the dark hours are few. The storms that surged at his depositing were said to be as fierce as the very end of the world, but afterwards was peace, like the deluge subsided. Only for some weeks in the spring and autumn do the locals lock themselves away, when the watery tomb is unfrozen, but the sun is sufficiently delayed to allow Pontius Pilate his pursuit of crimson life-force.

'Everyone is forbidden by edict to climb Mount Pilatus, on pain of execution,' the librarian told the emir, 'but I have uncovered secrets that will allow a man intrepid to speak with Pilate, and to gain his power of life over death, without his equal curse to return each sunrise to his mortal remains.'

IV

The emir's Swiss mercenaries accompanied the caravan, when it finally quitted Akhkanstan, who of course had made this long journey once before, though in the opposite direction. Many of those stalwart halberdiers there were, who had long dreamed of returning to the mountains and lakes of their homes, and all were now wealthy men from their years in Akhkanstan.

The travelling was harder than any remembered, though, the scorched desert's usually faithful oases failed and many camels and riders alike perished upon the first paces of the long route.

Of the three ships that took the cortège across from Bayrut to Venice, two were sunk by storms as vicious as if Pilate sensed their approach. But adventitiously, the vessel that held the emir within its bowels passed safely.

In less pressing times, the emir would have liked to have lingered longer in Venice, a city whose decadence and depravity pleased him greatly, now his blood was invigorated with hope. A floating haram, it seemed, where flirtatious silhouettes beckoned from every window, lit by long cracked chandeliers; where whores plied their pleasures in salt-lapped lagoons, and strange dance and revelry echoed across unfathomable canals. But he supposed Venice's charms would still be awaiting him upon his return, when he might spend a century encarnalled with her if he so wished, with an eternity his to fritter.

Many of the depleted company, already weakened from travel and unaccustomed want of sustenance, remained in that city, dead from disease or too infirm to continue. But the emir, who had started the endeavour so frail, seemed sturdier with every step.

When blizzards blasted the mountain passes that form the dividing ring about the Duchy of Savoy, more of the retinue were buried by snow, exactly where they fell, unable to struggle on. Still more perished from rock falls and avalanches, limbs fractured, dashed over ravine edges, unrescuable even if alive. Though the emir was too bent upon his aim to squander time saving underlings in any event. The roads were so rough that rapid progress was impossible. But progress the wanderers did, slow and sure as creeping gangrene.

Upon the first night passed in the land beyond Savoy, stealthily, the whole Swiss guard deserted. Knowing well the wrath that might be enacted on any who persevered, in penance for his comrades' crimes, they had parted to a man. Yet the emir rose and journeyed onwards, with what vagabond viziers and ragged servants remained.

Even to the root-twined toes of Mount Pilatus they journeyed thus, unguided but by answers of the execrable peasantry they met. A month or more beyond estimation, they arrived at their destination the very day of reckoning: Good Friday. And so, without the time even to camp a night, they readied for the climb.

The dread remains of the once mighty band of followers said their prayers to Allah, for they feared the sight of the toppling crags and blasted pines above them. But were cheered when the emir chid them for their cowardice and bade them remain below – he alone would make the ascent. For these last servants were sickening to their prince's sight, more corpse-like than the truly dead they seemed, so suffered and rancorous from their travels. The emir could no more abide even the thought of their mortal stink. So, unperceived, he infused with poisons all their victuals, as his farewell.

V

The emir climbed upward, through bed of surging river, between immense rocks, along ravines that would have stumbled men less fiercely striving than he. Amidst gun-barrel torrents as violent as murder, he never paused. Until, just before the shades of twilight, he reached that mountain lake which had been his quest of a hundred score miles, the

Pool of Pilatus. Vaporous clouds arose from the valley floor, lapping at the emir's recent path like the foaming mouths of hellhounds, sulphurous breath already engulfing what in moments they would consume utterly.

The emir began at once to toss rocks into the pool, crying the while, 'Speak to me, Pontius Pilate, I have need of audience.'

And surely, from the pool arose, as if Neptune from the deep, a mighty throne of fiery gold. Upon it a being, manlike though not man, tall and military of bearing, clad in blood-red robes, with eyes that burned and lip that sneered, wrath and thunder graven upon his brow.

'Who disturbs my slumbers? Which are not slumbers for I never sleep, but think only ever on. Who dares call me into this torturous half-light, when my place on the earth is not until darkness cloaks all?'

'I, Sulemein Mohamet, Emir of Akhkanstan, call you, and bind you to my service, and command you to deliver me your power over eternity.'

'Behold the man. You need not bind nor command,' spoke Pilate, 'I share willingly that which I have been given. I only ask what purpose would you, with this power of life eternal? Speak truth, for see I wear judge's robes and have judged greater than thee as ye know well.' He stepped from his throne upon the water's surface and like this made path on to the land.

The emir, with the bravery of one who has known only his every whim obeyed, rather than contrition or attempt to hide his purpose, spoke the plain truth as instructed: 'By Allah, I seek your gift of life unending so that I may enact every paroxysm of pleasure and for all time. I would know such carnality as would make Sodom shiver. I would throw such feasts of excess as cannibals would refuse. I would make my own body a temple to Dionysius. I would seek out every concupiscible, terrible and infinite curiosity of enraptured sin, yet be never damned.'

'Fie! You speak well, though speak not of Allah - know you not who I am? In feeble form such as you now are, I had the mettle to scorn and mock the very son of the one God you call Allah. I jeered as my men scourged his back with a cat o'tails and diced for his clothes. It was I who wrote a sign to hang above his dying head and I who had him nailed to a tree. And I who crowned this king of kings with a circlet of shredding thorns and watched the blood trickle into His forgiving eyes. Even then I might have taken that forgiveness, but I cast it aside and I am indeed blessed with life eternal and the power to bestow it, but my blessing is also curse - would you truly live for ever and forfeit that forgiveness? What need man to live for ever, when he is chosen even above angels, to be forgiven every sin by only asking it?'

'I know what I do and have long decided it, heaven holds nothing for one like me, who can know more pleasure on earth,' said the emir, and waited in anxious and horrible solicitude, face set with the forced countenance of one used to demanding not enquiring.

'Then so be it,' spoke Pilate, eyes alight like a basilisk's with contempt, and he turned and washed his hands in the gloomy expanse of water behind him. Then from within his voluminous scarlet robes he produced a short many-thonged whip, which he handed to the trembling emir, and bade him bare his back and apply it.

The emir scourged his own shoulders till the blood flowed, as if a penitent, and Pilate with a goblet, as of the grail of

Christ, though all in dark silver and set about with stones of tenebrous ruby and black pearls, captured the flow of the sham contrition. Pilate raised the cup, his countenance slashed with a pale fat mouth that laughed without joy, his eyes agleam with exquisitely gratified malice. And when he supped the skies umbraged, and thunder rattled madly.

The ghastly procurator let slip some drops of blood also on to the floor and said: 'Through the blood of yours that I have imbibed and by the now ensanguined earth of this double-scathed place, you share in my curse. You are, like I, immune to death; though blows may pain you, they can never now end your life, nor will you age though mountains fall decrepit about you.'

He offered more dreadful words too, words in languages archaic and insufferable to the ear, words that drew a hissing from the air and produced a further darkening of the heavens, and for some moments it seemed the only light on earth was the piercing fire which shone from Pilate's eyes.

'Fool,' said the damned procurator: 'now you will see what you have truly sought, in attempting to command me,' and he looked deeply into the emir, who returned his gaze as if staring over the brink of a frightful precipice.

The emir prostrated himself, cringing like the basest of the slaves that he himself had tortured even until their lives could no longer be preserved by art of physician. 'Spare me,' he begged.

Spoke Pilate, grim visaged, with words of granite: 'You are free to leave, though not through my choosing, but on this day I am curst to release the debauched and wicked and to condemn the innocent. Yet answer, how thought you that your food would be less bitter by the tasting of perpetuity? All the mortal things that you saw as blackened and blighted before, can only be the more rotten by your knowledge of time. Even the magnificence of your marble statues and golden cupolas will be as nothing to you, for they too will crumble and corrupt. Human lifespans will seem as of a snowflake next to yours, but not beauteous, only more foul and fetid than e'er they seemed before you began this bedlam quest. And you will envy those who you cannot bear to couple with, for you cannot know their sweet comfort of demise. Death, fool, is a gift. Then on, far from here, go to your passions of carnality and vice; sup, drink, fornicate and weep. For your last lust will be for the only thing you have given freely in your life and the one thing you are now forever denied.'

The emir convulsed and shivered on the ground as if it were blows not words that shook his body, his posture like a pleading hound.

'Go,' said Pilate, with demoniac smile, 'I tire already of thee. You will dwell in despair and live for ever, that is punishment enough. Yourself shall be your prison, within you and without you and around you will be your hell. Oblivion forever denied, loins never sated, thirsts never quenched. You lived for your lusts and they shall be your fate; for lechery and hedonism can never fill the empty hole within.'

...when I would account to myself for the birth of that passion, which afterwards ruled my destiny, I find it arose like a mountain river, from ignoble and almost forgotten sources but swelling as it proceeded it became the torrent which, in its course, has swept away all my hopes and joys.

Mary Shelley, Frankenstein

February 17th, 11.42 a.m.

Itchy was once a cub-scout, swore a now reneged-upon fealty: to God; and to the Queen. But he was very likeable as a boy actually, if anything too likeable, because adults and children both were too willing to forgive his faults. Itchy knows, not just from photographs, but by memories of his treatment that he was a beautiful boy, way back when Snickers were Marathons and Michael Jackson was black. Even for a boy being too pretty can be a curse. For a girl it can be fatal.

The first experience Itchy had of sex, he was collecting newspapers for the cubs, which they used to do some Saturdays, the first recyclers – apart perhaps from the milkman – saving for a new scout hut or church roof or something similarly consequential.

This was before Itchy had any comprehension of what an orgasm was; he had only recently learned that the swelling in his pants could be called an *erection*, a word that still sounded medical and important, before it was blunted from overuse, like the only decent blade on his Swiss Army knife. Being allowed a knife was one of the main reasons for joining the cubs, and slicing the strings on bundles of collected newspapers one of the things you had to do to justify it.

Itchy can still remember the man whistling, as he led him to the garage beside his neat, new-build semi, where the papers would be heavy broadsheets most likely. The man whistled not with his lips, not even through his teeth, he just whistled with every movement. Talking as if he were laughing, and showing Itchy into the garage as if he were inviting him on to a yacht.

Probably cubs no longer collect the papers, certainly not on their own, not going into garages with strangers. But it would have been hard for Itchy to have distrusted a man so bursting with happiness in any case. A grown man on a Saturday morning, in a blue towelling dressing gown, full of a child's joy for life, which even at ten Itchy was already jaded to.

And then, as he was saying goodbye and thank you to the man with the smile in his eyes, who was returning into his house, Itchy looked behind him through the open front door and saw a trail of things: two ladies' black high-heels; a lady's silky dress; a black, even silkier dress that was probably worn under the first; and then a black bra. All leading up the gangplank from the front door to another door. And Itchy realised:

'This man "did it" last night, and now he is the happiest man on the street, maybe in the town.'

And the man looked where Itchy looked and he smiled broadly and invited Itchy, for the first time ever, into the world of men, which was a better place even than a yacht, and he grinned bigger still and nodded, which was all he needed to do to say:

'Yes, little brother, I got laid last night and yes, I am the happiest man on the street and maybe in the town. And now you've made my day even better, because I've just seen how in awe of that you are. And I've made your day better, because you have now met a guy who's just been laid.'

He shut the brass-accessorised door, leaving Itchy with the bundle of papers and the knowledge of all that was required to be as happy as that all his life.

And Itchy wasn't there when the man called the woman a cab, after a mutually uncomfortable coffee: him feeling foolish in a Christmas present bath-robe; her feeling slightly used, in lust-crumpled evening-wear. Itchy wasn't there when the cabman barely disguised his leer – and she wanted to dissolve into his jean-rivet-scarred plastic seats – but was too proud to show she even noticed. Itchy wasn't there, when the one-night lovers didn't speak properly for a month at work and were never again friends as they'd once been. Itchy knew only that to be the happiest man in town, and the most admired man in town, you had to sleep with as many women as you could. Which, at the least, had to be more than anyone else.

Itchy the man was never beautiful like the childhood him; puberty and adolescence tried hard to mark his cards. And now, approaching thirty, his jowls are beginning to lose tightness along the length of his jaw. The blood vessels of his cheeks are red mesh like a kid's minnow net, booze-brambled, although a skier's tan hides it most of the time. His face is fatter. His hair is thinner. He is just beginning to have the twinges of fear at mirrors shared by vampires, midnight druggies and the middle aged. He prefers the artist's impression of himself, that he still carries in his mind, to having to confront the reality so brutally.

This is at the best of times: currently Itchy's face is still a mass of swellings and bruises from the kicking he took in the carpark.

He has told everyone else the damage was from a mugging he resisted, unable to explain the intricacies.

He's been to the doctor and there is apparently no permanent damage. But Itchy is convinced that a piece of glass went into his hand through a stigmata gash on his palm. The doctor said it has gone, that if it was ever there, then it must have worked its way out, as these things do. But Itchy can feel it still inside, a cube of glass in his hand, affecting him, infecting him, like the shard of ice from the Snow Queen. Something that has already started to make him harder and colder.

There have been no posters up with his picture, as Itchy had feared. Nor have there been gendarmes looking for injured Englishmen. Probably his indecisive attackers never went to the police, realising their evidence was too tenuous to justify such a brutal assault. Itchy has not returned to the carpark in the week since. He has been concentrating his mind, trying to run through the facts of the night. Trying to decide whether it really was the rapist who rescued him. If he really doesn't have an alibi for any of the rapes. If he really was just trying to protect the girl.

It's Paris holidays now, Black Week, the locals call it, who tend to hate the Parisians even more vociferously than they do the English. Doc calls the Parisians 'French bastards', not of course to suggest that all the French are bastards, but the opposite: to differentiate them from the 'foreign bastards' who inhabit Chamonix the rest of the time. The crime rates soar in Black Week, graffiti appears everywhere, there are fights – not just in the bars, but also the lift queues – the slopes are so crowded, with people so uptight and irascible, it is barely worth going riding anyway. But you do it to pass the time. That's all. There is nothing else.

Paris is no worse than London, though, you can't be smug about it.

London nettles Itchy now. Pavements blasted with black spots of chewing gum. Weary immigrants holding signs for golf sales, like crucifixes, against the flow of uncaring crowds; people cheaper than billboards. The little souvenir stalls filled with plastic brat-tat and signs saying: 'We *sell* maps, we don't *give* directions' and cards in phone boxes advertising sex – paying for things you get for free anywhere else.

In London, or Paris, Itchy only ever pops out of tunnel-holes like a meerkat or marmot, never really knows where he is above ground. Doesn't believe anyone else does either, isn't even sure whether it's really there when you're not looking. But hates the tubes, windows reflecting zombie eyes; panes smeared with earmarks and face-scum; tags scratched in the glass, not even the finesse of a marker pen left now. Above ground the wealthy, trying hard to be happy with how prestigious their cars and houses and clothes are, even though other people have better ones. Even though there will always be other people with better ones.

Itchy, Aussie Mark, Sean, Daniel, Suzi, Vince, Josey, Crispin… the rest of the 'Anglais'. They're all legal aliens, fleeing a standard of living below what they've come to hope for. Pitching up in someone else's town, taking their jobs, fucking their sweethearts, often not even speaking the language. And Itchy has no illusions, there are those who will hate them for that. There are those who will abuse them and will abuse their homeland for that. And against those people, Itchy will defend Britain to the point of death. Gladly to the point of death. But not to the point of moving back there. Or at least not till summer.

The snow is awesome, which is almost a waste in Black Week, but means that you can stay away from the pistes. Away from the snowblades and the queues. Out in the backcountry where it's so beautiful that it hurts your eyes and heals your hangover. Even in the midst of wilderness, alcohol beckons to Itchy. Like the sea from a beach. Like the sea from a thirsty life-raft.

He doesn't even shout for Sean to stop, up ahead. Leaves him boot-packing his way up along the ridge, skis over his shoulder like a Napoleonic musket, footsteps making Itchy's own progress easier. Itchy takes out his hip flask and pauses while he has a swig, embarrassed in case Sean sees him drinking this early in the morning, weirdly, because he knows it's hardly something Sean would give a shit about.

The air glistens with snowflakes so tiny that you can only see them at all when the light catches them. It is either the barest hint of moisture, in cloudless skies too cold to hold any, or fairy dust. The air is so bitter that the wet of Itchy's lips starts to stick to the rim of his hip flask as he swigs, even though it's been inside his pocket. A strand of his lip skin stays on the steel while he fumbles to do the lid up with fingers already numbing out of their mittens.

At the top of the Arolette couloir they both stop and respect the view before they start down, not ruining the moment with much conversation, getting their breath back, sharing.

They may be in Switzerland, Itchy is never entirely sure where the boundary lies up here. The Emmosson Dam, definitely in Switzerland, is before them, an impressive man-made monster, surrounded by natural ones that dwarf it. Dinosaur footprints were found when it was built.

People like Chamonix the same way they like dinosaurs; it's all about superlatives: the longest; the highest; the biggest; the most dangerous. The slopes they are about to ski are reckoned to be the most avalanche prone in the valley, but Itchy is pretty confident about the risk, the snow pack seems very stable, even if the official scale is still on three out of five. The wind has carved the pitches and gullies below them into dunes, like a caster-sugar desert, but they don't seem overly loaded. Though Itchy is no real expert, and those who are – the high mountain guides – are statistically far more likely to die in an avalanche than anyone else.

As he is about to set off, Itchy notices the snowflake trapped on the black of his sleeve. And it is as perfect as the cliché. And unique – just like everything else.

The couloir snow holds. It's dense where the wind has packed it at the top, grinding the flakes together to become like river silt. Itchy grunts as he fights his way through it. Forcing jump turns that become more fluent as the snow softens, but it's still maybe forty-five degrees.

He sees Sean, ahead of him, let fly as the slope shallows and widens beyond the couloir. Releasing his battle cry and leaning to drag a hand through the snow as his skis open up. Bouncing over wind-blown waves. Arms and poles like high-wire balance tools, but flinging about at epileptic pace. Sean skis like a cowboy rides: untaught; uncaring; unafraid. But he is still elegance itself.

Grace comes through speed. Especially off-piste. If you are going fast and your body is in the wrong position you will fall. So constantly you compensate, dancing somewhere between boxer and ballerina. And this thrill of nearly falling is where the pleasure comes from, when the adrenalin pumps. And the better you get the harder you have to push – faster, steeper, narrower, deeper – to be at that point of nearly not making it. To feel the rush. The jazz. So the more devastating will be the consequences if you don't make it. But knowing this makes the adrenalin come fiercer. Furthers you, brings skills you didn't know you had. Animal instincts. And also ups the dosage. Heightens the addiction. Leaves you exhausted and craving more. And knowing that to feel this same level of exhilaration again you will need to be going a little faster still. A little closer to that edge you cannot infinitely stay the right side of. Terminal velocity.

Itchy suspects there is even a formula. That a mathematician of adrenalin studies might prove it is impossible for you not to fail catastrophically if you continue. You have to pull off the road, or carry on to the end. Only it's not really a road, it is a spiral driveway, like in a multi-storey carpark: but one that can only end in one place. Like a corkscrew. Like a life.

> ...it was time for him to perform the tour, which
> for many generations has been thought necessary
> to enable the young to take some rapid steps in the
> career of vice towards putting themselves upon an
> equality with the aged.
>
> *Dr John Polidori,* The Vampyre

February 26th, 9.46 a.m.

The best views in Chamonix are from Cham Sud, because from there you can't see Cham Sud. From where Itchy looks out, he sees only Mont Blanc and the forests that lead up the Aiguille de Midi and an old stone apartment block, beautiful in its way, which he has seen in sepia photos, standing alone like a monolith, when everything else around was just fields.

Itchy takes another sip of his breakfast: a vodka and apple juice. For the vitamins. Just as everyone comes to Cham eventually, everyone comes to vodka eventually. The warm embrace of the tasteless, carbohydrate-based, bland release that asks nothing from you, not even a hangover.

Itchy feels so much love for this place, but he has no ways to show it. The profound, antique expanse of Mont Blanc, the vastness of its excruciating beauty, makes him want to laugh, like a simpleton, with no provocation but gladness to be near it. To be allowed upon it, unharmed, is even more of a privilege, since

Mont Blanc has killed well over a thousand of those who have tried – more than any other mountain in the world.

While Itchy ruminates on this, a chough appears on the balcony balustrade. Its black eye framed in a Fisher-Price yellow which matches its beak. The bird stands on one leg; so elegantly that it might be a mountain stork – but possibly it only has one leg. Though if you assume that, maybe it only has one eye, since Itchy can see only the single blackberry pebble that also watches him; you have to suppose that the bits of the world you can't see are still there. The bird sings or squawks something at him, and then flies off before either eyes or legs can be confirmed.

Aussie Mark has gone out boarding already. Sean left early to do visits or some such rep's stuff, but he comes back in, while Itchy is finishing his drink.

'All right, son, morning,' Sean says.

'Morning, mate.'

'Do you fancy coming into town with me and getting a fry-up at Cybar?'

It has already occurred to Itchy that he should probably get something more substantial in him, however efficacious the power of vodka-*pomme*, so he agrees.

They pass out of the courtyard, past Spar, through the tunnel under a building that is painted artificial-limb pink, and out to the river.

'I've just got to pop into the ski school office en route if that's cool?' Sean says.

Reps never really clear their workload, there's always something, one of the reasons why Itchy could never do it.

'No problem,' he says.

The ESF office is in the centre of town up by the church, which has Gothic spars and buttresses, an Eastern cupola to its spire, Roman arches and smooth Savoie walls, as if it's got a full-on identity crisis. Itchy has never seen anyone going in and out of it, except for a wedding one time.

It seems like all the major faiths have mountains at their fundament, usually as the places where prophets receive enlightenment. And why would they not, when exhaustion, beauty and lack of oxygen can cause God to be sitting behind any given rock?

But Itchy himself doesn't really see any point in religion, and it seems that the world is increasingly dividing along those lines – fanatics and atheists – which is only natural; because the logical extension of belief in God is to be a priest or a martyr, anything else is meaningless. Normal life is pathetic and bizarre if you may be squandering the chance of eternal paradise. If you believe at all, you must surely pull out all the stops.

And if you don't believe, then the only certainty in life is that everyone loses, everyone dies and everything you do in the meantime is utterly futile. Except perhaps for the pursuit of pleasure.

Itchy used to say that if God was everywhere then you were just as likely to find Him at the bottom of a bottle, or in the arms of some dark-haired darling, as in a church. But it was just a line, just gallows humour. Because no religions say that if you are basically an 'all right bloke' you'll go to heaven – though Itchy may not have qualified in any event – they all lay down extremely specific and stringent rules about what is required. And it seems so statistically improbable, the leap of faith against evidence so great, that Itchy cannot help but to bet all his chips on God's non-existence. But occasionally, in his darkest moments, Itchy doubts his own disbelief, which for him is the worst scenario of all.

*

While Sean goes into the ESF office, Itchy heads upstairs into the Maison de la Montagne. Up steps matted with non-slip rubber stuff that reminds Itchy of primary school; next to traditional stone walls hundreds of years old. Some blackened with soot, survivors of long-ago disaster. Itchy likes it up here for the huge relief map model, with the whole of the Chamonix valley and the mountains on either side laid out in painstaking accuracy. He hasn't been up in a long while, but remembers getting a real buzz the first time he saw it: plotting possible off-piste routes and working his head around how the land all lay – where the different ski areas interconnect.

There are also other rooms, with information on weather stations and avalanches. But Itchy likes the map room, with its charts and planning tables and the relief model.

A sturdy but ancient ladder, once used for clambering over crevasses, runs along the wall, above the information point which is always manned. But today it is womanned, because there, behind the desk, is the nightingale. Her normally large pupils are shrunken in the window light she faces, emphasising their blue, which is startlingly bright, like in old films when they only had a few colours. Her pupils expand noticeably when she looks up to see Itchy. Her lips look as if they taste of Refreshers. And she smells of electricity. Not the steady crackle of a pylon, but hot and sweet like a running Scalextric. She smiles Itchy an invitation to say something, and when he still doesn't, she says, '*Salut*' – 'hello', or more accurately, 'salvation'.

'*Bonjour*,' Itchy replies, which is hardly stunning as far as opening gambits go.

'I know you, don't I?' she says, solemnly, like a child at prayer.

'Yes, you do, but I didn't know you worked here,' he replies, after two breaths.

'*L'oiseau ne chant que pour lui qui l'écoute*,' she says.

Which baffles Itchy, because apart from sounding like bad spy code, it suggests that she can read his mind, that she knows she is called the nightingale.

'*Pardon?*' he says.

'It is a French saying,' she says. 'It means that you do not find something until you begin to look for it.'

She is ripping the little holed strips from down the sides of printed sheets of computer paper, *dentelle* in French – 'lace' – and fixing the sheets together with paper clips called *trombones* – even offices are beautiful in France.

'Would you like to go for a drink with me some time?' Itchy asks her, surprising himself with his boldness.

She laughs. 'The *anglais*, always a drink. Never "would you like to go for a dinner, or a walk, or even a ski". As if you cannot think without a drink.'

'Sorry, a meal, then, or a ski?'

'No, a drink is good. I like drinking. *Je plaisante.*' And she winks at him, a sensation akin to discovering untracked powder days after a dump.

Itchy and Sean can't know if it was Vince or the frenchies usually to blame, but they notice on the walk to Cybar that several walls have been tagged with a spray-painted symbol – illegible; impossible to know even the language.

Language again. The carpark is called *le parking du fond* and *fond* means 'underground' – but also 'underside' or 'underbelly', 'essence' and 'end'.

Itchy is down there, in the darkness, in his fond underworld, in his fond lair; hanging out like the ghost of someone who died there once.

And he understands now why he does it, why the rapist does it: it's because he has to; because he has raised sexual excitement to such a level of morbid intensity that the sex itself is anticlimactic; it isn't the sex he wants any more, if he ever did, it's the raping; the act; the power; he doesn't desire the girls any more than an alcoholic appreciates fine wine; he returns because he has to. As Itchy does. Because the repetition is the only thing that gives his life meaning.

A Peugeot 205, with local plates, is lying sprawled between two bays. It alone has been selected for vandalism, a grudge message delivered. All four tyres are slashed, one headlight and all the windows caved in. A shopping trolley hangs through the hole where a windscreen once was, looking half devoured.

Itchy finishes the wine he brought down. The flagon is cheap plastic, wincingly fashioned to look medieval, like Euro Disney. He is just about to leave, when Vince appears.

Vince thinks himself alone in the carpark, Itchy can tell. Himself unsensed, only twenty metres away. There is a look of malevolence on Vince's face. He has the expression of someone who has discovered something very nasty, something that has troubled him deeply; but who is at least deriving satisfaction from the fact that others are soon going to suffer it too, only worse and for longer. And it becomes obvious: Vince is the rapist.

Which explains why Vince sees Itchy as a soulmate and Itchy hates Vince: because they are alike; they taste in each other the very lowest dregs of themselves; and these parts, which Itchy at least knows to be abhorrent, Vince exalts in.

But now it seems, if Itchy is right, if it is Vince, who is his friend and nemesis – *le violeur* – then Itchy has a chance to absolve himself for his past and to make another pay for their evil of the present. And all he has to do is wait. To catch Vince in the moment. Then to beat him to a paste. To finally kill that part of himself. Like when the good and evil Supermans fight. Like when Jekyll kills Hyde.

Suzi comes through the door. Itchy recognizes her walk, even from this distance; sees the same square fly's-eye view of her as he saw on Christmas Day, when he discovered his hideout. He feels sick, because she doesn't know, because she will fall prey to Vince, because the rapist will not be able to stop himself now. Not this far along. But Suzi knows Vince, she can identify him, so he will have to kill her. Which raises the pressure on Itchy too high. The need to succeed. His friend will die if he cannot beat Vince, who is stockier than him and must have a knife, if the stories are true. Itchy starts to look around in the darkness of his lair for a weapon, sees only the row of empty spirit bottles, takes two, the biggest two, weighs them in his hands, like a pair of imperfectly balanced martial art tools. Decides he will try to sneak as close as he can. Then he'll break one bottle, the left hand, on the ground, just before his strike; try to smash his enemy over the head with the other, and stab him simultaneously. Need to be careful of Suzi, though. Can't hurt Suzi.

She is still advancing on Vince, unaware of the fate that would await her if Itchy weren't here. Awaits her still if he fails. Except, even if he dies, she might get away and expose Vince. And to accomplish that would in itself be a justification for his life and death. An apology. And an ending.

Vince is waiting, letting her come to him. Itchy is ready to mount his attack. Arm poised to lift the grate. But needs proof. Lets his friend be bait.

Vince hasn't pulled the knife yet, he's watching her walk right up to him. His back to Itchy.

'Hey, baby,' Vince says, kind of menacingly.

And Itchy thinks, 'It's show-time!' and is momentarily proud of the thought, because it's the sort of thing a film hero would say and it makes him feel stronger. And he's starting to ease up the grating. Hands gripping the bottlenecks so tightly he can feel his nails biting into his palms. He's about to put in progress the launch of a tirade of blows from which no one could ever get up, when Suzi kisses Vince.

She pulls him to her, hands scrabbling their way up under his clothes, trying urgently to feel some of his flesh.

And Itchy drops the grate and slumps back and tries not to vomit, as Vince and Suzi walk hand in hand over to a white company van, which they both clamber into the back of.

Itchy doesn't even stop to wonder why she's doing this; to Daniel, of all the people in the world. Itchy knows, only too well, the effect of a small amount of charm and a lot of attention, plied over a long period, on a girl who has been in a relationship for ever. If you don't stop it at the outset, flirting can arrive only at one place.

Vince isn't the rapist. He's just an arsehole. Which is no news. He's a self-confessed arsehole, after all, as he's told Itchy before, thinking that the confession is funny, thinking that it makes him a player. Not realising that he is indeed an arsehole: a dirty, shrivelled, incontinent arsehole; letting itself and the side down daily.

But you can't kill someone for that, wrong as the world may be – you can't even break their legs for that.

The Last Day of Term

RAMSEY WOULD BECOME a pharmacist. Merrick an actuary, which is like a cross between a loss-adjuster and a mathematician which a mad scientist has been experimenting on. McCloughlin would become a lawyer. Khan an accountant. Reece an accountant. Davenport an accountant. Elliot an accountant. Smith would work for an oil giant in Nigeria, would one day face serious charges. After dabbling in business, Godard would become an MEP. Charlie opened a bookmaker's. Dillon would become a teacher.

Marty would become a statistic.

Itchy would become whatever it is that he is now: a barman; or a bum; a borderline alcoholic, with the border lying just behind him; a womaniser; a freeskier; a life-loving, living incarnation of *carpe diem*; a creature that hides in a cave cubbyhole, where the cold shuts out the tinnitus of life; a sponge for regret and self-loathing; a Chamoniard; a sham?

They would all become something else, for better or worse – but on that day, for one last day, they were a team.

The fair went on around them, the whole of the uni in the same place at one moment. More or less anyway; there had been the usual tales circulating of those for whom the pressure of final exams had been too great. Of course, the urban myth of pencils up the nostrils, claret ink blooming over the undoable question paper on the desk. But also, a quiet Chinese girl, wingless, from out of a tower window. A chemistry student who had made himself an experimental potion, from which he knew he would not return. A medic who scalpelled his wrists, longways, down the arteries, to make stitching impossible.

The team survived unscathed, in the sunshine, testing their mettle against each other on bungee runs, pointlessly trying to make it farther down an inflatable alley than all the others – for no prize but pride and to be sucked the more viciously backwards by the rope when their socked feet eventually flailed.

They drank champagne, from the bottle, sprayed it about at each other and anyone else who came too close. Itchy's hair was matted to his forehead, sticky and clumped and sweet smelling. But he tried not to get too battered – though he didn't drink so much anyway, in those days – because the team were having their final dinner in the evening. The last supper. A takeaway curry banquet with every spicy delicacy that Singh and Sons could supply. A private room in the science block secured, with enough wine and beer to unseat a dry-docked ship. And there was the slave auction to look forward to before that.

Not all of the Regulators were so abstemious. The bars were doing good trade. All for charity. The whole day was for charity. So some of the team gave their support generously, in buying beer, paying off a bit of the karma debt they had accumulated during the year.

There was a row of blue Tardis-like Portaloos out behind the strip of trestle bars. Close enough to be obvious, but discreetly in the distance, and new-looking, unruffled plastic; not battered rancid things like you get at summer music festivals.

A few of the team, thinking that one of their number had gone inside, thought it would be funny to roll the Portaloo over. They strained their muscles, trying to be as silent as drunk jokers can; until they got it to the tipping point and let drop. There was a girlie scream from inside, though, not the half-amused anger they had expected from their friend. And when the door swung open from the horizontal plastic coffin, it was a girl who stumbled out, trousers undone. Retching to breathe and vomiting down herself. Clothes already covered in faeces and lime chemical. She staggered about, dazed and hysterical, shrieking as if her lover or baby had died. Collapsing, eventually, into a heap – uncomforted, no one wanting to put their arm around such a sickening beast.

Eventually a fat chick arrived, never the bridesmaid and never the bride, her face registering disgust not with the sobbing mess, but with the Regulators, still standing about, unable to take ownership of the catastrophe. She told them all to fuck off, in a voice as virulent as years of knowing boys like them. And as they did, she pulled the jacket from Charlie, who didn't even protest, as she wrapped it around the unfortunate on the floor.

The perpetrators were quietened for a while, but tried hard not to let the event spoil their day. It was lucky in a way, because had it really been Dillon in the cabin, it would have been much worse. And shortly afterwards, in a bower of warm skies, beer and friendship, the incident disappeared entirely.

The slave auction was held on a plank-and-scaffold stage, where various awards and announcements had been made over the course of the afternoon. The DJs of Sheffield's student radio, voices unknown but to them and the small bands of cronies who listened to their shows, booming out over the PA. Announcements like the cancellation of the wet T-shirt competition, after combined petitions by the Feminist Society, the Women's Officer, the Society Against the Objectification of Females, and various Islamic and Christian killjoys.

The slave auction had the air of a last-minute plan – there was after all very little term-time left in which to be someone's slave – but the conditions were set for only two hours anyway. Most of the slaves were too drunk to be of much use as anything but a partner to get drunker with. The bidders seemed to be doing so in the hope of acquiring an end-of-term panic shag or out of pity for a mate who had foolishly put their name down.

Slaves could choose their own charities, though, so there were a few who appeared to have a genuine zeal for their cause, beckoning their hands upwards in the hope of summoning more than a pitiful few quid. Most would have been better off doing a two-hour shift washing dishes and giving the wages to their charity, or staying sober and giving the saving.

Itchy noticed that the only bid that broke substantially into the arena of folding money looked like a grudge match between two girls over a boy. They were raising the price against each other with grim looks and neither acknowledged the other, only a few metres away. The bloke was a gangly loping wolfhound, grinning through his embarrassment, apparently unbothered as to which would win. Presumably guaranteed a root whatever.

Despite the best attempts of the MC, the event was low key and lacklustre. The only real excitement was when the compère called out the name of the next slave and everyone waited for a moment while they mounted the stage, briefly interested to see whether they were vaguely recognisable and whether they were vaguely fit.

Marty said that 'fit' came from 'survival of the fittest', but that did not mean, as commonly supposed, the healthiest or strongest, it meant *fitting*: the most appropriate. Darwin's theory revolves around the best adapted, not the most domineering. So *fit* means *suitable* more than it does *athletic* or *fierce*: proper; right; the one for me; the one with whom I would like to share my genes, to make an even better us.

And while Marty was wittering on, the MC called out the name of the one for Itchy: *Tina*. The one with whom Itchy wanted to share his genes.

As she appeared from the crowd her expression was almost emotionless. To those who didn't know her soul as well as Itchy, it might have looked as if she were trying to suppress a laugh or a smirk. But he could see that she mounted the steps to the scaffold as if it were indeed a scaffold, as if she went there to be hanged, but head high, with the martyr's faith that, after a temporal pain, hers would be eternal paradise. She walked as if she were already there, like an angel. She walked as if she were Paradise itself.

Itchy stuck both his hands into his pockets, enquiring of each cotton corner as to precisely how much his maximum bid was going to be. Knowing that, even if it was everything he had and could borrow, it would be a bargain.

Marty recognised something from the look on Itchy's face. He did not know the depths of Itchy's passion, love some would call it, but he had heard his friend recount, through many a late-night sofa Kronenberg, tales of the unattainable Tina.

'So that's her, is it?' he said. 'I can see why you like her,' and he stuck another twenty into the scrumpled bundle that Itchy was studiously counting.

Tina walked to the front of the stage and looked out, over the heads of the crowd, into the hills. She wore jeans, dark indigo jeans, that clung to her Madonna-svelte hips, and a tight light jumper with the sleeves rolled up to present slim, pale wrists. Fingers tucked, just tip deep, into her front pockets.

'Tina is giving her proceeds to Amnesty International,' the DJ said. 'Let's hope it's a lot.' Then he added, 'Matter of fact, I'll bid twenty quid myself, how's that?' and a muted cheer went up from whatever section of the crowd housed his mates.

Tina smiled, courteously, slightly aloof but unpatronising, in the way Princess Di could, but the rest of them can't manage. This was back when Di was alive. Itchy had liked her when she was alive, cuckolding a king; lost his sympathy when she inadvertently unleashed that plague of vacuous mourning on the nation's inane.

Tina didn't look like either Diana, though, not the hunted queen of hearts, nor the huntress goddess. Tina looked like more than either. More than the sum of their parts.

'Forty,' Itchy shouted out, his head tilting slowly, as she looked at him – finally looking at him with something approaching real recognition.

There was a volume in that look from afar, over a tipsy mob, which he had never seen sitting spaces away in class. A glint of interest, which he had never received for his most erudite musings on the historical subtext of Shelley, gleaned with impediment from little-known geniuses in the library periodicals.

Itchy could feel his excitement rising. This was going to be it.

'Sixty,' said someone else.

Itchy recognised him, in a flat, leaden way; their paths had crossed at some drunken after-party. He could picture this rival bidder, scraping coke with a gold credit card, in a squalid student bedroom unused to such conspicuous consumption. And the rival wore clothes sufficiently similar to Itchy's own for him to know they cost a hell of a lot more. Which suggested he was in trouble.

'Quick, lend me some more money, man,' he whispered to Marty, who passed him another twenty with palms face out, to show there was no more.

'Seventy,' said Itchy, leaving space to manoeuvre.

'Ninety.'

Tina looked at Itchy.

Itchy gazed back.

The rival pulled chewing gum out from his mouth, like a long lizard tongue.

'A hundred pounds,' Itchy said.

There were some cheers at this. Well over double what the highest previous slave had gone for. A fortune in student funds. A good cause. A fit bird. It was actually starting to get exciting.

The MC began to milk it a bit. Itchy watched him walk the stage to close by where the rival stood and hold the mike out.

'It's got a bit too rich for my blood,' said the compère, 'but any advance on one hundred from you, sir?'

Itchy cursed. His rival had looked as though he would probably have let it go at this point. A realisation it was getting very silly. But the mike thrust into his face was like a challenge-slap from a fop's glove.

'One hundred and twenty,' he said.

Itchy turned around, couldn't see Marty. Marty had no more money anyway. Couldn't see any of the rest of the guys, was surrounded by slightly amused strangers. Couldn't believe he'd come this close just to fail.

The MC strode back across the stage. 'One hundred and twenty pounds going to Amnesty International, one lucky guy going to spend a couple of hours with the lovely Tina at his beck and call. Any advance on that from you, my friend?'

'Give me a minute,' Itchy said, looking at Tina, not at the microphone holder. 'I need to get more cash.'

'I'm afraid it's an auction,' the compère said, 'not hire purchase. It seems she's out of your league, mate. Going once. Going twice, for one hundred and twenty pounds. Going…'

'A hundred and forty,' a voice shouted out, Marty's voice.

Itchy turned around, could see him now, near the back of the growing crowd, with most of the Regulators about him.

'A hundred and sixty,' said the rich kid – richer kid – but half-heartedly, wanting to lose now.

Itchy hoped that Marty had spotted that, and would raise just a tenner. Itchy didn't want to have to pay the guys back more than that.

'Two hundred pounds,' Marty said.

'Shit,' Itchy thought; he was broke already.

But he grinned up at Tina, who smiled back; fuck, what a smile. Letting her know it was his bid. He was flying anyway. Who says money can't buy love?

The rival must have made a sign he was out of the dance.

'Going once,' the MC said, 'going twice, going, going…Sold for two hundred pounds to the man at the back. A round of applause, please.'

Marty came forward with a bundle of notes. Itchy went to meet him.

'Thanks, mate,' Itchy said. 'You know I'll pay you back,' and he started to hand over his own cash to Marty.

'Forget it,' Marty said, 'and don't worry about that, just give me back my forty. I persuaded the guys we needed a waitress for tonight. You'll just have to ply your charms there. But she's been bought by a conglomerate. She's everyone's slave.'

Mont Blanc is the monarch of mountains;
  They crown'd him long ago
On a throne of rocks, in a robe of clouds,
  With a diadem of snow.
Around his waist are forests braced,
  The avalanche in his hand;
But ere it fall, that thundering ball
  Must pause for my command.
The Glacier's cold and restless mass
  Moves onwards day by day;
But I am he who bids it pass,
  Or with its ice delay.
I am the spirit of the place,
  Could make the mountain bow
And quiver to his cavern'd base –
  And what with me wouldst *Thou*?

Byron, Manfred

March 9th, 11.22 p.m.

Itchy is looking in the mirror made by the darkness on his flat's balcony-door glass. Where the light catches his face from the bright hundred-watt bulb, it has divided it exactly in two, like a voodoo mask, half of him in black. Only he can't properly see his features at all, the things that he once recognised seem to be dissolving, leaving only what others think of as him.

Outside it is snowing, heavily and steadily. The ground is already thickly plastered. As is Daniel. Itchy sees him weaving his way along the street, still in his ski boots and uniform, kicking snow high as he staggers home between parked cars.

Itchy is only just drunk enough to quell the need, is long before any pleasure. He's just fixing another gin and tonic when there is a knock at the door. It's Daniel; apparently he was coming here, not home. His face says why. At least it says sufficient for Itchy to know the rest, knowing what he already does. But he has to listen to the story, because he should have told Daniel already, he can't just reveal his knowledge now. Not when he didn't have the heart or the strength to say before.

'Suzi's fucking Vince,' Daniel says, commandeering Itchy's gin and tonic and taking a drowning-man's gulp.

Itchy had hoped it was a one-off, the thing he saw in the carpark.

'How do you know?' he says.

'She told me – well, not that it was Vince…but I knew, I asked her, because I knew there was something…and she told me.' He sits down on the sofa that is Itchy's bed, spent.

Itchy doesn't know what to say. What is there to say? So he lies; because there is a comfort in lying, for them both: 'I didn't know,' he says. 'How long?'

Daniel just shrugs, exhaustedly, drunker than Itchy has ever seen him.

'Doesn't matter…it's over, isn't it? Doesn't matter how long it's been wrong, just how many good years we had. I loved her, Itchy, I love her.' And he slumps over on the bed, the hand in which he still holds the drink trailing slowly down to trickle gin along the floor.

Itchy covers him with the Union Jack duvet, which feels kind of weird, as if it's a military funeral. Daniel is as still as death too, totally passed out. Blissfully allowed freedom from his thoughts for a while.

Sean is long gone, off to the airport, it being Saturday. Daniel is the last awake and the god of small mercies has allowed him the luxury of it being his day off. He sits up on Itchy's bed, clutching his head in his hands, partly from hangover, but also, no doubt, because he feels his new knowledge of Suzi with Vince rattling about. A small-calibre bullet that had the force to pierce his skull, but cannot blast its escape, so instead continues to ricochet.

Aussie Mark has a fried breakfast ready to go and starts cooking, while Itchy gives Daniel a cup of tea, two brufens and a pint of water. Even though there is fresh powder and blue skies in wait for them outside, they are not going to go without Daniel.

The Aiguille de Midi lift broke just about every record in the world when it was finished in 1955: highest; fastest; biggest; more Chamonix superlatives. The cabin itself is McDonald's red, but the walls are carpeted like an old-school French flat, floor rubber-painted like the flat bed of a pick-up truck.

On the second stage, despite his best efforts to remain by the door for a quick exit, Itchy is hustled to the front window, where he stares through the ski-scratched perspex. The cables on which they are carried loll slackly, slumped with their own weight, then suddenly soar upwards, like an optimistic line graph.

Ahead are the *aiguille*'s peaks, the *needles*, sharp spikes everywhere, except for the smooth, sugared, illusory comfort of the Dôme de Gouter. Some of the *aiguilles* look like pyramids, others like rampant leering spearheads; all are lined and scarred like half-rotted ancient hunks of wood. Though in fact these are the youngest mountains in Europe, which is why they remain so jagged and so high. Erosion has only just phoned through his estimate, for the work required to make this range as blunted as the rest.

Dark glacier ice shows, where the slopes are too steep even to hold snow. It overhangs like a fortress bulwark, blocking ascent up gullies too vicious to be climbed anyway. Though of course they all have been climbed, it's all been climbed now.

Out of the window to the left, spindrift swirls, from the narrow ridge along which they will shortly have to walk to get to the start of the skiing. To the right lies Mont Blanc and the Bossons glacier that flows down from it. Words are inadequate to paint the staring, sheer massiveness of the glacial landscape. Ocean surf, frozen solid at the very instant of breaking, perhaps, but only if you were as small as a phytoplankton. It looks similar to the surface of the moon, only even less hospitable: colder; fiercer; harder to get to. The truth is that glaciers look like nothing so much as themselves; there is no image in common human experience comparable to the vast uncaring enormity of these barren, crevasse-strewn, ice-bouldered wastes.

The cable car docks, and its passengers dutifully troop out, like Vulcan's dwarfs on their way to work the mines. The tunnels they pass through are partially concreted and cold-stained like ancient cellars, skewed with rust-bleeding bolts; partially left as hewn rock, where you can still see the dynamite blast rod marks, like fossils of long smooth proto-eels. Real fossil fish have been found up here, and higher, which the creationists once argued proved the truth of the biblical deluge, that the oceans had reached to the very mountain-tops. Until geologists showed that actually the reverse was true: that these mighty peaks were once flat seabeds.

The bridge that joins the two rock towers and their tunnels is a place too starkly beautiful to be real. It looks computer animated, a location that must be defended, a place where good and evil will fight, one on one, with light sabres or long-swords. Skywalker and Vader, Gandalf and Balrog. An old man is standing staring down into the drop below, a yearning chasm that could swallow a high street, and he is crying to himself. Itchy watches him, wondering whether it is for loss or pain, or just the unbearable smallness of himself up here, that the man sobs.

Perched on the cliff behind, swathed in platforms, gantries and cold-buckled gangways – looking every bit like a Bond villain's base – there is a restaurant and gift shop.

When the weather's been too crap to ski, Itchy's gone up there sometimes, with Sean or alone, just to cane a few cans of Heineken. The extra effect the alcohol has at this altitude is more than worth the slightly inflated prices. And you're often above the clouds, you can sit and stare down at the rolling billows, as if you're a god. If Itchy was a god he'd be Bacchus, patron of booze and orgies.

The final tunnel is ice, with blue sheeny walls like Santa's grotto; they come through it into the blinding brightness of the outside, painful on the eyes even through goggles. This is the highest lift-accessed skiing in Europe. The thinness of the air, to Itchy, tastes like an over-diluted vodka, the important bit missing. The peaks around in the near distance are all named: the Shark's Tooth; the Crocodile's Tooth; the Giant's Tooth; the Capuchins – after the dark-hooded monks; the Scissors; the Black; the Mallet; the Accursed; the Raven; the Ogres; the Devil. The names are not just descriptive of the peak shapes, they are specifically chosen to be ominous.

The guys put on their equipment for the ridge, the arête, one side of which looks as though it drops to Chamonix, two and a half kilometres straight down; the other side goes only a few hundred metres, still more than ample to mangle a faller.

Daniel struggles with his crampons, through the haze of his

hangover and his new-found anguish; he has them on the wrong foot to start with. Itchy rolls his trousers up above his boots; baggy pants have a liability to get spiked by the crampon of the other foot, which is a good way to go tumbling towards a final impact. The guys are all wearing harnesses for crevasse rescue, more vital than ever for Itchy after his New Year's Day escapade, but they don't rope up for the ridge.

Around them, weather-worn mountain guides are clipping in their groups, on to pre-tied loops on ropes. Other strings of tourists are already edging their way down, skis in one hand, gripping the frozen thickness of the balustrade fixed line in the other. Edgy steps, shaky, slipping ski boots. Unable to appreciate the magnificence of where they are, because the arête is demanding all their concentration. Behind, nonchalant guides shouting orders and encouragement, bandoliered with excess rope.

The guys step past them, easily able to overtake, untied and with sure cramponed feet, spikes biting through the powder into the hard-pack beneath, skis and board strapped to backpacks. Below them clouds are flying past, whipping along the valley in a hurry to be elsewhere, though the air is portentously still on high.

Where the ridge widens and flattens, guided groups of holiday-makers congregate, congratulating one another on surviving the ridge, unclipping from the ropes, properly taking in the view for the first time. From here they will all peel off to ski the Vallée Blanche, the run for which they followed the ridge, for which some have come to Chamonix in the first place. Twenty-two kilometres of off-piste. Digital pictures of today will be shared around dinner tonight, will appear as computer wallpaper at work on Monday, will be shown to friends for years to come.

But the Vallée Blanche route is strictly for punters and picnics, not for a powder day. Itchy, Aussie Mark and Daniel swap their crampons for skis and board, but continue to follow the ridge, upwards now, the first to do so since the snow. Itchy's skis disappear into the deep powder; he pants as he pole-pushes and kicks himself forwards uphill. Daniel follows easily, even hung over. Aussie Mark struggles behind; boards are not built for this; despite his collapsible pole and one of Daniel's he is forced to unstrap a foot, which keeps sinking up to his thigh.

At the top, Itchy and Daniel wait for Mark to reach them. Daniel looks shrunken, but he's still bigger than Itchy, and Itchy knows his friend will be all right as soon as they start skiing. You can escape things when you're skiing, the pain and the pointlessness can't catch you. Like when you're fucking, whatever position you settle on, you turn your back on it all. And when you're drunk, it can't catch your eye, as if you're an aged maître d'. But when you stop, it's there, and Daniel at the moment is in its full glare.

Daniel knows this as well as anyone. He is anxious to be going, sets off as soon as Aussie Mark gets his board on. Leading them down the steep first slope of the Col du Plan, fresh, loose snow sloughing behind him as he skis. His style is beautiful, if anything overly so, like many instructors. Up to his purse in powder, on thin piste skis. But bouncing himself free, through skill and sheer power.

Itchy and Aussie Mark follow down, but taking it one at a time, paying respect to the mountain. Picking their lines carefully over the bergschrund at the bottom of the pitch. You have to be careful not to forget you are in crevasse territory up here. Which is all too easy to do on a powder day, when everything is hidden, and the snow intoxicates you to the point where you'd like to stop measuring and evaluating and just let rip. And there is the old other danger: that you could cease to care – start to think that there could be no finer day to go than this – because everything after this point will never be as good.

But Itchy reins himself in, and Aussie Mark accepts that the others know more about the mountains and especially about these mountains than him, and he follows their lines. And Daniel is the most sensible of them all, he leads them like he'd lead a group – though he'd never take a class up here, and isn't qualified to, even if they were good enough – but he watches the others in, as if he's still responsible for them. Smiling through his hurt, sucking in some of the mountain's spare strength.

And Itchy thinks that seeing this brain-maiming beauty in nature must be a sort of survival instinct at its fundament, because days like this make you want to live. The mountains make you want to live. And he'd like to think that this feeling, the appreciation of their awesome beauty, came before the religion and the bullshit. But he knows, from those long-ago studies, that the love of mountains was an invention of the Romantic period; before that they were mostly feared and loathed. And so, to some degree, his love must have been learned as well.

Daniel sets off again, turns flowing as he flies, snow as pure as angel wings bursting from behind his skis. Itchy feels giddy, he can't focus on the floor, it's as if he's going backwards up the slope, even though his skis are set sideways and he knows he can't be moving. Then it hits him, with a sudden lurching nausea, that it's the ground that's moving: the snow is sliding away from him and Mark, beneath where they stand, down towards Daniel. Avalanche!

There has been no crack, no warning. Itchy shouts. The word. That word. 'Avalanche!' But by then Daniel is already aware. Must be gripped by fear. Yet keeps skiing, unpanicked. The snow slides past him, but doesn't sweep him off his feet. As if by miracle he stays upright on his skis. He's swept downwards, then backwards, but the flow is already slowing. The slope spreads out into a small valley. Daniel is buried up to his waist, but the danger is over. He scrapes at the snow with a hand, only it's set like cement, the guys will have to dig him out. But the slide was mercifully small. Itchy and Aussie Mark high-five in relief.

Daniel looks placid, as if he's offering a silent prayer of thanks, or cleansing himself. His hands no longer scrabble at the snow. He's just waiting for rescue, meditating. Probably feeling the absurdity, that such a feeling of deliverance and happiness should come on a day of such anguish.

The second avalanche signals properly, with a thud like a dropped bowling ball and then the rumble as it rolls to scatter the pins. There is a rush of wind that even Itchy can feel way up above, but Daniel remains calm and still, seemingly oblivious. The snow powers down in a cloud, with every vengeance of gravity. It bursts like Old Testament wrath. Smashing down the slope behind Daniel, the opposite side of the cleft in which he is entrenched. It pours like hate from angry heavens. Like a thunderous flood. Daniel looks either at the guys or the unruffled blue skies behind them, serene as Buddha.

Aussie Mark erupts with a shout that lingers in the air, longer even than the last of the airborne avalanche blasts. A shout that seems to cover every moment of the event, from the instant of the first crack and slide, to the point where Daniel's still-smiling face is enveloped by the stuff for which he lived, on which he worked. Even until the snow is settled and motionless and all is silent, except itself, that shout lasts. And Itchy will never know what Mark yelled. Will never ask. But will never forget the soul-rending noise.

The valley has become a terrain trap. Though they track Daniel's transceiver in minutes, the snow is set too hard and piled too deep. Pisteurs have arrived on the brow of the slope behind them, the point from which they watched their friend disappear, by the time Itchy and Mark have reached Daniel with their shovels. Finally found him, in a lonely well of snow.

Itchy's tears are frozen on his face, despite the exertion of digging. But they are like fire next to Daniel's cheeks. Which are the coldest thing Itchy has ever touched. The coldest thing he has ever held and kissed and wished it was him and howled.

'Whom the gods love die young' was said of yore.

Byron, Don Juan

March 16th, 12.30 p.m.

Suzi has fled to Britain, she hasn't taken all her stuff, but Itchy doubts she'll be back to Cham. She has been invited to the real service, held by Daniel's family, who don't know what Daniel discovered in his final hours. No doubt she will wail and wring all the harder for what she's done. None of Daniel's other friends have been asked to go, particularly not Itchy and Aussie Mark, guilty of survival.

They have their own service instead. On the Midi, where it happened, though not precisely where it happened, not next to the now wind-smoothed bunker where Daniel was buried. The ceremony is held at a safer, flatter place, on an easy route, so that anyone who wants to can be there. They hold it on Saturday, so all the instructors from Daniel's school can attend. Even Sean has been allowed the day off. The occasional sliders-by stare at the strange circle gathered there, but do not stop, sensing that this is something they cannot be a part of.

Everyone up there can say something if they want to. Religious words or words about Daniel or anything; poems and lines of oriental and Native American philosophy get read; and a promise by the ski school that each year an event will be held in Daniel's honour, a freeride competition most likely.

Sean struggles through his strangled tears to tell a story about a time when Daniel made them double back three miles further down the road, because he felt too guilty about not having given a lift to a hitcher, who of course had disappeared when they got there, and then they got fined for speeding trying to make up the lost time.

Josey asks those who want to, to join her in a prayer. Itchy doesn't pray, Itchy can't pray, and if he could it would be to St Jude, but even those ears are long closed.

Aussie Mark says that from now on he is going to pick up every bit of litter he finds on the mountains, because that's what Daniel used to do, and every time he does it, he'll think of his friend, and he suggests that they should all do that. And it doesn't sound like much, but this chokes Itchy, and that's a long speech for Mark.

When it is Itchy's turn, although there are no turns as such, he reads from a book: *A Farewell to Arms*. A passage that he remembered and tracked down, and a book that he thinks Daniel might have liked:

'If people bring so much courage to this world the world has to kill them to break them, so of course it kills them. The world breaks everyone and afterwards many are strong at the broken places. But those that will not break it kills. It kills the very good and the very gentle and the very brave impartially. If you are none of these you can be sure it will kill you too but there will be no special hurry.'

Itchy closes the book and looks up, at the peaks and the sky, at the black rocks, which appear so only next to the white that surrounds them.

'Daniel was all those things,' he says. 'I mean, he was good and gentle and brave. He probably wasn't the best guy in the world...

only because you have to admit that the chances are against that. But he was the best guy I ever met. He was the best of us.'

There are more readings and memories, more people containing their weeping, or not bothering to.

Normally it is hard for Itchy to feel emotion, without booze and a soundtrack – sufficiently soaked, moments in a film have provoked tears when the same incidents would never move him in real life; except for lust and loathing, those he can feel – but he has never lost someone like Daniel before. There has never been someone like Daniel before. Daniel mattered more than other people somehow, he offered something to life, he was less redundant.

Everyone has a glass of wine after their home-grown service is over. Except for Itchy, who feels as if it marks the occasion better if he doesn't.

There is a tiny stone in Itchy's shoe that has been there for days. It niggles him constantly but slightly, just enough to irritate when he walks, but not bad enough to be worth taking off the trainer and shaking it out, or to remember when he removes them at night. It may well stay there for weeks.

He walks beside the nightingale now, though, on the side of the cars, to shield her from the meagre traffic. Her presence not only erases the pebble, it also soothes the knowledge of Daniel's not being and eases the general strain of existence. The ice on the street is dark like quartz, with diesel fumes and dirt, but it glistens in the lamps as if there might be diamonds in there.

Their drink date has been long delayed. Itchy took her number that day in the Maison de la Montagne, but did not call it at first, afraid of finding she was not the possibility he'd half dared hope. And then Daniel died.

*

She drinks Cosmopolitans, he drinks Caucasians; sat in Elevation, on the same stools he sat on with Wendy that night all those weeks ago, when he first saw the nightingale. Wendy might be back soon, she said she would have another holiday to Cham near the end of the season.

The nightingale is not called that, of course; she is really called Marietta. And Itchy tells her his real name too, but explains that nobody calls him by that, not even his parents, that nobody has called him by it for years. It has become only a sound to Itchy now, the name he was once christened with, it has ceased to be attached to the object that is him.

She isn't a Chamoniarde by birth, it turns out, she's from Sète, down south, where they think a glacier is someone who sells *glaces*.

'But I am living here since I can walk,' she says.

Her English is made more beautiful by imperfection. As she is, by the scar that runs along her shoulder, slightly pinker than her pale skin. From a climbing fall, she says, she spends her summers here too; unlike Itchy, who has always drifted back to a homeland that he's not even sure is any more.

Inside a white top, the visible portions of her breasts are pale and quiet like sleeping faces and Itchy wants desperately to wake them, but he is mesmerised by all of her. She is more than he should even aspire to, up close. She allows him to believe in myths long since dismissed.

But she is no goddess. Though she would look good on a pedestal, her slightly inward-facing feet rest firmly on the floor. She noisily slurps the dregs of her Cosmopolitan through the straw when it reaches the bottom, then rubs a cube of ice from Itchy's drink around her lips in a mock-sexy way, like a parody of an advert; tiny drops cling to her feather-faint moustache.

Being a bartender, you notice certain things, conversational traits, similarities that strangers share. For example, people who say that what they are about to say is 'interesting' are almost never correct. But on the other hand, people who say that their conversation is boring are invariably absolutely right.

When walking her home, Itchy can't really think of a single thing the nightingale has said to him, but he knows he has dangled from her every word, like a spider from a cherry blossom.

Her door is at the other end of town from his, along the old road to Les Praz. The parked cars they pass en route have ice flowers frosted on to their windscreens. She still lives with her parents; but they are either out or sufficiently liberal that they don't mind her having guys to stay, because she asks him whether he wants to, after they kiss.

Baiser means to kiss and to fuck, the two meanings only divisible by context and the contexts often similar.

The kiss is calm and perfect, not clutched and charged, but like a contract. Itchy's bottom lip tingles with the freezing night air on the nightingale's saliva, when she shifts momentarily to sucking in his top lip. Eskimos rub noses only because they would ice together if they used their mouths and rend flesh away when they parted. Her hips jut bonily into his hands, like those of a sixteen-year-old, whose body has not yet been discovered by fat. It is a kiss like a full stop. A thing that ends something, so that another stage can start. And because of this, Itchy finds himself declining her invitation to stay the night. Because he has one more thing to finish, before he can begin another stage.

'Not tonight,' he says, like Napoleon. 'Maybe next time, and I really want there to be a next time. There should definitely be a next time. But not tonight.'

And he takes a last good look at her, to carry home with him, then walks away into the black.

Entry Number: 2895

Narrator: Shelley

Entry Title: The Monk's Child, or Every Good Tree
Bringeth Forth Good Fruit

On a rocky prominence, part of that far-extended chain of
mountains called the Alps, there is a summit col, where
travellers have trod for centuries along the devious winding
paths, to trade and to make the distant pilgrimage to Rome.
It is a desolate pass, where eternal squally winds tear
frantically from rock to rock, blasting the stunted shrubs
and buffeting the craggy granite heights.

At one extremity of the col there are scattered remnants,
piles of orphaned stones, the sombre time-dismantled
splendour of what was once a temple to despot Jove. At the
opposing end there is a Catholic monastery of arched roofs,
impermeable grey walls and undefined shadows, filled with
dark and solitary cells. The dim lights which pierce without
its shuttered windows are all that break the otherwise
uninterrupted gloom of this remotest waste.

Between these two tabernacles, in the middle of the
pass, there is a mountain lake and in the lake there is a
small island, too small almost to be called such, barely an
assemblage of jutting rocks. It contains nothing but a single
unadorned wood cross. But perhaps more properly there
are two crosses, since the profile of that first and physical
cruciform creates a second cross, upside down, in the glassy
surface of the bitter-chill waters.

And who is it that sits upon a flinty seat looking on
this reflection amid the deepening twilight? Habited as he is
in black-cowled vestments, we might correctly suppose this

young man to be a monk, but there is no fire of religion in his eye. And yet he has an invincible mildness of mien which is suggestive of saintliness. More suggestive perhaps than the chanting requiem that yet murmurs from the monastery, mingled with the banshee wind.

For a time, the monk remains sitting there alone, on that projecting lump of stone, until the monastery bell mournfully declares the end of evensong and another figure, similarly attired, though haughty in demeanour and with golden chain of office, approaches him.

Abbot- You were not at prayers, Brother, are you ailing?

Monk- Not from physical ills, Brother Abbot, but I have come upon a problem, a paradox rather, which I cannot pass.

Abbot- And what is the nature of this problem?

Monk- It is the evils which we know to be in the world, the perfidies which men inflict upon their fellows and the horrors which nature inflicts upon all.

Abbot- Thou speak truth, but our purpose in the monastery is to rise above such things, to do what we might to ameliorate them and to pray to our Heavenly Father, the Lord God Almighty, for His forgiveness.

Monk- I beg you to forgive me, Brother Abbot, but therein lies my problem, this is the paradox I have encountered. Since if God wishes that this evil was not so, but cannot prevent it, then He cannot be omnipotent. But if He might prevent it, and chooses not to, then surely He is malevolent? He cannot be both willing and able to prevent such evil, or else whence cometh it? And if he is neither willing nor able, then how is He God?

Abbot- You venture into deep blasphemies, Brother, and yet you have been the most noble and devoted of our community these past five years, so I will grant you this transitory window of grace. God allows evil that men might wilfully avoid it; in the absence of choice, we could not decide upon His love and salvation over eternal damnation and hellflame; to be devoured, skin and sinew, by furious fires and for evermore. The which fate you strongly risk now by your words. You struggle perhaps against the frenzy which accompanies a fever. Repent of such talk and return to the monastery's warming room and to the fold, before it is too late.

Monk- Alas, in hell too I see unreason, for what can be the purpose of rendering the body capable of indefinite excruciation? How can that fit with a God of love as Christ spoke of, and what use can there be in punishment which is inflicted, not to correct, not for the moral improvement of the sufferer, but merely as revenge without any view to future good? How can God command man, who is in His image, to forgive any trespass against us, if He meets such trespasses with eternal tortures? Torments which serve not even as a warning to others, since they are never seen save by those already sainted, who Aquinas wrote are permitted to gloat from Heaven. The hollow folly of revenge has been condemned, not just by Christ, but by theosophs of every creed. And so, alas, my mind cannot but derelict from such plainly fraudulent faiths as those which preach infernal perdition.

Abbot– You are confirmed in apostasy then, former brother, and must look forward to what punishment it will solicit, in this world and the next.

Monk– I cannot command belief and I cannot longer believe in a deity who would punish me for what it is not in my power to enact. Belief or disbelief are not acts of volition. How then could a just God hold me to account for what was beyond my will?

Abbot– You mistake, for God's ways are more mysterious than man can know, and yours is not to interpret them with human logic. Did not Mark write that Jesus came upon a fig tree, when he had great hunger, but the tree bore no fruit, because it was not the season for figs. You might say in your sophistry that it was beyond the will of the tree to produce fruit in the wrong season, but Christ withered and condemned it just the same. So will it be for you, and all who do not believe; for every tree that bringeth not forth good fruit is hewn down, and cast into the fire.

Even as the abbot spoke these words, the monk felt that insolence in the face of peril which peril can create; the desire to meet it headlong and defy it, through the hope that conquering its ills, rather than fleeing them, will eventually be proven the better course. So he lingered on his seat, beneath the overhanging brow of a colossal misshapen precipice, after the abbot had departed. And he was there still when presently a body of black-clad monks arrived, the minions of God's red right hand, to lead him to his destiny.

The monastery of St Bernard having no gaol, the monk was thrust into the charnel house. That stone sepulchre where in winter the frozen corpses of those who have perished fighting the mountain passes are stored, until the ground thaws sufficiently for them to be buried, which was still empty in early October's first snowless bitters.

They allowed him no lamp to cast against the dismal darkness and no blanket to fight the chill. The tile floor so sapped the heat from him that eventually, though enhorrored at the prospect, the monk was compelled to lie upon one of the wooden biers, where so many bodies colder, stiller and quieter than his had lain before. He surmised with terror, that the abbot intended this mortuary to be an oubliette; that they would leave him here to perish with what algidity or starvation or death from dread would seize him first, and then bear him away with the other accumulated corpses in the spring. The despair which pervaded his soul accorded but too well with the gloom surrounding him in that ghastly inhumation chamber and his mind became jaundiced with ideal terrors.

He thought he felt the shades of those who had passed their first season of death in this sepulchre, those travellers who had expired, feet frozen, toes blackened and gnarled, cheeks spattered with waxy frostbite, on the impenetrable winter roads. The sound of the wind as it groaned through the crack beneath the time-worn, locked door seemed to the monk like the doomed ghost cries of those once stranded, too weak to force their way farther or back through the crippling snows that had hindered their way. He sank into an ecstasy of terror, where every undefined shadow, every chill breeze, each shriek of night-bird and low hissed whisper of movement struck forcibly upon his senses and made him shrink farther with affright.

Such was his state of mind already, when he heard the scraping on the door. A noise like nails or claws being drawn against its surface, their bearer desperate to enter, accompanied by the low whimper of a tortured soul. The monk was almost bereft of sense, so afraid was he, his whole frame thrilled with tenfold terrors. Then began a pounding upon the door, which shook it against its casement. A force which could only be created by an immense beast, and one which must be impervious to pain, throwing its own self at solid wood with such might. The monk drew himself back against the wall; there was nowhere he might flee and no weapon he might wield, though that were not in his character. The ancient portal splintered open and a gigantic dark-furred form plunged into the tomb, jaws dripping.

But even through eyes stricken with horror, the monk recognised that this beast was no monster, but only one of the monstrous Barryhunds – those dogs which the monastery breeds to seek out the lost and the weary in the night and guide them to safety. And this one, the monk recognised as Theseus, a brave and noble hound that he himself had helped to raise from pup. Theseus must have smelt his fear or sensed the creeping death from cold, which would surely have come upon him in the tomb, and the dog had forced the door just as it had forced fallen rocks and tree trunks from many an ailing pilgrim in the past.

The monk wrapped his grateful arms around the warm beast and bade it follow, as he fled away from the charnel house and into the dense vapours which overspread the night air.

From the summit border of the St Bernard Col, the monk could flee to the Kingdom of Piedmont to the south or the Duchy of Savoy to the north. Both routes lay down treacherous mountain paths, dangerous even by daylight, and the orb of day had long since gone. But the monk knew well that the inscrutable evils of the Inquisition held stronger sway the closer they were to Rome, that domain founded upon fratricide and rape, whereas past Savoy lay the independent city state of Geneva, which had long been a seat of religious dissent and protest, where one like he might perhaps begin anew. To what hopes of futurity he knew not, but with the lolloping Theseus by his side, he started the descent to Savoy.

The skies were gloomy, as if with broad strokes of charcoal they had been filled, and few transitory moonbeams broke their shade. But even by this faint light, the mighty hound knew his way along the narrow mountain paths and guided well, bred and trained for such tasks as these. The monk kept his hand always upon massy Theseus's short-furred shoulder-bones and like this could tell the inclination and direction, though frequently his steps faltered upon stone or branch. The zenith soon was far behind them, their paths leading through desolate heaths, and lower still to pasturelands where cows tolled their churchless bells in the blackness, competing against the sound of swollen mountain rills, whose water trickled often athwart the paths. On through the night the strange pair travelled, their pace quickening as dawn allowed at last the weary monk to watch clearly where his boots would tread.

When finally the monk could proceed no farther, he slept with bosom curled upon Theseus in a cowshed, nested in the hay stored against winter's inexorable approach. The monk was stirred from sleep at dusk, by the sound of muleteers upon the nearby path and through the stable's slit window saw that messengers from St Bernard had overtaken his progress. So instead of heading towards Aigle, Montreux and the lake along well-travelled roads, as his former brethren would expect, the monk took smaller paths still, the rocky windings of the shepherds and the silver panners, towards Argentière and Chamouni.

Since his dereliction of the monastery the monk had not taken sustenance, but for the swift chill waters of brook and burn. Yet when he approached inhabitation in the following days, he found that the noble peasants, taking him for a mendicant holy wanderer as of yore, would gladly share with him and Theseus what meagre meals they had. He in turn would bless them, and his words were heartfelt, free of hypocrisy, for though he blessed in Latin, he used not lines of prayer-book and Bible. Instead he blessed them for their generosity and human kindness. He sometimes used the word 'Christus', which even those uneducated mountain minds comprehended, but the monk said only that if Christ was simply a man like us, perhaps we could all strive to become men more like him.

And so the monk spread much happiness as he made his way from hut to shack to humble cottage, for though the impoverished goatherds and hunters were well used to the Church taking its tithe of their bread, none were accustomed to monks breaking it with them. When he was brought water by his hosts, to wash away the toil of days on the trail, he would always first take the bowl and clean the bare hoof-tough feet of their children, who shrieked with joyfulness or stared in quiet awe at the strange act.

And the smallest of the children, Theseus would bear upon its back, loving and unbegrudging as any disciple.

Whether they had been informed by the abbot and it was feared he was preaching atheism on his meandered wanderings, or whether more temporal dissent was suspected, the monk would never learn. Yet as he entered the village of Chamouni, men-at-arms of the Duc de Savoy closed in upon him. Theseus snarled and lunged as their intent became clear, but the beast was pierced by a score or more of crossbow bolts, porcupined like St Sebastian in Renaissance frieze, and its four mighty legs collapsed beneath it. Life left the Barryhund with its brown eyes at peace, even through such a violent end. Its master was restrained with heavy chains and sat backwards upon a mule, and like this was led to Château Chillon, seat of the Savoy dynasty.

That grey-turreted castle is built upon a rocky outcrop into Lac Léman, isolated and impenetrable, from where it commands the route to Piedmont; a road which eventually passes the very monastery and col from which the monk had fled, exiled from home and happiness.

The first sight the monk had of Château Chillon's dark expanse, the unholy coupling of Gothic and Bernese architecture, filled him with dread. Gargoyles and other grotesque forms jutted from atop narrow arrow-slits and broad embattlements, the projection of ruthless inherited rule. Fretted roofs were surrounded by high ivy-mantled walls, rearing up from the lake and into the sky. On the highest tower was painted a sundial, where the black shadow cast by a cruel iron spike pointed out the hours, as if they too were owned by the castle's masters.

But the monk could not see the sundial from the dungeon

into which he was cast, down slimy and precipitous steps, and so the days passed even more lingeringly slowly. Only a scant ration of blackened bread and brackish water each morning served the prolongation of his existence in that place. Only a wretched pallet held his weak and emaciated frame from the flinty fundus at night. Even by day, the light from treillaged windows hardly served to dissipate the darkness, and shades still lurked in the arched distances of the ill-carved rock. Damp clung to the prison walls, like the cold sweat of death on a corpse, and slithering lizards were the monk's only company in that place.

Past the door, locked and strongly barred from without, the hangman's use-worn black beam was dressed with rope ready knotted, a final reminder, as if one were needed, that on the duc's word your life would be ended, who cared not for judge nor jury. Everything belonged to the duc, all about were his perquisitions, nothing but misery was the monk's.

And yet from the grille of his window, the monk stole some pleasure. He looked out with fixed serenity upon the lake and on Mont Blanc's imagination-staggering immensity, from the foot of which the duc's house-carls had snatched him. He inhaled the saltless sea's morning breezes, which belonged to him as much as any man, and watched the red glare of the setting sun on the mountain peaks and the whitened waves of the lake. He listened to the lapping of water on the rocks which bound him in and the shrieking chatter of gulls and ducks and the doves which nested in cotes more comfortable than his own home. The enchanting harmony of the scene gave much solace to his hapless bosom, nature became his divinity, nested in his heart from whence thought of God had been dissolved. And in the unvarying sombreness of his gloomy gaol, he remained freer than his captors. For all souls are imprisoned which follow falsehood.

On Sabbath days the monk would see the fishermen in their small skiffs, sailing their pilgrimage to church, looking for God rather than themselves. And on these Sabbaths he would often also see a young maiden, alone in a rowing boat. An almost ethereal form of loveliness and grace, kindness irradiated her most symmetrical features and her hair floated unconfined about her shoulders. She would appear, shortly after the hollow bells had called the castle's other residents to chapel, and would read in her little craft, until after the service had finished. When she rowed past the monk's metal-latticed window, she would smile to him and swiftly look away with retiring modesty.

Inconceivable it may seem, but such is the way of love, its movement more mysterious than any erroneous God, and over many months this maid, who was named Julia, began to feel the Sunday looks she shared with the matted-haired prisoner as the greatest balm upon her. She found that a warm sigh would arise involuntarily from her bosom whenever she thought on him and the tender softness of spirit which she read from his love-beaming eyes. She talked to him but briefly at first, scared by what she did and by her own dilated and fluttered heart. Then over time their conversations would fill the entire void left by the chapel service she truanted, and ever longer. And by then it was too late to turn back from the road, though the monk tried to dissuade her still, since he could offer her no hope of future delight; but they were bound by a true harmony of souls, though tyrant's walls kept them apart; cemented by mutuality of sentiment and maddening love, separated only by a treillage of metal.

Julia told the monk that she was his gaoler's daughter and had no love for her father nor his profession, she had a contrivance of how she could get the keys to the dungeon to flee with the monk. The danger of failure would come from the strong chance of her being seen by guards on the corridors or steps after nightfall. The monk begged her not to make the attempt, for though the black pall of imprisonment whittled his life, yet would he not have hers risked.

The night which Julia had designated for escape, for reason she would not reveal, was to be the feast of St Jude, patron of the desperate; near two years the monk would then have been captive of the dastard duc. The monk lay awake, in recumbent posture, watching the shimmering moonlight reflected from the waves, which seemed to animate the spiderous cross-vaults of the prison ceiling. He was palsied with cold and fear, his breath in the frigorific air rose like smoke from a condemning censer, as the terrors of his mind augmented.

At midnight's tolling, a key turned in the dungeon door's lock, and the monk awaited with anxiety the fate of one he loved more than himself. Would the entrant be Julia, come to free him, or a guard, or her gaoler father come to mock that their scheme was shot and he would never see her more?

The awful figure that floated through the door seemed more frightful almost than that ill-news would be. It was a grim ghostly vision, white-veiled and draped with galling chains, purple gore staining its chest; it seemed to scintillate, through the circumambient darkness. Chilled with horror, delirious with affright, the monk feared he must have been driven to intellectual derangement. Yet there was something familiar about the slim waist and equal footsteps and when the vision lifted its veil, Julia's liberated tresses tumbled out.

Julia explained why she ported the strange disguise of this wedding gown, so discoloured with blood.

Julia– A barbarous ancestor of the present duc murdered his own daughter in jealous rage on her wedding day, upon the feast of St Jude. The very next year he himself died of affright, that same night. Ever since, it has been said that the murdered maiden haunts these corridors, upon that uncalled-on Saint's Eve, and any who impede her path will die. Two watchmen have I met on the lonely walk to free you and each but crossed himself and stepped aside to hide his eyes. Thus they have been tricked by their own vulgar superstitions, and now we shall away!

A darkling way she led him, down antiquated passages and through a door into the same small rowing boat as she had floated on through the many months of their curious courtship. Though his bones started almost through his skin, yet had the monk much power still within him and he drew upon the oars knowing well that every stroke was taking him farther from hell and closer to heaven.

Like phantoms they glided across the vast lake, under the sparkled concavity of night. And as he looked back at the château, where torches, like comets, gleamed upon the battlements, the monk could swear there was a bride-pale figure at a fenestration, waving their small craft mournfully on its journey.

Abandoning the boat at Geneva, they fled into the Jura Mountains beyond, out of Savoy's dominion. Julia had with her not inconsiderable sums, larcened from her father, and they procured a mazot-hut in the farthest reaches of the highest habitation, cloaked by trees, alone but for their goats and the intoxicating evening zephyrs. There they thought them beyond any reach and lived a life as pure and joyous as any children of Rousseau's.

The ardent fire of their mutual love kept them warmed more than wine or stove through snowbound winter's shivers. And as days lengthened and heated, they shared with excessive and unaffected delight the luxuriant meadows and odiferous pine groves. Not a pair of songbirds took such pleasure from life on that mountain and asked so little from it as did the monk and Julia. Not a pair of songbirds lived with such nuance and harmony, so naturally and purely married, by love alone.

Alas, would that the story might end here, but there must be more. Julia had spoken true to the monk, when she said she was his gaoler's daughter, but her words lacked fullness. For fear of his rejection, she had neglected to include that the gaoler she spoke of was not the man who turned the key and brought the scanty nourishment, but rather he who owned the gaol and the château about it and indeed the very lands which spread between the lake and the mountains. Her despised father was the Duc de Savoy himself, against all intuition, for how could such loveliness fount from such loins?

The duc's rancorous will to have Julia returned and her eloper punished had not been mellowed with time, nor would it be, even had he known her happiness. The dark colours of his character were immune to conscience, he dreamed only of the utter and ignominious destruction of the monk, and the return of his daughter to his thrall.

Julia had thought them to be beyond his grasp, when they had passed from her father's land into those cloud-capped mountains, but the duc's agents were everywhere. Perhaps they would not have been safe even had they travelled to Bordeaux or Munich. At summer's tail the clatter of steel-shod horses signalled the return of Savoy's dominion. The monk was once more cast in chains by men-at-arms and he and Julia were retracted to the rock-rooted, black and barren turrets of dismal Château Chillon.

There the monk was again immured in the stone-carved fissure of the dungeon, but this time fixed by immense iron pinions to a pillar, denied even his window glimpses of the world beyond. Julia, though big with child, was cloistered in the highest chamber of the ivy-clenched keep, as far from her love as was possible within the castle's compound.

It was four months later that the papal inquisitors arrived at the lofty drawbridged portal of Chillon. As holy and insensate as those angels who approached the gates of Sodom, that they might bear unaiding witness to the rape of innocents and then murder the entire populace in revenge.

Cast another glance at the countenances of these most righteous religious men. Cast another glance, so that when you see another visage like these, you may know the owner as a sanguinary, remorseless fiend.

They had been summoned by the duc, inasmuch as even he had command over such as they, because he sought confirmation, before the inevitable execution, that his prisoner was condemned to immortal agony, endless and irremediable pain; as well as the furies the inquisitors themselves might heap.

But the inquisitors discovered that their tools of torture were unrequired, the monk beheld them with composure, when they were better used to accents inarticulate from terror. Yet he answered their questions with such obdurate atheism, that there could be no doubt but that he was tenfold damned. He felt no contrition for his sins nor his blasphemies, indeed he questioned their own faith with such fixed serenity and unsettling sense, that they decided it were good the deviant be executed, the more swiftly the better, lest his forked tongue speak to any less able to resist than they.

The monk forgave them, as they slunk away, though he could see that they knew what they did: they condemned him to calm their own doubts. A man cannot be a zealot about certain truth; to exercise his dedication its object must perforce be suspect. No pietist murders the heretic who refuses to recant a belief that the lake is dry or the glacier warm. Fanatics can only be so because a great dark veil of qualm hangs over their dogma. The first and greatest evil they enact is to silence their own inner voices; it is but a small step after that to cut out the tongues of the entire world.

Ere four and twenty hours had elapsed, a pyre was built in the courtyard. Pines, dragged from the happy seclusion of the flowery mountain steeps, honeysuckle and jasmine still twined amidst their boughs.

As the monk was led forth into the blinking daylight, his gaze fixed on Julia, guarded within the massed crowd, and the blanket-wrapped baby girl she held aloft for him to see. His look parted not from them, as he was chained amid the trees; it was an image which would last till the destruction of the intellectual particles which cradled it.

Even as that insupportable fire scorched his resolute eyes to blindness, he saw still the implanted image of his daughter. Even as the craven flames crept about his manly limbs, he knew that he lived on in her. As every man, the monk was immortal to himself; for though he faced the certainty of death, he would never know that he was dead. But his true immortality was the parts of him that now howled in Julia's slim staunch arms, parts that would one day know peace and joy. He would not perish in fire, as those celibate hypocrites who had lit it surely finally would, he had brought forth the best fruit of all: he had created a child through whom he survived.

Christians have burnt each other, quite persuaded
That all the Apostles would have done as they did.
Byron, Don Juan

March 28th, 11.13 p.m.

The end of March marks a turning point, the warmer weather is arriving, even the pistes on the mountains have started to soften to slush in the afternoons. Over the past few days the snow and ice in town have melted away, revealing three months of now defrosted dog shit; Chum-flavoured chunks dissolved into splats of kidney-brown sludge on the pavements.

Itchy is advancing into town, past the building work in the centre that has been going on for years. They are making another underground car-park, it says so on the billboards, but the images on those optimistic illustrations are still a long way off. At the moment there is only a colossal ragged-walled pit in the ground, foundations fit for a ziggurat. The kind of excavations where it would be easy enough to hide a body, if you worked for the Mafia, or were just so inclined.

On the site's plywood wall someone has spray-painted *'Rapist go home!'* in French and underneath, in the same hand, is *'English go home!'* As if it is certain these will amount to the same thing.

Outside the L'M restaurant there are burning torches that look like the lonely start of a lynch mob; a gathering point for the Ku Klux Klan, or the villagers massing to burn Frankenstein's malformed child. Itchy is hunting for prey of his own.

He finds Vince in the Clubhouse, drinking with his usual gaggle of acolytes. Itchy orders a vodka martini, shaken not stirred, and starts to chat, masked behind glib banter. The cheesy choice of drink earns a deserved smirk from the barman. But Bond likes his martinis shaken because the friction melts the ice, waters down the drink; it is important not to get too drunk if you don't know when you might have to fight. What wouldn't Itchy give for Bond's ruthlessness? This is the hardest part, though, feigning friendliness to Vince. Itchy feels his hypocrisy slicing into his stomach like a knife. Every smile he swaps with Vince takes a year from his life. Sicilians say that the price of revenge is a season in hell.

After a while, Itchy whispers to Vince that they should slip away from the others, that there is an invitation-only party going on at the Cantina. Vince agrees readily, always anxious to ingratiate himself into what he thinks might be a cooler crowd. Itchy sends the text message, stored ready to go on his mobile, a single rubberised button pushed.

Vince has no idea what's coming. Walks alongside Itchy without a care in the world. Skating over melting ice. When they are level with Aussie Mark's Land Rover, Itchy has a quick scan about the street to make sure they are alone, then punches Vince with his full strength in the face. It doesn't work as it would for Bond – Vince doesn't drop senseless to the floor, but he is sufficiently stunned for Itchy and Sean to be able to bundle him into the back seat and hold him there between them, while Mark pulls away.

'What's going on, what are you doing?' Vince croaks out.

'Shut up, cunt,' Itchy says. He doesn't like the word, but language has been so devalued that 'fuck' no longer begins to convey the malice he feels.

'Do you see that white dot?' Sean says, pointing a gloved finger to a fresh spot of Tipp-Ex, applied for the purpose, behind the Landy's handbrake. 'If you take your eyes from that spot before I tell you, I'm going to break your nose.'

Vince lets out a strangled moan.

'Oh, come on,' Itchy says, 'you must have seen something coming. Did you really think you could get away with it?' Itchy adjusts his position on the seat, which is slippery, because of the clear-plastic decorator's sheeting it's covered in.

Vince doesn't ask 'Get away with what?', which presumably means he knows exactly what this is about.

There is a car in front of them, on the back road out to Les Praz. Aussie Mark keeps his distance, but Itchy notices it has a Corsica sticker on it, you see them a lot in Cham. The symbol of Corsica should by rights be Napoleon Bonaparte, its most famous son; instead, it is a black-skinned head in a bandanna. When Moorish invaders attacked the island, they were executed without mercy, and the carcass-heads were put on poles all along the coastline to remind others. No one fucks with Corsicans these days either – the stickers are a warning, same as the original heads on spikes.

The car in front turns off and leaves them alone on the shadowy road up to Argentière. The passenger-side wing mirror on the Land Rover is loose, it twitches with every bump, and because human eyes – predator's eyes – have evolved to notice movement, it is distracting Itchy, even from the back seat.

Vince keeps starting to speak. Itchy knows what he's trying. He wants to talk to them, make conversation, to make whatever they're going to do to him harder to do. But every time he opens his mouth, Sean tells him to shut up and punches him in the ribs.

After the lights of Argentière's high street, they follow the road onwards, away from Montroc and the memorial for those killed in '99 when an avalanche swept away half the village, up the Col de Montets towards Switzerland, into the Aiguilles Rouges Nature Reserve.

Mark chugs the Landy off the road, into a sheltered and deserted summer carpark, lit only by the polar moon.

They pull on IRA-style balaclavas, which will hide their expressions from Vince and each other, and that will make this easier. They will become the task and not the people. All of them are already wearing gloves, a criminal advantage in the mountains.

They make Vince get out and kneel, and they cable-tie his hands behind his back. He is moaning constantly now, a horrible damned moan – that Itchy has to try to shut his ears to – and making a helpless rocking motion, which reminds Itchy of himself when he was beaten and trapped in the bin. Suffering does not ennoble.

Sean produces a can of lighter fluid and squeezes it, spraying it on to Vince's mouth and nose. Vince is really shrieking now.

Itchy plays with a Zippo lighter, flicking the case open and shut.

'Go and get the petrol,' Sean says.

Aussie Mark goes to the Landy and pulls out a battered green jerrycan that sloshes audibly as he walks.

Sean sprays more lighter fluid on to Vince's lower face as Mark empties the jerrycan over the rest of him.

Vince is screaming like a girl now, he tries to get up but his legs collapse under him, his jeans are drenched in his own piss along with the other liquids.

'There was this emperor,' Itchy says, 'or an emir or something, who used to punish people by soaking them in a barrel of brandy all day, while their family was flayed alive in front of them, and while he reminded them of whatever they'd done wrong. Then at night, when it was dark, like this, he would fire them out of a cannon and their burning body would light up the sky. Pretty cool, huh?'

Sean pulls out a packet of Lucky Strikes; he doesn't usually smoke Luckies, but Itchy can see that they have a certain cool befitting this occasion.

'Smoke?' Sean asks Vince.

Who only sobs and whispers, 'Please don't, no, please.'

Sean takes a cigarette anyway and tries to push it between Vince's quivering lips, but it won't stay there, just keeps dropping to the floor.

'All right, guys,' Itchy says, 'that's enough, let's put him out of his misery.' And he lights the Zippo and tosses it at Vince's legs.

There is a scream, but no flames. As of course there wouldn't be, since the jerrycan held only water.

Vince is lying on his side, chest heaving. Silent. Itchy grabs him under the armpits and helps him up, puts a hand around his shoulder.

'It's over, Vince,' he says, 'we're not really going to kill you. But we couldn't just let it go. Not with Daniel dying and everything.' He starts to lead Vince back over to the Landy.

'What are you doing?' Sean asks. 'Let's just leave him here.'

'He's soaked and it's about minus five,' Itchy says. 'We might as well kill him, if we're going to do that.' He cuts through the cable-tie that binds Vince's hands and helps him on to the back seat, puts a blanket over his quivering shoulders.

The others get in, pulling off their balaclavas, Sean in the front now.

Itchy pulls off his own ski mask. Vince is looking at him with pathetically grateful eyes, which makes him feel worse than he already did. Ashamed of Vince's shame and his own. But once you start these things, you have to see them through.

They dump Vince in the Place de Poilu back in Cham, by the memorial for soldiers who died in the First World War; the *Great War*, as it is unfathomably called, when from what Itchy knows of it, it sounds like the worst of the lot. Then they drive on home.

Itchy is both sated and sickened by their revenge. He knows it's not what Daniel would have wanted. It's probably the last thing that Daniel would have wanted. But Daniel's dead. That's the point. Daniel's dead.

I fear thy kisses, gentle maiden;
Thou needest not fear mine;
My spirit is too deeply laden
Ever to burthen thine.

Shelley, 'I fear thy kisses, gentle maiden'

April 7th, 2.55 p.m.

Three o'clock is the perfect time in Cham, because anything is possible. You can still ski, but also respectably start drinking; the shops have just reopened, the sun is still up. Three o'clock is never too late or too early.

Aussie Mark has lent Itchy the Landy for his date and even the carpark is cheery today – you could hardly believe this is still the stalking ground of a beast – the broken glass below looks like the last of the shattered icicles in the warm streets up above.

Itchy passes a group of Scandies as he pulls out past the barbershop-striped barrier of the carpark. They are carrying a metal BBQ and crates of beer, evidently for an impromptu party in the square. One of them is wearing a Daz-white 'I love Sud' T-shirt. A lot of these shirts have started appearing in the last few weeks, and badges and hats, an ironic reference to the I Love New York stuff, when that city had a reputation for rapes and violence; ironic, but carrying that same pride.

Itchy runs his hand through his hair, which he has decided to grow a bit now, like Daniel's. It is always at its softest and its thickest just after he has washed it. Itchy doesn't have a pension plan, but he does use a shampoo that promises to fight the decline into baldness, at least making some provision for the future.

He picks up the nightingale from the road outside her work, where her thirty-five-hour week has just finished, both of them precisely on time. She kisses him on the cheek like a little girl's curtsy and he doesn't even beep his horn at the car that abruptly stops in front of him. They are at the back of the cinema here, it has murals painted on the walls, silhouettes, like the ones that appear in the garage, only these are funny – crowds of happy cartoon people in top hats.

'Ça va, Itchy?' she says.

And he smiles yes, loving the way she frames his name, her voice making the mundane exotic.

'Why do you collect me up in a car?' she asks.

'Because we're going for an Italian meal,' he says.

'But we need to drive there?'

'The best Italian restaurants are in Italy.'

The seracs on Mont Blanc, above the tunnel, are falling down, like London Bridge, but so languidly no one would sing about it. Even one of those speeded-up films in which flowers open and close like Mexican waves would produce only an imperceptible slow-motion creep if featuring the glacier. Itchy can't help holding his breath, looking at the chastening bulk of ice and snow as he swings the Landy up the hairpins towards the tunnel's entrance; passing the bronze-and-granite memorial to those who died in the fire.

The tunnel runs on for eleven kilometres under the mountain. An idea almost preposterous at its conception, but now slotted comfortably in the lowest echelons of the marvels of modern life, above radio maybe, but below so much else: thousand-ton aircraft that look as unlikely to fly as anything you could think of; bullet trains that float on air cushions; monster mice with ears on their backs; cloned sheep, like herds of peaceful Hitlers; robots so small they can swim about in blood vessels; digital cameras, TVs, MP3s and computer games all inside mobile phones – things that we accept as givens, but have no idea how their ordinariness works.

The tunnel is just not that impressive now, as a concept; not as impressive as the mountain it goes through or even most of the cars that go through it. But it still costs thirty-five euros return. Itchy pays, mentally converting the sum back into pounds, after all this time; to know value he still has to think in sterling.

There is a camper van beside them in the next toll cabin. Lime green, split-screened, painted with flowers, a proper old-school wagon, low on its axles with universal love. Itchy can't see its drivers for the booth, but he hopes there's a kid in there with them, a little blond boy with a rat's-tail at the back of his hair.

The nightingale's presence makes Itchy long for such a boy of his own. A boy he could teach to ski. A boy he would tell all the secrets to: that nothing's impossible and nothing is true. A boy he would invest with no expectations except absolute freedom, and who would probably rebel into a banker or a bureaucrat. Which would still make Itchy proud, because freedom only means not doing what's expected of you.

They follow the camper into the tunnel after the digital space-launch countdown that separates all the vehicles, for safety, these days. Itchy doesn't recognise the camper's registration origin and it has no nationality sticker, just a smiley face. The tunnel ceiling is a wispy grey, like an old tie-dyed T-shirt, which seems appropriate to the hippy-happiness Itchy finds himself surrounded by today.

The walls are plated in slats like an armadillo's tail. Slope-sided, like the tunnel that still couples the Thameslink station with the rest of King's Cross; sides that Itchy and his mates used to try and skateboard up – on their way to adventures at the South Bank of the Big Smoke, far from the small suburbia they grew up in.

The nightingale puts her hand on his thigh, an act charged well beyond its light touch; more than sexual, in a less-than-it way.

'Do you believe in free love?' he asks her.

'No,' she says, 'I believe you should pay for it. Things you pay for are worth more.'

And because he has to look back at the road, rather than still into her eyes, he can't tell whether she is joking or misunderstanding him.

Out of the tunnel they are in Italy. This side of Mont Blanc is totally south-facing and windless; it feels as if you have appeared suddenly in the Mediterranean. Bright beyond belief, after the strip-lit burrow. Spring is two weeks closer over here, Itchy can smell it, the soil's scent is drier, the air has the first whiffs of pollen in it, signatures of subtly different plants and trees than those over the other side of Europe's largest natural border. The evidence of the planet's warming is more blatant here too; the glacier reaches only halfway down the gigantic ravine that its vigour once ripped into the mountainside. But being warm doesn't seem like such a bad thing, today.

Itchy parks the Landy farther down the spooling mountain road in the town of Courmayeur, slinging its battered frame casually between a Porsche and a Beamer.

Hand in hand, Hansel and Gretelled, they stroll around the bleached old streets. Among the dried sausages and Prada. In a courtyard, under a canopy, white linen like biblical robes, they have a beer each, served in giant glasses like expensive vases. The nightingale reclines, hands folded over the bare brown flesh of her stomach, a half-inch of invitation between her T-shirt and her jeans. Her eyes shut, thick lashes lulling over Egyptian gold cheeks, the lids kohled black like those of a temple priestess; she could easily be a vestal virgin, or a sacred prostitute. But there are more varied roles available now; she needn't be at either pole. And he is stabbed, suddenly, by an unsought similarity to another girl he once knew. As different in complexion to the nightingale as a silver-birch tree to her teak, but just as demandingly desirable. And anxious to flee these thoughts, he leans over and kisses her closed calm lips.

She opens her eyes and says: '*Attention*, Itchy, if you wake the sleeping beauty, you might have to marry her.'

They wander through Courmayeur, idle as aristocracy, peering into windows; passing the time till dinner, which would doubtless pass in any case, regardless of their activity.

Itchy gazes into the weapon shop. He has always been interested in tools of destruction and still has a small boy's fascination for blades and bullets. They have similar shops in Cham – the Europeans generally have a franker approach to this sort of hardware. But the shop in Courmayeur is particularly explicit. Shuriken-throwing stars mingle with shotguns as if they would be equally useful for hunting birds. There are also metal truncheons, which telescope out from pocket convenience to an unhealthy baseball bat length. Switchblades, replica SS daggers, electric stun guns, mace spray – a catalogue of equipment completely illegal in the UK, lounging here on the sort of vinyl mown-grass traditionally associated with greengrocery.

Normally Itchy longs for these things – though never enough to buy them, he is sufficiently astute to realise that for him to own weaponry would be too hazardous for himself and others – but with the nightingale by his side the longing seems to be banished, he doesn't feel the need to stroke and weigh. Somehow, having for once something worth protecting has reduced the desire for these articles of supposed protection.

They eat meats so good and sliced so thin that cooking them is an irrelevance. They drink a champagne that is made somewhere near by and so of course is not champagne as such, but next to it the real stuff would seem like an expensive imitation. Cheeses from goats and mountain sheep, dusted with Mediterranean herbs. Served in sunshine that lasts longer over here.

This time Itchy stays with her, in a sturdy oak bed that has been hers since childhood. He takes his time, lingering like a glacier upon each uncovered stage of exquisite skin. The jut-bump of collarbone that sticks out next to her shoulder scar, where calcium has formed around the break to make it now stronger than the rest. He licks gently and diligently along this scar-valley, feeling the slight ridges ripped into her flesh. Her nipples are brown and round as two-pence pieces, remind him of home and childhood. Her eyes burn into him, even when they're closed. They make him ache to be better than he is, and laugh at himself with the knowledge that, coming from his level on humanity's ladder, that can't be hard. Her ribcage frames itself so prominently against her flesh – sucked in, in anticipation of his fingers – that he could count the bones with his eyes. And when his hand sinks lower she opens to him with murmurs into his shoulder and a sensation like he can only imagine a mother must feel suckling her child: so urgent and so meant to be; so right.

With her, he feels as if he might actually become a prince. No longer a toad, in the crown it wears only to trick kisses from princesses.

He wants to cry as he slides into her, with the goodness she forces on him, as much as the pleasure. And he eases out, finally, born again. Doubly sure that there is no God and that He is her.

Afterwards they talk. About family at first. Her father is a forester, which makes the nightingale more fairy tale and builds Itchy's hopes for a happy ending. But her mother works in local government – waste services management – which even in French sounds unromantic, and Itchy's memories of vault-bins make him shudder.

Her favourite film is *La Haine*; her favourite author is Camus; her first pet was a cat, bizarrely called Chien; she skis 171s. She hates her feet, though to Itchy they look beautiful; and he kisses her malformed little toes, to show her so. She has an older brother, who returned to the South when he left home and now manages a restaurant in Montpellier. She wishes she could see his child, her nephew, more often.

Something occurs to him, so he asks her:

'If your family aren't Chamionards, aren't from round here, why were you laying flowers on that grave in Argentière – is it a friend's grave?'

She shakes her head, black tresses like the subject of a sonnet.

'He's just a man, who has no one else. I saw one time that no one cares for him. He's an Englishman like you and he is far from home and cold up there. So sometimes I go and I take care of him. I like the people who have got lost and left behind.'

Itchy has been flailing in the wake of something for years. A ship he jumped off for a swim, forgetting that he can't. Waving so enthusiastically that even he didn't know he was drowning.

'Can I ask you something?' the nightingale says.

'Anything.'

'The place where you work, do you know what it means, the name, what the name means?'

'*Derapage*. It means to slide, of course. Like skiing or boarding, or even, I guess, in a car on ice,' Itchy says.

She kisses him and looks into him, as she speaks; her eyes glint with something: a knowledge of him, deeper than his own.

'It means that, yes, but as well a different slide, Itchy, like *la chute*, a fall.'

'Like a fall from grace?' Itchy says.

'*Exact*, it means a slide away from your *moralité*, Itchy. Like you. You are full of truth and good, but you hate them, and you hate yourself. How did you become this you? If I can be the place where your slide stops, first you have to tell me where it begins.'

Itchy is stunned. Her words, so softly spoken, hit him like a telescopic metal club. And so, not knowing what else to do, and knowing well the spot, Itchy takes her there. He tells her about the place where the wheels locked and the skid started.

The Last Supper

SOME OF THE Regulators took a tactical nap before the final meal, sobering themselves sufficiently to make the most of the mountain of booze they had accumulated for the curry feast. Itchy paced about his student-hall room, small as a monk's cell, not wanting to keep drinking, too edgy to sleep. The walls were white breeze blocks, thickly grimed at the joins, and he stroked his fingers down them, not sure why. All his stuff was packed up in looted cardboard boxes, ready for a getaway to a Hertfordshire home, far from Sheffield.

The hired function room of the science block was like a laboratory sketched by Mary Shelley; shadows played on cabinets filled with glass jars – formaldehyded body parts and creatures, fetuses of felines and simians prematurely womb-ripped. A long, black, benched trestle table ran down the centre, built in an age of stronger things, a table that could support cavorting orgies, or bear monstrous bodies, to be dissected or rebuilt. Tonight stacked with foil and cardboard packages from Singh and Sons, oil oozing from every crack.

Itchy was nervous, waiting for Tina to arrive; he stared into the cabinets to keep a semblance of control. Marty mistook this study for a genuine interest and, always ready to expand on his favourite subject, he gestured to a fetus that Itchy was looking at.

'The problem with birth is our heads,' Marty said. 'Look how small a monkey's skull is compared to a human's. The modern *Homo sapiens* infant's head is too big, on account of how big its brain is. Most women need assistance with birth, if they and the sprog are going to survive. Which means, effectively, that human beings can no longer function in a natural environment; we're like some crazy science fiction species, artificially kept alive. And that overlarge brain that causes so much problem in birth also forces us to face the certainty of our death. We are the only animals who spend most of their lives knowing they will die, knowing that death is in fact the only certainty we have.'

'I guess so,' Itchy said, not wanting to be rude, but trying to discourage any further conversation along these lines; Marty could go on for days, once he got warmed up.

Marty didn't seem bothered that Itchy wasn't up for some of his theorising. He opened a can of wife-beater and mooched off to another group of the guys, whose laughter suggested they were probably also talking about reproduction.

Some of the Regulators wanted to start on the food, but the general consensus was that since they'd all chipped in for a serving wench, they should fucking well hold off until she turned up and could serve them.

They didn't have to wait long. Tina arrived bang on the nine o'clock they'd asked her to. She had her hair up in a ponytail and wore a plain white blouse and black skirt. She looked like a waitress, but still throbbingly beautiful, even in that dowdy outfit – like a film heroine, who's pre-transformation plainness is not fooling anyone.

Ramsey was the captain, inclined to lead off the field as well. He tried to start a chant of 'tits out for the boys', but it was still a bit early and the song petered away. Tina dealt with it like a pro; she smiled at Ramsey and waggled her finger like a primary teacher.

'I'm not going to like you, am I?' She winked.

'Don't be fucking ridiculous,' Ramsey said, 'everyone likes me.'

A row of shots was already lined up on the heavy table; green spirit that didn't try to disguise its potency, stuff distilled by backwater inbreds, brought here from a holiday by one of the most over-privileged of the mostly over-privileged team. Behind that row of glasses was another line, like trench reinforcements, just as sure to fall as the first wave. Behind them another. And another. And then the fortress they protected, a staggering tower of spirits and beer.

They didn't really get Tina to serve them, only in a jokey, good-natured way, of passing this and that. A few of the drunker ones made the odd grab for her arse, but they were slapped away by hands well used to it. Hands that had worked their way through this first year, in cheap restaurants that the team had visited only to get drunk.

They did persuade her to join in the drinking games, though, games that gradually became more important than the eating. And she matched them shot for shot, and doubled everyone in punishment shots, being unused to the rules familiar to the Regulators.

Itchy tried at every opportunity to stick up for her, finding it virtually impossible to make his mark any other way, through the Viking bawl the team put out. He was just one among many trying to catch her eye, though; most of the Regulators were now inebriated to the point where getting laid had become a sudden priority, and Tina was the only game in the room.

Soon Tina was swaying even when sat down, waving like washing-line knickers in a warm wind. She had failed to get her booze-battered head around the last game at all, and now sank every shot presented to her without protest. Already fractured with liquor. Eyelids drooping and drawling her words.

Itchy tried to say she'd had enough, did say it, but failed to reach her in time to stop her doing another knock-back; this one with something white fizzing gently in the alcohol's midst.

'What was that you gave her?' he asked Merrick. 'There was something in that.'

'Relax man, just a pill, ecstasy,' Merrick said, leaning back, out of Tina's earshot, though she looked well past keeping up with much around her.

'No more,' Itchy said, though thinking he wouldn't have minded the pill himself.

Merrick agreed. But only ten minutes later, Tina had to do another shot, poured by someone else, and this too had a starchy look to the liquid, also drunk too quickly to be analysed.

Another game was started – Ring of Fire – one better suited to Tina perhaps, because the downfall was luck, on the turn of a card, not on the skill or practice or sobriety of the participant. And the forfeits were not all drinks either. Though some required items of clothing to be removed. The Regulators were sufficiently chivalrous to let her off the first couple of times, but luck wasn't with Tina that night. Or maybe luck isn't really a lady. Maybe luck is a bloke.

Soon Tina was in her bra. A black bra. Lacy. The sort of bra women wear for a special date, where they know there's a good chance someone's going to be able to appreciate it. Itchy did, and judging by the applause and open jaws, it was pretty clear that the others did too.

And Tina seemed to be enjoying the attention; she was grinning, as far as her drug-gurning jaw allowed. She stood up on the bench and did a twirl when she pulled the Queen of Spades and had to take her skirt off. Luckily, a couple of the guys caught her when she toppled off. She was not nearly so methodical about slapping the over-helpful hands off her as she had been a couple of hours back. But then it was probably only the pills which prevented her collapsing, from the amount of booze she'd put back. She must have weighed half what some of the Regulators did, and had done more shots than any. McCloughlin, the goalie, the biggest of the lot, had a hand on her arse now, and it virtually covered it.

Itchy's stomach was knotting, seeing Tina mauled like this.

'All right, guys, that's enough,' he said. 'She's done her two hours and then some, and we've all had our money's worth. I'm going to take her home.'

'Are you fuck,' said McCloughlin. 'Nice try. She's all right, aren't you?'

Tina looked blankly. 'I want to dance,' she said. 'Can't we go to a club?' At least, that's what Itchy figured; her words were as slurred as those of a gutter-tramp shouting at the heavens.

'Come on,' Itchy said, 'let's get you dressed and get you home.' He took her arm, the first time he'd touched her dreamed-of flesh, trying to lead her away from McCloughlin, bare chested, who was staring him into a fight.

One of Tina's snow-pale breasts came out of her bra, the nipple erect – the effect of being nearly naked in a room full of men who wanted her, or more likely cold, or maybe the ecstasy – but Itchy felt his blood streaming away from his brain, down to where it could be better used.

'Don't wanna go home,' she mumbled to him, 'you don't know what girls wanna do, d'you even like girls? I always thought you jus' liked poetry and books.' And she looked up, with her lips parted, as begging to be kissed as anyone Itchy had ever seen.

Charlie said: 'Wear a condom,' and pressed one into his hand.

Merrick said: 'That's so eighties.'

But Itchy did anyway, rolling it over a cock engorged, but lolled to three o'clock with booze and self-disgust.

He was pumping her and thinking that this was all he wanted to do. Thinking that this was all he'd been thinking about for months – for near enough eight months this was all he'd wanted. But not here, not like this, not in front of all the guys. Not with her the only one not present.

And as he was pumping, as he was slipping in and out of her, hopelessly far from any possibility of coming, he couldn't take his eyes off a scar that lay across her belly. The most perfectly beautiful girl he'd ever known was naked under him, but all he could look at was a scar. Across where her womb might be, but probably wasn't, because otherwise why would the scar be there?

He was looking at the scar and all the while he was pumping, automaton, like one of those corny mechanised mannequins, at a museum or something, which is doomed to carry on doing the same thing for ever. Only as if this were its first day on the job, where it might still feel an edge of freshness.

And all the while, the guys were cheering. Smithy was actually filming it, on the camcorder he had rented to record their last supper, a copy for posterity to be made for them all. None of them seemed to get it. No one seemed to realise what this was, what they were doing. Except for Itchy, who knew and carried on anyway. A cognisance that should entail an extra level of guilt. But at that moment Itchy couldn't feel guilt, he only felt a rage, a hatred for this girl moaning under him on the solid slab table.

He hated her for being so blind and so weak as to let this happen, for not being stronger than the combined will of fifteen footballers. He hated her for not having been more worthy of the love that he could have given her. And for not accepting it when it could all have been so different. He hated her for making him become this monster. He hated her and loved her and fucked her through them both.

And while he did it, other hands were on her, hands she didn't make any effort to remove. And her own fingers reached out for any part of anyone they could find.

When Itchy finally came, he roared like Prometheus, like a man utterly blasted, who still shouts his wrath at the gods. Defying their damnation, almost desiring it.

Itchy came like a tiger. But he slunk away like a bested cat, into the shadows that lurked at the back of the room. Into himself, away from the team.

No one noticed, because they were all crowded around Tina now, all taking their turn with her hands and mouth and hungry mound. Her high on drugs and booze and atmosphere and almost insensible to what she was doing. Not insensible to pain or pleasure, but her moans could have been for either. Her eyes were elsewhere, pupils as big and black as LPs, nothing going on behind them, strung out.

The video – which would be circulated around college next term, its own alibi – would only show the wanking and sucking and fucking. The lens couldn't pick up how far her mind was from the proceedings. Barely, if at all, conscious of what was happening to her. Lost in a forest of pills and alcohol. Feeling for anything that might help her find her way out. Finding only further dicks. Ridding them from her path as best she could. The oldest chore of the slave.

It should have made Itchy treat women with respect, what happened. It should have made him want to spend a lifetime dedicated to apology and atonement, but for some reason it didn't. The self-loathing slithered into his bloodstream, like a shard of ice from the Snow Queen, or a cube of glass from a carpark; something that numbed and needed numbing.

Itchy left the team behind. Alone, sick and sober. Very, very sober. More sober than he'd ever felt before, and ever intended to feel again.

Relect on *this*, ye libertines, and, in the full career of the lasciviousness which has unfitted your souls for enjoying the *slightest* real happiness here or hereafter, tremble! Tremble! I say; for the day of retribution will arrive.

Shelley, St Irvyne

April 15th, 11.21 a.m.

Itchy is now thirty. The time of life when Jesus faced his trials in the wilderness. The year that Sartre's *Nausea* came on. The age of Shelley when he died.

'Live each day as if it's your last' had been Itchy's drunkenly roared maxim at his birthday party the previous night. And now he is in bed, in pain and alone; which he believes is how he deserves to spend his last day.

Normally Itchy would start drinking again as soon as he rose, to break the back of a hangover of this magnitude. But for some reason he decides that today he will suffer his way through it like a penance. A bit of mild martyrdom to mark his ascent into the age at which society says he should know where his life is heading.

He struggles out of bed and spoons five teaspoons of coffee into a mug. Stares at the coal-heap of granules, while he waits for the pan of water to boil. The pan is unwashed from making someone's pasta or potatoes; the water is nearly clean, but still leaves a film of oil on the coffee. There is a bottle of unopened and undegradable UHT in the fridge and a stack of liberated sugar cubes, from the Derapage, in the cupboard, but Itchy drinks the coffee's cheap bitterness black, like further flagellation.

He meets the nightingale for a late lunch, feeling shipwrecked and still scarcely able to comprehend that she wants to keep seeing him, after what he told her.

She holds his hand across a pine-slatted table, flypaper-sticky with the morning's spillages. He is shaking with withdrawal symptoms and too much caffeine.

'Itchy,' she says, 'one ugly work, no matter how bad, does not make ugly your whole life; you are not evil and your liver is not evil too. You do not have to keep punishing you both.'

'It was my birthday,' he protests, enfeebled with his alcohol illness.

The nightingale hadn't wanted to come to his party, and he hadn't pleaded, knowing that her presence would limit his excesses. Immoderation is expected of Itchy, his capacity for self-abuse is legendary. In a land of hedonists, he is the head. And he is too typecast now, and too weak, to let his public down.

The nightingale has wine with lunch, she has wine with every meal out, except breakfast; but Frenchly: to enhance the experience, not to get drunk. Despite having told himself he wasn't going to, sunlight on the carafe winks at Itchy, until he has a glass as well. The nightingale watches him take the first thirsty gulp with a smile halfway on the stairs between love and pity. Itchy silently worries about which way she's travelling.

There are gendarmes outside one of the entrances to the carpark when Itchy walks home. There has obviously been another attack.

He avoids looking at them, feeling twitchy and guilty, but they have no interest in him anyway. They are studying the ground outside, with surgeon gloves on and those little plastic baggies that drug dealers and TV cops and button sellers use.

There is something automatically intimidating about gendarmes that they use to their advantage, a thinly veiled threat of violence. Their name actually means 'the guys with guns', as does the Italian *carabinieri*, more or less.

Britain used to celebrate the fact that its police did not have firearms, but Itchy knows from airports that those days are almost over. Now British police carry Heckler and Koch sub-machine guns with double-clip magazines, laser sights and mini-Maglites attached – all painted glint-proof matt black – sporting bulky Kevlar body armour and earpiece mics. That is not someone you ask for directions. And you don't call him 'Bobby', you call him 'Sir'.

Sean says the latest victim fought back, and she was stabbed for her trouble. She is alive, but in intensive care. In French *victime* is always feminine.

Mont Blanc is as rose tinted as the apocryphal spectacles, a beautiful pink in the final light of the day. Is it beautiful, though, or is it only different? If the mountains were always this delicate shell colour, would an occasional white be more sublime?

'The guys here now,' Doc says, at work, later, 'they just slide over the surface of things, they don't know the depths of these mountains.'

Doc's hands on the bar-top are rough and look as if they were carved from wood, but each scar contains the memory of pitched battle with a summit.

Itchy's worst scar is also the slightest: a scratch on his cornea's lens that he no longer notices, but through which he watches the whole world.

He sips at a White Russian, beginning to feel whole again. The calcium from the milk pours into him with the vodka's potatoey goodness and the chocolate pudding of Kahlúa – a White Russian is a meal in itself.

'There was a time,' Doc continues, 'when everyone came to Chamonix for the peaks. Now this town is full of people, most of them *anglais*, who never get up there even to go skiing, never mind to make *alpinisme*.'

Itchy is momentarily offended by the slur on his nation, but he likes Doc too much to take it personally. In fact, he is embarrassed by the affection he feels for Doc; it makes him suddenly sullen inside, like a teenager expressing love for his father with anger. But he resists the urge to snap at his boss and just says:

'I guess you're right.'

But then he thinks for a bit and asks: 'Doc?'

'*Oui. C'est moi.*'

'Am I one of them? The "sliders over the surface", I mean.'

'*Non*, not you, Itchy, you're not that lucky. You'll end up on the high mountain, maybe, but more than likely underground,' and old Doc chuckles away to himself, a noise like pebbles clicking together.

...if he has indeed taken refuge in the Alps, he may be
hunted like the chamois and destroyed as a beast of
prey. But I perceive your thoughts; you do not credit
my narrative and do not intend to pursue my enemy
with the punishment that is his desert.

Mary Shelley, Frankenstein

April 28th, 1.51 a.m.

Underground.

It is nearly time for Itchy to leave. The season is coming to a
close. Already the tourist numbers have dwindled, to a trickle
scarcely more than the Chinese-water-torture drip-drip from the
dungeon ceiling down here in the *parking du fond*.

In a few days Itchy will unpin his existence from the walls of
his flat, take himself from the shared shelves and cupboards, pack
his portion of the wardrobe, and finally disintegrate his presence
from the resort. But before he leaves that place, he wants to say
goodbye to this one, to the den he has inhabited down here.

In *Frankenstein*, the monster hides out in Chamonix, up on
the Mer de Glace. But real monsters don't like it on the mountains.
Monsters don't like the exposure, the light. Monsters like the dark
valleys; crevices; caves; and carparks.

Itchy saw a marmot, the other day. Up skiing with the
nightingale. She skis almost as well as she sings. And as if she is

singing. The marmot was perched outside its winter hibernation burrow, sniffing the coming spring. It's time to give Cham back to the marmots, time for the monsters to leave.

Chamonix is perfect camouflage for an alcoholic and so is working in a bar. Drinking heavily every day is so normal that you can even fool yourself, for a while. Itchy swigs from a now almost empty bottle of neat gin that he has brought with him. The alcohol hardening his arteries and his heart. After he says goodbye to his den and his flat, he will have to say goodbye to the nightingale.

There are a couple more painted figures down here now. A couple more girls have been attacked. The frequency is increasing. They say that's how it ends for all psychopaths. Running out of control. Beyond their own cunning. Their want spiralling down. Like a corkscrew. Everything ends at one point.

The carpark itself is closing soon, indefinitely – Itchy has read the printed sheet left on all the doors and entrances and all the car windscreens down here. Closing, the management said, *Pour des raisons indépendantes de notre volonté*: for shit we can't control. Probably the gendarmes are trying to flush the monster out into the light. Or maybe someone has finally realised that the carpark itself has become the problem: that if you let somewhere rot and stink and be daubed with paint and piled with refuse; if you let the fire extinguishers be stolen and the alarms be smashed and the sand buckets get so filled with filth and litter that they could only add to any conflagration; if you don't fix the bulbs, or mend the rust-fucked gates, or hide the trailing electrics, or patch the leaks, or repair the vandalism, or shift the dumped cars and broken fridges, or put the doors back on their hinges; if you let a place disintegrate to the point where it looks and smells and feels like a brutalised environment, then brutality itself will sooner or later arrive. Even in Chamonix.

It rained today, heavily. Normally it's depressing when it rains in a ski resort, strips the snow away like ice cream on the lawn. But the snow is long gone down in town, and at least the water cleaned away the dirt and the dog muck. There was a smell of newness just before it happened. A fresh heavy smell trapped by the pressure, close to the ground.

The woman who is making her way across the carpark now doesn't need to fear the rapist. She isn't his type. Too old and too big. From this distance, you could barely tell she was a woman, except for the hair and the skirt. But then who knows how far down his spiral the rapist has slid, maybe he no longer has a type. She is striding away from the circle that Itchy can see through his grille. Soon she will be in the catacombs and the labyrinths.

Just as she turns the corner, Itchy sees a new figure appear. A man, slipping out from the slide door of a shadow-parked dark-tinted van. A figure dressed all in black, as black as the murals on the walls. A figure that follows her.

Itchy has had his dress rehearsal for this role: the part of saviour. For which he is perhaps ill suited. But here and now there is only him. He grabs two bottles from his collection and rushes at the grating. Dents his head. Falls back stunned. Raises the rusted grille and goes through again. Dizzy now from the self-dealt blow and staggering from the gin and all the previous drinks of his night. He lurches to the gateway the other two passed through.

Itchy can no longer see in this gloom, he needs to be somewhere better lit. The strip lights leave trails on his blurred eyes like meteors. He can't tell where the woman and her stalker have gone. But thinks he hears the clip of high heels, so pitches his disobedient legs towards the sound. The best replication of a run he can produce.

Another junction leaves Itchy suspended between options.

Dangling like Damocles in the minotaur's maze – his brain not making sense. Useless as the overturned crowd-control barrier that lies in a puddle of sludge in front of him.

He hears a scuffle off to his left and heads there. Cursing himself for the drink that has smashed his coordination and thought. Slurring even those words. Flucksucking blooze. Ricocheting off bins as he tries to run onward. He has already dropped one bottle somewhere. The second smashes on a wall. He can hardly stand. There is a shriek and a gargle. Then the noise of someone falling. Not Itchy. His own fall was long ago. This was his chance to atone. And he's fluffing it. Fucking it. More shrieks. Someone still alive, but in deep pain. Sounds that can mean only one thing: the time for Itchy's atonement is either over, or very, very near. He rounds the corner one-legged. Like an unfunny cartoon of himself. Sees the body on the floor. Writhing and bleeding. Sees the knife in the perpetrator's hand. Itchy readies the meagre remains of his bottle. His own puny blade. He is poised to launch the attack that must certainly fail – the state he is in – but may fail gloriously. To cease in an instant of goodness is surely better than to exist for ever in pointlessness. He is ready to blunder his will against this nemesis. Who he realises now he recognises. This standing figure with bloodstained blouse and knife. This red-handed, broad-backed, familiar villain…in a skirt…

'Itchy,' Wendy says, toeing her prone and still-shrieking, black-clad attacker, 'thank God I've got a witness. This bastard tried to stab us.'

Hope you enjoy all your prizes, including this
book. Give my love to Geneva and Chamonix.
I'll see you next term to hear all about it.
Dr Henry Ragworth

The Pyre

There is no smell more dire in sweet sickness than the stink of burning human flesh. Except, Byron discovers, the stench of burning flesh which has previously floated for ten days in the Mediterranean and been buried nearly a month in quicklime in the sand. No smell could be made worse than this, except by the added tang that it is your greatest friend, Shelley, who you burn.

It is a pagan send-off. An atheist's funeral. Only the old gods or no gods look on. It is how Shelley would have wanted it. But there can be no joy in a young man's death.

Younger have died, of course. Allegra, the daughter of Claire Clairmont and Byron, or perhaps Claire and Shelley, has already gone from the world, in the bleak comfort of a stone-arched Italian convent. A suitably Gothic ending, for a life barely begun.

The children of Mary and Shelley, even younger, only babes, have been left upon the route their lives have taken since that dark summer under the shadow of the Alps: daughter buried on a salt beach in Venice; son in Rome. Shelley's baby by their Italian nursemaid died in Naples.

Claire and Mary's sister, Fanny, has taken her own life:

an overdose of the same laudanum that Shelley took for his nerves. Death for unrequited love of the poet; even his largess was not boundless.

Shelley's first wife has killed herself too, and the unborn she carried, deserted by husband and family; drowned in the Serpentine, down a set of dock stairs, having already descended the steps to prostitution. The court generously avoided declaring suicide, to allow a decent burial.

Another accommodating coroner, a year ago, gave verdict that Dr Polidori 'departed this life in a natural way, by the visitation of God'. But it seems unlikely it was God who supplied the poison. Polidori tried to join a monastery, but was rejected for his scandalous literary acquaintances. So he left this cruel world of every day another way: with a self-prescribed dose of prussic acid. A horrible way to go; but then, as a doctor, he must have known that. Is there a good way to go? Hope so. Perhaps that's all we have.

Maybe Shelley's way is best. He has sailed his way out of existence. On his siren-beautiful, sylph-slim, twenty-four-foot, twin-masted, quick-rigged craft; his last happiness; the *Don Juan*. Named, of course, for Byron's epic poem of picaresque conquest, which still sweeps the high society from which its author is still exiled.

Some mariners claim it is an ill omen to name a vessel after a man, particularly, perhaps, a man damned to hell. When Shelley first saw his schooner, the shipwrights had painted *Don Juan* black and thick on her sails, overzealous or on Byron's instruction. Shelley vacillated, he had the towering words cut out and new cloth stitched in; he wondered whether he should call the craft *The Ariel* instead – as if the ghost from *The Tempest* would be a better portent to put to sea under.

Shelley's sailing had progressed greatly since the days of

Lake Geneva. He had grown tanned and lithe on board the *Don Juan*, which was his sometime study and house, as well as his passion. Yet for all this, he never learned to swim. Among ancient tars this was customary; men who knew that even the strongest swimmer could never recatch a sail boat in a storm. They had no wish to prolong their agony in floundering for breath against the inevitable. But isn't that what we do, isn't that what we all do?

Shelley set sail with his crew of two on a clear and calm Mediterranean day. The Italian summer had been as hot and bright as that far-off Alpine one had been black and cold. But there was still space for a storm. A sudden shrieking witch-gale lunged from inexistence to become a malevolent gauntlet, as soon as the *Don Juan* left sight of the Italian coastline.

All the local vessels fled to harbour, knowing that no journey save to Davy Jones's locker could be accomplished in such a fury. Shelley's schooner sailed on.

In the later inquiry, one captain claimed to have seen the *Don Juan*, pounded by waves as high and white as cliff faces. He said he yelled to them through his loudhailer, to put to port or to board his larger ship or, at the least, to reef their sails. His suggestions were all forcibly declined, and turning to land himself, it was the last he saw of them. Naively, or stubbornly, or with one final finger raised to authority, good sense and godless nature's blank cruelty, Shelley and the *Don Juan* went to the depths under full sail. His body was found days later, so ravaged and bitten by the sea and her creatures that it was only identified by the handwritten book of his friend Keats's poetry, still buttoned in a pocket.

So now Byron feeds the pyre. He throws on salt to make the flames grow blue against the black of night. And he throws on frankincense, present for a God-child, to hide the stench of mortality.

As if to dare the sea, Byron takes a swim – before the fire has yet burned away – into the tenebrous night waves he plunges. They do not swallow a swimmer so strong as him. No mermen or sharks come to attack so fierce a fighter. He returns to the beach unharmed, unchallenged, lame once more on land, but victorious. Yet something he has swallowed out there, or the cold he has encountered, will make him sick in the days that follow. Not as sick as poor young Keats, who has lately died of consumption in Rome, spitting up bright arterial blood. But a shaking fever hard to shake off.

Shelley's heart does not burn. Even with additional fuel, it will not disappear. Eventually they cease to try, and Mary takes it with her, the last husk of her husband.

Byron tries to lift Shelley's skull, when the flames trickle away, but it disintegrates beneath his fingers. It was an unusually small and frail skull, which once protected such a mind.

In the near future, apparently recovered from his fevers and agues, Byron will set sail on his own final voyage. His twenty-two-ton schooner, named *The Bolivar*, will be equipped with cannon, and another ship, the hundred-some-ton *Hercules*, will be hired and loaded with the provisions a lord requires to make war. With guns, powder, artillery, sabre, enough medicinal supplies to last a thousand men two years, uniforms in revolutionary scarlet and noble gold, crested helms and coin – plenty of coin. The cash will be raised by the poet selling his possessions and properties, his prized Napoleonic carriage, even a part of his animal menagerie – though the dogs must come, of course, bulldog for fighting, Newfoundland for swimming – and every ship needs a monkey. But the cause will capture the imagination of Europe, there will be a new smell of freedom and big donations will come in, as word spreads from newspapers and orators: Lord Byron is leaving his openly dissolute Italian life, off to the land of heroes, to Greece; to free civilisation's founders, the creators of the only true democracy the world has ever known, now enslaved to vicious Turks, who massacre and extort at whim.

Byron is to be the figurehead and commander of a stand for liberty, a fight to throw off foreign oppression. He will be, once more, the man of the moment. Even repressive England will be behind the Hellenic struggle and Byron's sins will be forgiven. Sins are things of mortal men, not demigods, who may judge themselves. Goethe, the age's sagest head, will write honour verses when he hears of Byron's intent. And Byron will rise to the self-designed station, be once more the man that captures the world's hearts. The man women want and men want to be. He will become a slimmed-down super-him, sparring and fencing his way to fitness, leaving behind the brothels and the brandy that have characterised his life of late. Europe needs a hero, and Byron needs to be it.

He will die in the endeavour, of course. History demands it. He needs to die, and it's inevitable. But he shouldn't die as he will. And since this is still a future of which we talk, let us suppose that Lord George Noel Gordon Byron will die as he should. Let us suppose he will go roaring like Hector, among fallen enemies, having fought too ferociously to have realised his mortal wound. Or perhaps he will end, with his rapier held high, crying liberty, Fletcher by his side, as the *Hercules* sinks beneath them, from volleys of Ottoman cannon. No, wait, maybe he will perish thrusting a new pan-Hellenic banner into Athenian earth, at the very steps of the Parthenon

– long turned into a mosque – Byron will be cut down by a last sniping musket of his vanquished foe, his hand still on the flagstaff, his lips upon the sacred soil. Let us suppose he will be remembered for ever like that. Because, perhaps, how we go is all we have. And Byron is not a man who should die of a never-shaken illness; a fever first contracted on the night he burnt his greatest friend. Byron is not a man who should be bled to death, in an already weakened state, by incompetent doctors. So let us suppose he won't be. Just for a while.

And back on the beach, between the mountains and the sea, Mary Shelley and Claire Clairmont live on. Byron too, for the moment. Claire will become a governess, taking some dram of contentment in helping to raise the children of others, now that her own daughter is gone. And Mary, blessed Mary, Mary still has a last surviving child: the youngest, Percy Florence Shelley, named for his father and his birthplace. He is her comfort and her purpose now; he will be her light, in this darkness, till it is brightened by her own pyre.

All tragedies are finished by a death,
All comedies are ended by a marriage;
The future states of both are left to faith,
For authors fear description might disparage
The worlds to come of both, or fall beneath,
And then both worlds would punish their miscarriage;
So leaving each their priest and prayer-book ready,
They say no more of Death or of the Lady.

Byron, Don Juan

July 14th, 9.29 a.m.

Love and death, always close and final, are made more so in the French – *l'amour* and *la mort*, pronounced properly, are almost indistinguishable to untrained ears; but Itchy is now approaching the stage where he can divide such subtleties.

Recently he has bought a diary, just a whim, but it seems to give more substance to each day to see its historical surrounds – the diary is the sort full of those interesting events in the past, as well as the perhaps less interesting results of Itchy's daily jottings.

Today is Bastille Day, of course – tonight Cham's streets will be lit by flags and fireworks – but also the day, in 1867, when Alfred Nobel first demonstrated dynamite; the substance that was to change the shape of mountains and the world, to catalyse industrial revolution and found the Nobel Institute. In 1933, today, Germany outlawed all political groups except the Nazi Party. In 1958, today, King Faisal of Iraq was assassinated and a republic proclaimed. In 1959, today, the USA launched the first nuclear warship. In 1967 Britain legalised abortion. In 1972 Gary Glitter and the Glitterband performed their first concert. In 1989, down the road in Geneva, the world's first particle accelerator was unveiled – as if particles don't move fast enough.

But all these happened on this day on other todays; today, Itchy is going to go for a walk, with his girlfriend.

He has to go and meet her first. She is still living with her parents at the moment, though Itchy and she have talked about getting a place together. Not to buy. Not to start with anyway. Prices in Cham are way too high. The rents are much cheaper in the summer, though; Itchy doesn't even have to live in the Ghetto. But he does anyway, and he's enjoying how it's changing.

Many of the summer residents are Alpinists. There's a couple in the square now, preparing for an expedition, Gore-Texed and jangling with assorted spikes and axes, checking each other's backpacks. Bags big enough for a curled-up nightingale to fit inside.

There are also walkers and hikers, ranging from the elderly riverbank strollers to motivated, plus-foured, wool-socked, route-tickers. In the winter, people with tick-lists can get themselves killed. In the summer it's a joy to witness such enthusiasm.

Rock climbers are in abundance, of course, shoes like ballet pumps, muscles like Nureyev not Stallone, dancing up impossibly stern cliff faces and making them smile. Chamonix hosts the world climbing championships every summer.

Itchy's favourites among the new immigrants, though, are the families. He never really noticed any kids in the winter, but now they are everywhere he looks. On the way to meet the nightingale, he passes a little boy in dungarees, with a blond basin-cut that

Itchy aches to ruffle like an uncle. But he knows that the days are long past when a man could muss the hair of any child but his own. Gone with the Jackson Five and the Glitterband.

A postcard is lying on the pavement in front of Itchy where he walks, a picture of a husky dog in sunglasses, the height of tinselled tosh. He picks it up and reads the biroed words, oddly fascinated by someone else's irrelevance. And Itchy finds his usual disdain for tourists has slipped away, he is touched by the stranger's banal best wishes for a friend. So he makes a stop at the post office, to buy a stamp, slots the kitsch epistle on its way.

He meets the nightingale at the start of the path they are to walk. She's already waiting there; upright and motionless, she doesn't even wave hello or smile at him. As he draws closer he sees why: a wasp, striped with nature's warnings, is making sharkish circles around her. The nightingale is justifiably afraid of wasps, and irresistible to them. One more sting in her life and she might forfeit it. So she sits there immobile until her satellite nemesis departs; so still she could be a piece of the landscape. The brightest, most beautiful part. Itchy plumps down on a stump beside her, where a tree has been cut down. A sprig of green is sprouting from the blackened, dead-looking lump, a slim chance for regrowth.

The paths are dotted with chamois poos, in blackberry clusters, and fir cones open and inviting – a feast for the scampering, black mountain squirrels, which in the winter can only huddle and shudder. In occasional places the grass grows in thicker little patches, fairy rings people once called them. Itchy knows that these are the spots where creatures have died, where the ground has absorbed their nutrients. But they remind him of the crown-clump of pillow-hair that Daniel had at the back.

Itchy and the nightingale follow the stripes on the trees, like Indian warpaint, though of course she knows these tracks like the way to bed. Ski poles, broken or clumsily dropped from chair lifts, have been used to support an electric fence, where the path crosses a farmer's field, and Itchy can't help but smile at them, looking so solemn and helpful in their little rows.

Whenever they pass a cairn, they add a couple more rocks to it, in the same way that mountain folk have for ever. The cairns are reminders of existence more than they are direction markers. For lonely shepherds and chamois hunters, it must have been comforting to know that other people were not just dreams.

For some reason this makes Itchy think about The Game. And he thinks that perhaps it is as much a cairn as a competition. He finds now that his tired legs feel stronger when he thinks of his friends. He sends out a text, while he walks, but just to say hello, he doesn't mention The Game; if they're winning, let them win.

A young man is coming down the same path they walk up, with a baby on his back in place of a rucksack; it gurgles and grins at Itchy, as he steps aside to let them by, flaps its doughy arm in a way that might be a first wave, or an attempt to fly. And the nightingale calls Itchy soft, when he waves back; though her moistened eyes suggest that she is softer.

They sit down for lunch at Le Panoramic, the restaurant where Itchy ate with Wendy all those months ago. The ultimate big game caught, Wendy has a new tale added to her legend now, and a bounty from the police to fund next year's ski trips.

And what of the rapist? Who was it that Wendy overpowered and stabbed with his own blade? All Itchy can remember, through the alcohol blur, is an everyman, a nobody. A blank-faced, featureless fiend, who could be your next-door neighbour or your customer. But the story that has gradually emerged is of an ambulance driver, a man who lived a commonplace life in Cham. Who must have done some good, indeed, by day. But maybe he was too close; perhaps contact with all the frightened beautiful girls at work eventually touched a vestigial tail in his mind; reanimated a primeval lobe we thought was dead. Or maybe he was broken in a place that wouldn't heal. Or just evil. Itchy might find out more when he has his day in court. But looking back, the most disturbing thing of all for Itchy was the ordinariness of the monster, once he finally fell unconscious; a mundanity far more chilling than the contorted rictus of fear and pain and impotent rage, while he fought against it.

The rapist's capture brought Itchy no lessons. No great epiphany. No catharsis. Not even the feeling of atonement he had hoped for. Maybe it did mark the end of something, but then again, maybe that was just the end of the winter.

Itchy offers the nightingale the wine list; she knows more about wine than him, even though he's an ex-barman. But she puts it back down on the table again.

'I do not think I am going to be drinking for a time,' she says.

And Itchy thinks that sounds like a good idea. 'You're right,' he says. 'Let's dry out for the summer, like the mountains. I don't think I'm going to be drinking for a while either.'

There is still a bit of wine in the cheese fondue they have, but only enough to stop it sticking. You can taste it, but the warmth you get is from the cheese, not the small amount of booze – a measure the old Itchy would have considered homoeopathic. Cheese fondue is probably the most calorific stuff in the world, and Itchy is hardly surprised when the nightingale stops eating and looks into his eyes and says:

'Itchy, *je suis pleine*,' and she pats her tummy, for some reason nervously.

Pleine of course means 'full', but this is an unusual phrase for the nightingale to use. Women generally favour a different form of words when they want to say 'I'm full' in the sense of 'I have had enough to eat', because *je suis pleine* also means something else entirely. Brit girls are always being ribbed for falling into that one. But then the nightingale is French…Itchy frowns, confused…She looks worried, but he is…weirdly…hopeful… Because *je suis pleine* also means…

She says it again, only this time she uses his other name, his real name, which nobody uses, not even his parents. Apparently, Itchy's dad had wanted to call him Byron, but his mother had put her foot down, so he got a more sensible name instead. Albeit one the world seemed to have agreed didn't suit him. But now the nightingale uses it: 'Dan,' she says, and she strokes her womb, not her stomach, 'Danny, *tu comprends? Je suis pleine.*'

Notes on Authenticity

The Chamonix portrayed in this novel, while largely accurate, is a kind of a 'dream time' Chamonix, rather than that of a specific year. Those who know the town very well will probably have noticed that there are some aspects of a slightly older Cham along with newer ones. For example, Elevation and the Clubhouse were opened long after the pole and post barriers to the Chamonix Sud carpark were replaced by card-operated security gates.

All the entrances to the Cham Sud buildings are now pin-code protected as well, and with the launch of new bars and businesses it is an even more vibrant community than ever and a fantastic place in which to holiday or live. At the time of writing, however, the carpark, where so much of this book's action took place, has been closed entirely for three years, owing to a combination of neglect and arson.

The Derapage is a real bar, but it is a popular cosmopolitan spot rather than the quiet haunt depicted in my novel. Doc is of course fictional, as are all the other characters; though I have met some of them.

Considerable new investment has also been made in the lift

structure in the past couple of years, as befits a station with the deserved renown of Chamonix.

Where this novel focused upon the town's darker underbelly, I hope it will be appreciated that this probably highlights only the preoccupations of the author. Where I tried to show the sublime splendour of the Chamonix valley, I can assure you that all my words fell short.

Fiction
Crime
Noir

Culture
Music
Erotica

DATE DUE

dare to read at serpentstail.com

Visit serpentstail.com today to browse and buy
our books, and to sign up for exclusive news and
previews of our books, interviews with our
authors and forthcoming events.

NEWS
cut to the literary chase with
all the latest news about
our books and authors

EVENTS
advance information on
forthcoming events, author
readings, exhibitions
and book festivals

EXTRACTS
read the best of the outlaw
voices – first chapters, short
stories, bite-sized extracts

EXCLUSIVES
pre-publication offers,
signed copies, discounted
books, competitions

BROWSE AND BUY
browse our full catalogue,
fill up a basket and proceed
to our fully secure checkout

oyster

FREE POSTAGE ... ALL ORDERS...

sign up today – join our club